IN THE BACKSTREETS OF COCHIN

Into The Shadows of a Corrupt Underbelly

PRAMOD GROVER

INDIA • SINGAPORE • MALAYSIA

ISBN 979-8-88704-889-5

Contents

Contents

Chapter 1

Shyamala and Shanker were in the office, drinking tea when the operator called.

"There is a well-spoken gentleman here at the receptionist who wants to meet you. He looks a bit of a dandy."

Shanker was a little surprised and checked his diary, but there was no appointment listed there. He was nonetheless curious and asked the receptionist to let him in.

The man made a graceful entry and dandy indeed he was. He looked about 55, with an appearance smooth yet timid. He shifted a bit and seemed nervous. Introducing himself as Mr. Ramesh Pratap, the Managing Director of a well-known, international consultancy firm. Shanker observed a well-manicured hand as Mr. Pratap handed him his visiting card; his hand shook slightly. His salt and pepper hair were thick and neat on this head with no sign of balding as it shone beneath the light. He was not a fat guy, just a hint of a paunch around the middle. He smelled expensive and looked the part too. His hand-woven, embroidered, long-sleeved blue and cream silk tunic collar shirt and khaki pants did not have a crease in sight. His shoes were made of fine black leather and were polished until they shone.

"What can I do for you, Mr. Pratap?" Shanker enquired. He had seen Mr. Pratap in business magazines and the photos emanated arrogance and a shrewd businessperson but the man that stood before him certainly did not give that impression. He shifted from one foot to the next, looked nervous and had a worried look in his eyes. He wore glasses and a thin moustache and beard around his mouth and jaw only that had a few grey patches between. He kept pinching the bridge of his nose again and shifted from one foot to the next, raking his hand through his hair which fell neatly back into place. He carried a small brown pouch in the other hand.

"Save my life! I am getting these threatening letters for some time. Just got another one yesterday as well." His voice was low and pleading. It shook slightly as he spoke. His eyebrows knitted on his forehead as he took a small step forward and then back to his original position.

Shanker was confused as questions formed in his head. He glanced at Shyamala, who looked just as baffled as he was.

"But why should anyone threaten you," Shyamala asked in a confused voice.

"I don't understand," Shanker stated looking even more baffled than he was before.

Mr. Pratap exclaimed, "Well when you are successful, you make a lot of enemies in your line of work. We bid for the consultancy of large companies, we specialize in banks and financial houses, in particular. Recently, we put a tender for a well-known bank which is keen to take on our consultancy services to reorganize their working system."

A still confused Shanker asked, "Then, what is the problem? I still don't understand. This is quite routine, and you must be tendering for jobs all the time; you have a large staff, don't you?"

Still looking nervous, Mr. Pratap answered, "Around 600 highly qualified engineers and MBAs from top universities and institutes."

Shyamala glanced at Shanker who was now looked bewildered. He blinked through his glasses just as Shanker glanced at him then they both looked at Mr. Pratap. Shanker cleared his throat in an effort to calm his frustration and asked, "So, why this issue now?"

Mr. Pratap, sensing their confusion explained that the company, whose re-organization his firm was bidding for, happened to be controversial and it was partly owned by public sector banks. This RMC Bank was involved in several frauds in the past and had recently figured in a very large fraud wherein the management members quietly left the country for U.A.E. He added that should his firm be awarded the contract they will be exposing a lot of corruption in RMC Bank's system which would lead to unearthing the names of the those involved in the fraud.

Mr. Pratap's shifting from foot to foot was becoming too distracting to Shanker, who motioned him to sit while Shyamala, in her ever-gentle way, assured Mr. Pratap that any other consultancy firm would have to expose any form of fraud or corruption including the consultancy wing of large accountancy firms as well.

Mr. Pratap scurried nervously on his feet turning around on the spot as if he was looking for a sweet spot in the chair before sitting. His brows came together again with worry as he continued explaining that accountancy firms would not be bidding, as it was decided by their management. However, his firm had a reputation for integrity which his competitors lacked. He added that a group of senior executives would be most unhappy if his firm got the contract.

Now the picture was becoming clear to Shanker as he nodded and asked to have look at the letters. As Shanker read the letters, a flurry of emotions spun across his face revealing his surprise and shock at the venomous tone, hostility, bold presumptuousness, and the possibly fake accusations against the firm - P.D.L. Associates. The threats sounded vile, desperate, and serious. Clearly, they would stop at nothing to keep their corrupt practices from being exposed. It was clear to him why Mr. Ramesh Pratap had come seeking his help. Shanker sighed heavily as he looked at Mr. Pratap advising him that nothing could be done at present and that he should go ahead with the bid, and in case he was awarded the contract, he could call again since the real danger would begin then.

Shanker assured, "I think the officers of the RMC Bank, who would be concerned with your enquiries, will probably approach you and offer a bribe, or threaten you; that is how it works."

"Yes, I agree with you, but I thought that I should come to seek your advice. If you think it is too dangerous, we will not bid; there are always other contracts and we do a lot of work overseas, particularly in the gulf countries and Malaysia," said Ramesh in vexation.

Shanker reassured Mr. Pratap not to back out of the bid at this stage, that his chances were good and to tender for the job. With that, Ramesh took their cards and left.

The next morning, the operator got a call from a lady called Anupama, who, in an urgent tone, insisted on speaking with Shanker stating that her husband had met with Mr. Dayal the previous day. Upon hearing this, Mr. Shanker Dayal told the operator to immediately connect him.

"Ms Pratap, I hope nothing is wrong. Your husband was very worried that something bad may happen," a very anxious Shanker enquired.

She sounded close to tears as she related, "Mr. Shanker, my husband met with a serious accident last evening while returning from the office. He is presently in a private hospital in Saket in the emergency wing."

"Oh, my goodness, what has happened!" he thought. Shanker could not believe his ears. He felt anger, sadness, and disgust but pulled himself together. He told Anupama, "I will meet you at the hospital in 20 minutes. You can recognize me as I and Shyamala will be in our police uniforms and will arrive in the force's official car." He had his suspicions about the accident.

Shanker was pleasantly surprised to meet the elegant and very attractive lady, Mrs. Pratap.

She was in her early 50s and was standing near the reception, looking very distraught. Her quavering lips though perfectly shaped carried a hint of lip gloss. She was very beautiful, pleasing to the eye in every way. Her sad brown-grey-green eyes looked tired from the tears shed. There was a slight bit of darkness beginning to form beneath her bottom eyelids. Her thick wavy black hair had a dark burgundy tint that skilfully camouflaged the grey strands and was folded neatly at the nape of her neck. A few had escaped and curled softly framing her pretty face. Her fair skin looked smooth and creamy soft to the touch. She wore a beautifully tailored milky brown knee-length skirt suit that accentuated her curvy mature figure. Clearly, she was still a head-turner at this age. Her jewellery was simple, stud teardrop diamond earrings and a fine chain with a similar teardrop pendant. Her perfectly manicured hands carried her proof of marriage on the left third finger. Her shapely legs gave way to perfectly shaped ankles in a simple but fashionable pair of low-heeled pumps.

Turning, Anupama recognized them as they walked through the ER's wide swing doors towards her. After introducing herself, she said, "He is still critical and not allowed visitors. They may have to operate on him due to the severity of his injuries; the extent to which I don't know, but you could talk to Dr. Arvind Basu, who is his attending doctor." She led Shanker to his cabin; he was reluctant to let her in but after seeing Shanker and Shyamala he relented.

An anxious Mrs. Pratap asked Dr. Basu to explain her husband's injuries. In the presence of the police officers, she was told that the accident was actually a case of a hit and run. It seemed as though a large van had collided with Mr. Pratap's car smashing it badly in the process. His driver was killed on impact. The doctor indicated that further details could be received from the Saket Police Station and the officers would be able to see the wreckage. Looking at Mrs. Pratap, Dr. Basu assured, "He will recover for sure, Mrs. Pratap, but some injuries on his legs may not heal and he might require crutches or a wheelchair." She relaxed a little.

Anupama sighed with relief and said, "Thank God, he will live!" She added that hopefully, with advanced treatment in London, he would also recover the use of his legs.

"That is a possible option but our hospitals here are just as good, in fact, many doctors in London are of Indian origin, and some are from our hospitals. We will let him recover first. But he is in no position to talk or communicate, we have just removed his ventilator," Dr. Basu said.

Anupama came across as a gracious lady, but she still seemed concerned for her husband's safety even in the hospital. Shanker comforted her saying that he would post a police guard near her husband's room, for security reasons. He then headed for the police station with Shyamala.

The SHO, Suresh Kumar stood up upon recognizing both Shanker and Shyamala and greeted them. Shanker stated why they were there and the SHO informed him that Mr. Pratap was lucky to be alive. He explained that some good Samaritan had called the hospital for an ambulance which came almost immediately. Mr. Kumar mentioned that the scene of the accident was a short distance from the hospital and immediate attention was given by the paramedics after recognizing and confirming that it was indeed Mr. Pratap who was the accident victim. Also, two senior executives from Mr. Pratap's company were at the scene handling the formalities. They also made contact via phone with the Managing Director of the hospital seeking the best medical treatment and care for Mr. Pratap indicating that money was no issue.

Mr. Suresh Kumar took them to where the crashed vehicles were- the van and BMW. Mr. Kumar confirmed what the doctor had said to them earlier that the van had crashed into the BMW. What they saw made Shyamala gasp and Shanker stop in his approach to the vehicles. The van had its top practically pushed halfway back in a mangled mess taking with it the entire windscreen and bonnet leaving the contents beneath exposed in a twisted wreck. The two side windows were broken and also both the front lights. It looked as if the green HULK had attacked it with an angry slap in the front of the van. Both front wheels were blown out and the tires were a twisted mess around the wheels. The strange thing was there was no blood visible on the van. Meanwhile, the BMW seemed to be curled in a semi-foetal position. The car had its inside rearranged; it looked shaken, stirred, and then dumped with a bang. The entire driver's side was smashed in and pushed back and in at the same time indicating a head-on collision. Both airbags were out and the one on the driver's side seemed to have exploded. Both the vehicles were now good for nothing other than scrap metal. How could anyone have possibly survived this mangled wreck thought Shyamala as she asked in a sad but curious voice, "What happened to the driver of the van?"

Mr. Kumar responded saying, "Oh! We don't know, but the bystanders said he exited the van a few minutes before the accident which was at the traffic light. They saw him running away like the devil was after him. He must have got someone waiting for him. The driver of the BMW died instantly. His body was removed from the scene by paramedics, and his family claimed it later and took it away for cremation."

It is obvious that this was not an accident, but a plot to kill Mr. Pratap, who had somehow defied the odds and survived the accident.

Mr. Kumar went inside to his desk drawer where he retrieved photographs the police had taken at the scene of the accident, photocopied them, and gave the originals to Shanker after taking a receipt from him. He added that the word was out asking the general public if anyone had taken photos at the scene of the accident using their mobile phones to kindly forward those to the police as soon as possible as this would aid in the identification of the driver of the van.

Shanker questioned whether they were able to ascertain the identity of the owner of the van and was told that it had a false number plate; it was not on record with the Transport Department. Mr. Kumar was of the opinion that sooner or later, someone would provide a photograph or some recordings from their mobile phones. Those he promised to forward to Shanker, adding, "These youngsters are pretty quick to whip out their mobile phone to capture the slightest thing they see happening."

After Shanker and Shyamala left the station a little disappointed, they called Mrs. Pratap advising her not to leave her husband alone, even through the night. Shanker was baffled by what had happened and felt guilty about the advice he had given to Mr. Ramesh Pratap. He hadn't expected this level of violence to happen considering that his company had not even won the contract yet. 'Was it a warning to them to withdraw,' he wondered. 'But they did have a very good chance of winning the contract because of their good reputation.' Just at that moment, Shyamala decided to check her mobile phone for the latest news updates and there it was - all about the accident, which had happened minutes after it was announced that Mr. Pratap's company had won the bid for the contract.

She gasped, flashing the mobile device in front of Shanker and he replied grimly, "Well, that speaks for itself. They had been given the work they bid for, but the opposition acted very swiftly. They almost got away with it. But I don't understand why Ramesh was attacked, even if he had passed away, the company would have appointed someone else as the Managing Director and they would have executed the contract under a new team. After all, it is a fairly large consultancy group with international connections."

"I agree, it is not a one-man-show or proprietary company," nodded Shyamala.

Chapter 2

Shanker and Shyamala went to the hospital to see Mr. Ramesh Pratap. He had been moved to a large and expensive room of the hospital, akin to a suite with a sitting room and two bathrooms attached to it. The bandages were all off now and scars were visible but healing. He was dictating something to an assistant, who was recording the same and was being corrected by Ramesh when he wanted to add or delete something. It was the latest machine, and, after all corrections and Ramesh's approval, it would be printed out on a special computer with voice recognition. This was very different from the way they worked in Shanker's office, where they dictated to a stenographer who then typed the contents. The only modernization that they had caught up with was that they used electronic typing machines instead of the old manual ones.

"So, Mr. Ramesh, how are you feeling now? I hope better!" said Shyamala.

Mr. Pratap replied, "Yes, better, but I still have a long distance to go before I fully recover. I am likely to stay a week in the hospital before getting discharged.

I may not be able to attend office for 3 weeks at least." His leg was still bandaged and still very swollen, but he could move it much better than before. Ramesh wasn't worried on that count as he had a very competent staff, and his deputy who was younger was very helpful and efficient.

"Could you tell us who would be wanting to kill you or injure you? We don't know as of yet, but my feeling is that you were targeted for killing," said Shanker.

"After checking thoroughly, this act was done before the contract was awarded. The driver of the van must have been given instructions and if I had been eliminated before the award, they may have had to reconsider. As it is, mainly my efforts and contacts were responsible for bagging the contract. The results were confidential, they could not be disclosed to anyone and were made open only when it was publicly announced," said Ramesh.

Shanker considered what Ramesh had just said carefully but he needed confirmation, so he asked, "Let me understand this properly. Were you the key player in getting the work? Would it have made a difference if you were eliminated? Would they have had to reconsider their decision?"

"I think so, because the Executive Director of that company is very close to me", replied Mr. Pratap.

"Come clean, Mr. Ramesh. We know how these contracts are awarded and there must have been some other considerations which were at play because it was a large and much-coveted contract," commented Shanker.

Ramesh said in a low tone, "If you know the answer then why ask me? Our main competitor would play the same game. The question is who in the group was backing them. Obviously, they were extremely ruthless to have gone to this criminal level of trying to eliminate me. All companies have directors who are strong rivals and, in this group, two wanted the contract very badly and had made a deal of a substantial figure with our rivals."

Shyamala was quite surprised but remained silent while Shanker kept his cool even though he sensed more was to be uncovered. "I can't investigate further unless I have more information. I can come next week to your residence and maybe we can discuss it further. It will not be an easy case to solve Mr. Ramesh unless you give us the full information. It will be difficult for you. Take my advice and don't talk to any journalist or even to your colleagues, particularly your fellow directors as they may expose you to take your position. In the meantime, we will try and trace the driver of the van."

As he was leaving, a message flashed from the SHO to meet him at his office. When Shanker and Shyamala arrived at the office they were first offered tea that was too sweet and too milky, before the SHO took out his mobile phone showing them a recording forwarded by some bystander or shopkeeper. The recording revealed how the accident happened and how and when the driver of the van jumped out and escaped. Even though the image of the driver's face was not very clear it was recognizable. The SHO enlarged the image on the computer and forwarded it to Shyamala's email. They also took a print-out for circulation. He was possibly a truck driver, dressed up as a professional driver, and was carefully and skilfully used by the rival camp. Shanker asked Shyamala to circulate that photo hoping that someone would recognise him and respond.

After contacting Mr. Pratap and arranging a time in the afternoon, Shanker and Shyamala went to Ramesh's house in Westend Colony area. The home was very large and expensive looking with a mini horseshoe driveway that sported an antique fountain similar to the ones C. Bhogilal had on sale with nature come to life through water image. There were 4 steps up to the front glass door of the three-story building which sported a roof garden. They were greeted by a servant who directed them to a fairly large office on the ground floor of his mansion residence. His office was separate from the main house, a type of annexe, with two small rooms attached for his secretary and another middle-aged lady who probably arranged his appointments with his business clients. The walls, bookshelves, and desk were made of polished wood giving the room an expensive antique look. The room sported all the modern electronic communication systems that an office would have inclusive of a printer/scanner along with a widescreen monitor for business or conference calls. Mr. Ramesh Pratap was seated behind his desk. It was a solid mahogany hand-carved wooden desk with a rustic look, like the ones you saw in movies that had secret compartments and hidden spaces that blended skilfully into their carvings.

Shanker felt the need to get straight to the matter leaving out the pleasantries of a greeting stated in a matter-of-fact way, "Mr. Pratap, you better tell us more if you want us to help you, as there are chances you may be attacked again." He paused, then continued, "Never underestimate your own staff, there may be someone who is ambitious and wants to take over your seat."

Ramesh Pratap leaned back in his executive chair and looked regarding Shanker wisely. "While in bed, in the morning, I was thinking of the same thing." There was an uncomfortable weighty silence that a broken by the ringing of a phone. "I have to take this, it's my son calling came from New York." Shanker and Shyamala went to the small conference room to allow him privacy. After the call had ended, Mr. Pratap apologized and explained that his son, who was working with an associate company in New York, was very worried and kept ringing after every 3-4 hours.

"That is very understandable," answered Shyamala and gently asked, "He must be very close to you." Mr. Pratap's face took on a pensive look as he answered, "Yes, so is my daughter, but she is presently working for a multinational company in Mumbai. She recently joined them, so I told her not to come; we talk on video calls."

Becoming all serious again, Mr. Pratap related that when the tender was floated, a college friend of his, who was working for RMC, came to see him and they discussed business. The friend offered to help them win the contract for a price. He did not disclose the amount but only stated that the bargaining was quite substantial and that it would have to be built into the tender price quoted by his company. He indicated that the friend said he would like to give it to Mr. Pratap's firm as their main competitor Singhal & Co. was also bidding very aggressively. They too had contacted RMC Bank and had done some consultancy for them some years ago, which was not that well appreciated. Their main office was in Calcutta, but they had a large branch in Delhi and Bengaluru.

"You also have a fairly large branch in Bengaluru, I understand Mr. Ramesh; it's the I.T. hub of India."

"Yes, you are right Mr. Shanker. We would need to get consultants from our branch in Bengaluru to assist us, or we may even outsource it to our branch."

Shanker was blunt as he asked Ramesh, "Let's get to the point, it is all about kickbacks and maybe you quoted higher kickbacks than them and got the contract."

Ramesh Pratap admitted as if he were at a business meeting, "Kickbacks were not the only issue, I think our tender was better prepared and we also showcased the competency and qualifications of our staff, which was more impressive than theirs. We also have better associates, and we can count on our overseas partners. All these do matter."

Shyamala remarked while glaring at Mr. Pratap, "Yes, of course, but money is the biggest factor." Ramesh kept quiet for a moment and then continued, "Well, we eventually did win the contract. Now who tried to kill me, we have to concentrate on that. It could be someone from inside our own company, an overambitious executive who wants to take my position and who saw this as an opportunity. But he has to be connected to someone high-up in RMC Bank. This is also an angle we have to investigate." Shanker remained quiet as he thought there were a lot shadier dealings involved that Mr. Ramesh Pratap was keeping close to his chest. He looked at Shyamala and could tell she was thinking the same. He thanked Mr. Pratap for his time and they left.

Shanker was sitting in his office when the SHO of Saket called informing Shanker that they were able to trace the driver of the van. He disclosed that the driver was from Rohtak in Haryana, and worked for a small trucking company, which operated vans within the city and adjoining areas delivering provisions and food to grocery shops. However, he seemed to have gone underground disappearing without a trace even though considerable efforts were made to capture him. It had been the manager of the company who identified the driver and the van that was apparently hijacked. The manager disclosed that this driver was well paid and one of their best and he had to have been handsomely paid to do this job. He was not married, as per their knowledge, and had come from Ambala, which he claimed was his hometown. "We can ask the Haryana police to check up his antecedents from Ambala, it is possible we may be able to trace him."

Shanker and Shyamala still had their routine work to attend to in the police station and decided to get down to it since the Ramesh Pratap case had taken up a lot of their time and they had to catch up. Shanker was busy reading a file when the operator called saying that there was a gentleman from Calcutta to see him - Mr. Singhal. He did not have an appointment and wanted to know if he was free. Shanker was surprised but told the operator to send him in and asked Shyamala to join him.

In came Mr. Singhal, a typical Marwari looking, modestly dressed man in his 50s, with a good personality and a pleasant smile. Shanker looked at him and smiled having a fairly good idea why this individual wanted to see him and needed Shyamala to be present. "Now, Mr. Singhal, what can I do for you? It is regarding the contract with RMC Bank, I suppose?"

"You are right. It is about the contract and the subsequent accident that took place and was highlighted by the press."

"Yes, we are at it," said Shyamala. "What is it you want to discuss with us?"

Shanker offered him some tea which he refused. "I have a sugar problem and in government offices, the tea is loaded with sugar," he laughed.

Shanker laughed back, "Can I get you a cup without sugar and you can put your own *sugar-free* in it?" Singhal agreed and the tea came.

Mr. Singhal got right into it. "In business, you can be competitive but maintain good relations. It is the most important thing. We have jointly done some work in UAE with them for an Indian company, and I didn't have any problems collaborating. It is sometimes difficult to do a project by yourself, you need expertise from another company. I do not know who plotted this vicious accident, but it was not me. But I can't speak for my senior executives as they may have been involved, as you well know, kickbacks are part of the game. No contract is awarded without some form of money being given under the table." He continued, "It could also be some ambitious executive working under Ramesh Pratap, who could have plotted it."

Shanker looked at him cautiously, "There are many possibilities, but we have to start somewhere. If we can find the driver of the van, we may be able to get some positive leads."

Mr. Singhal nodded in agreement admitting that is very important but only the police can find the driver. Mr. Singhal spoke very aggressively and said, "Mr. Dayal, we had nothing at all to do with the accident. We didn't hire any van driver to do what he did. That is not our style of working. We have many works in hand and a large staff. We lose some and win some. It is part of the game. But never have we indulged in any form of criminality. I know PBL must have raised a finger at us, as their M.D. was almost killed. Mr. Ramesh Pratap was lucky to have survived such a serious vehicle attack, but I am very glad that he survived. We are competitors, but we are also good friends and meet often at parties. His wife and mine are also close and she always telephones Mrs. Pratap. She and Anupama have coffee together."

They thanked Mr. Singhal for coming in as he departed.

Later, Shyamala received a telephone call from the police headquarters in Ambala. She got all excited when the officer said where he was calling from. This meant they could move forward with the case; the driver of the van had been traced. As the officer continued, her heart sank; what they actually had was his body in the morgue as he was dead. Apparently, he had been stabbed through the heart. They too were trying to trace his family but had not been successful. One of his cousins, who was also a truck driver, had last met him 5 years ago, as he had left Ambala and was doing a driver's job at Rohtak in Haryana. His parents had died some years ago and his brother was also working as a driver in Saudi Arabia. Shyamala thanked the officer for the update and ended the call with a heavy sigh. Shyamala related the conversation to

Shanker. They had come to a dead-end again, this left both Shanker and Shyamala disappointed.

Shanker telephoned Ramesh Pratap and told him the details. Ramesh was disappointed and so was Singhal when Shyamala informed him.

Mr. Pratap mentioned to Shanker that Mr. Singhal went to his office to see him. He told Shanker that even though Mr. Singhal and himself are competitors they still have good relations between them, particularly at the personal level. "He was, of course, unhappy at losing the contract, but said that they had plenty of work in hand, particularly in Eastern India - Assam, where we don't operate," Mr. Pratap explained.

Earlier that day, Mr. Ramesh Pratap went to his office and was not expecting the staff to be waiting to welcome him, with flowers and sweets and garlands. The senior executive, Ashok, garlanded him and shook his hand vigorously, congratulating him for getting the contract. Ramesh modestly said it was a joint effort and the tender had been prepared by the staff. Ashok had coordinated it; he had only gone through the final copy. It was a day of celebration and Ramesh said that when the contract money would come, he would distribute a portion of it to the staff in appreciation of their efforts. "We have a lot of work to do," said Ramesh, "and there are other contracts which are still to be completed."

Having said that, he went into the office he occupied and saw beautiful roses in a huge vase. The sweet aroma permeated his office. His secretary,

Deepika was there waiting to greet him with a passionate kiss. 'Heavens, this woman smelt good always,' he thought. Her kindness and thoughtfulness were what had pulled him to her, apart from her sexy figure. She was always thoughtful and made him feel like he was a KING, the only man on earth. The good Lord Vishnu knew he had a beautiful wife at home who truly loved him but no longer made him her number one. He wanted that passion, excitement, youth, and naughty sensational romantic bliss but she was busy having tea with the corporate wives and heading off to one or the other charitable event. She was very ladylike and shy, smart, and came from a very cultured and respected family. She made him look good in society and stood by him as he built his empire. She made their mansion look luxurious. Deepika on the other hand was more beautiful with a tight body that somehow made him "ZING" at this age. She had been careful to lock the door and clung to him in a loving embrace, but he brushed her away cautioning, "Someone is bound to come, you better unlock the door and get me some tea in a pot. We will continue later." She threw him a sultry look and shook her firm backside just before she went through the door. "Oh Kamadeva, this woman has got me crazy", he muttered as he felt the discomfort in that part of his anatomy. He muttered again as he sat behind this desk… "Oh, Lord Vishnu, forgive me, I love beautiful women."

A few minutes later, his three senior executives came in, greeted him again, and sat down to discuss his fatal accident. "You were very lucky sir, as someone was desperately after you, and was so ruthless that he even got the driver of the van killed in Ambala." They theorized about who it could be but couldn't come out with a definite lead. Mr. Pratap remarked, "I agree with the police that it may not have been Singhal, as they don't indulge in such behaviour and we have competed with them in the past, winning some, losing some, and Mr. Singhal is a personal friend of mine."

"I think we better try and solve the mystery before another incident takes place, and this time it could be lethal," said Ashok. Navin looked at his old friend, and said, "I am as surprised as you are, and have been thinking about it day and night. In fact, I have not had proper sleep for quite a few days. My wife is also worried, and my daughter keeps asking me, "why are you worried Papa, you don't have many shares in the company, and it is making profit anyway, so why do you have to worry, to which I have no answer for her."

Shanker Dayal sat in his office thinking aloud; he couldn't focus properly. Running frustrated fingers through his thick mane, sighed and tried again. He theorized, "Navin, do you think it was an inside job in your organization, Singhal's organization, or PBL's organization? There may have been someone in your bank who was connected to Singhal and badly wanted the contract, as we all know money was involved." Shanker stood up and begin pacing in the office. "Now, who in your company was going to benefit from a deal with Singhal CEO? It could be you or one of your directors or some senior executives." He stopped, looked at the water jug on his desk with narrowed eyes, and mumbled, "It is all guesswork right now. We need to investigate more."

Chapter 3

Shyamala was sitting on her chair and daydreaming about this charming young man she had met at a tea party, who worked with some multinational company. He was a few inches taller than her and had a handsome face with pleasant eyes. He had kept talking to her about good things without being personal, which she liked. He had requested her to get him another cup of tea without milk, which she willingly did, and he thanked her and gave her a big smile.

Vikram was quite surprised that she was an IPS officer and remarked that she didn't look like one to which she asked, "What do I look like?" "Oh, that is difficult to answer", he smiled. "You are too soft and elegant to be an IPS officer. I can't imagine you arresting someone. Please give me your card in case I need your help". Shyamala laughed but gave him her card all the same just before one of his colleagues called him away. She was confident that he would telephone her and ask her out for a date.

As she lingered on with her daydreaming, her phone rang. It was him. Not wanting to make her excitement apparent, she answered pleasantly, "Hello?"

"Hi Shyamala, this is Vikram, how are you?" 'Oh, my goodness, his voice sounds so hypnotic and soothing', she thought. "I am well thanks."

"Shyamala, how about having dinner with me tomorrow?"

She agreed to the day after that, and he fixed the rendezvous at the 'Oh Calcutta' the restaurant in Nehru Place for 7:30 p.m. She rather liked that restaurant; it had very good Bengali food, particularly seafood. She couldn't sleep that night thinking of him but then realized that it would be their first date and it takes long before things 'gel' if they do at all.

The 'Oh Calcutta' Restaurant was a nice cosy place to eat with its ever-warm inviting window-like glass front. The lights behind the chairs against the walls made it seem like square yellow diamonds sparkling behind you while the basket-designed shades on the lights above cast a rich glow over the place. The glass chandeliers gave the right amount of light for friendly conversation and enjoyment. Its walls were lined with seating accommodation as well as down the middle. There he was, waiting for her. Looking all casual and cool as if he has just stepped off of the catwalk in Paris, like a male model. He wore a silky light brown shirt with a black leather jacket over it. His jeans clung to his thighs expressing masculinity and power. His physique demanded attention as he shifted his weight from one leg to another moving with a graceful yet sensual swag. His comfortable brown leather loafers matched this shirt. The man looked like a real-life Greek god.

His face was smooth and neatly shaved showing the hint of dimples on both sides, just that sexy beard along the edge of his jawline and around his mouth and chin. Damn ... those lips, full plump and ... ever distracting. His eyes, like Hrithik Roshan, took in every detail as she approached him.

Shyamala had taken extra care with her appearance opting for a saree instead of casual attire and makeup. She was quite satisfied with her appearance in the mirror, which showed no trace of being an officer at all. She was looking stunning in one of her favourite sarees, bought in Lucknow. The blouse was light rust brown cotton, and a chiffon saree complimented the blouse with rust-brown stripes in the skirt and a rich embroidered pattern across the body and shoulder. She used simple costume jewellery and low-heeled sandals with a matching clutch purse to complete her accessories. She had brushed her now open shoulder-length hair until it shone, and the natural big curls relaxed like waves around her face and shoulders. Vikram smiled and held her hand as he guided her to one of the tables in a corner. He kept gazing at her, and eventually gushed, "You are very pretty. I could never have imagined an IPS officer like you." 'Oh, wow,' he thought, 'brains body and beauty; the entire package.' 'I don't mind being arrested by her any day or night for that matter.' She blushed slightly embarrassed.

They placed their order before easing into comfortable conversation. He told her about himself and that he was from a highly educated family.

His father was a professor of Economics at a leading college and his mother a headmistress in a well-known private school, where he had also studied, before joining I.I.T.

Several times she had to remind herself to look down and not gaze at his ever so kissable lips. It was a struggle to concentrate on what he was saying. He told her that he now worked with this consultancy company, whose office was in Gurgaon, and he commuted daily from Vasant Vihar which took him 40 minutes to reach but more time on the way back. After dinner, he offered to drop her back, but she politely declined, stating she had her official car given to her, in case of being called in for some emergency. Vikram could not hold back his emotions anymore and to her surprise, he took her round the corner away from the bright lights of the restaurant and gave her a deep long kiss. He had been waiting to do this all night. 'Ohhh… she's so beautiful, so feminine, so smart, oh goodness, and an officer of the law! … was he dreaming …', he wondered. He had never felt this way about a woman before. He had been around women and knew he was good-looking and financially strong and could have any woman he wanted but this woman right here … ooohh… there was something about Shyamala that he just couldn't help himself. He kissed her passionately and, to her surprise, she also responded. This passion was blissful and engaging sending off an alarm. The kind of passion that would trip an alarm on a bank vault. 'What was that sound,' she thought. There it was again. It was her mobile phone.

They were both breathless as she reluctantly eased away. His eyes looked dreamy. He chuckled nervously as did she; both were slightly embarrassed at this point. He gave her a quick hug as she nervously retrieved her phone. It was the driver calling to find out if she was ready. She told him she was and to pick her up at the restaurant. Vikram was reluctant to let her go. "I don't feel like leaving you, but we must meet again soon." She assured him that she was ok as they walked into the light of the restaurant. He stood like the proper gentleman until her car came and opened the door for her. She nodded in agreement to meet again soon and gave him a peck on the cheek as she seated herself. At this point, the driver's eyes grew a little round since he had never seen Shyamala in such close company of a man before. He closed the door as they wished each other good night. She reached home all moony-eyed, in another world.

The next day, her neighbour and friend teased her. "Where did you go Shyamala, all dressed up and looking pretty? Who is this boy you are dating?" She felt a little embarrassed but gave her friend a hint. "Can you remember the guy I was talking to at the tea party? Well, that's the one and I like him a lot." Her friend seemed a little surprised but happy for her saying, "I hope it works out, Shyamala. He would be a great catch."

The next day, when she was sitting in the office, Shanker came and looked at her and said, "You are looking different, Shyamala. How did your date go?"

She blushed at that. 'He must have come to know of it because of that tell-tale driver, she thought.' Shanker continued, "You deserve a good boy and I think you appear to have found one. Don't give him up or get disillusioned like you generally do, no one is perfect. Why don't you call him for a cup of tea at the office to let him see where you work? He will be very impressed."

'So, there it is', she thought, 'he wants to gauge Vikram's intentions.' "You want to meet him, that is why you are suggesting it?" she asked.

"Well, you are like a sister to me, so I have to see to your best interests."

'Hmm ... he did have a point there and maybe it wasn't such a bad idea.' So, she decided, "OK, I will call him soon, and then we can go out for lunch." Shanker looked at her with a wide grin and stated in a brotherly tone, "Oh no, you go. I don't want to spoil things by coming with you. Three is a crowd, remember?" Shyamala laughed and telephoned Vikram to invite him to her office and then to lunch. He remarked that it was Saturday and why was she in the office to which she replied, "You don't work on Saturdays, but we do, you see." He agreed to come and Shanker looked forward to meeting him.

Vikram came dressed casually but smartly, in a flowery silk shirt, and dress pants, and shook hands with Shanker firmly. Shanker gave him a big smile and motioned him to sit and wasted no time getting to know more about Vikram. He asked, "So, you are an IITian. What is your father's name? Did he teach there?"

"No, he was with Delhi University at the Delhi School of Economics, Prof. Manohar Sharma is my father. A lot of his students joined the I.A.S, I.P.S. and multinational companies."

"Oh, I attended his classes when I took a short course in Economics, though it was a long time ago. I remember him clearly," Shanker replied. "He was a very good teacher and because of him, I took Economics as my subject later." "Please give him my regards. I don't know if he will remember me. Is he still teaching?" Vikram explained that this father had retired but was with a coaching academy and quite satisfied with teaching students for admission to colleges. "He can never stop teaching. It is his life." "It is good to have professors like him who are so dedicated," commented Shanker.

A bit later, they slipped out for lunch to Pandara Road and just managed to find a table in a restaurant that served tandoori. The manager recognized Shyamala as she had eaten there before with Shanker and moved them to a better table. They slipped into a comfortable conversation with her asking about the type of consultancy Vikram did. He told her that it varied since the company did things like the reorganization of offices, the development of new operations systems, and improved communication operations, among others. He teased saying, "It will be quite boring if I tell you everything." She smiled but encouraged him to continue. He indicated that the company did a lot of work for foreign companies, particularly in the U.K., and Australia, the U.S.A., but he was not in that division. He lamented that in the US, one would have to be there for a period of 3- 6 months on a temporary visa and then, one is required to work 10-12 hours a day to finish the assignment at the earliest time frame. He indicated that it was a tough job, but they paid well and, by now, having gotten used to it and he had started enjoying it. He commented that he might be going on a short assignment to Australia next month. "I really like the country, particularly, Sydney, their main city. Why don't you take leave and join me there? It is a fun city," he said all enthused. "Your ticket and stay will be on me." He sounded excited. "You could take two weeks off easily. You will love it." She maintained a facial expression that he couldn't read. "Think about it, Shyamala. These chances don't come easily," he laughed.

She laughed heartily and cautiously said, "I know, but I think it would be difficult for me and scandalous too. We in the police force, still have some ethics and everyone in the building will be gossiping about it. After all, we are not married, not even engaged."

"I understand. I should not have made the offer." He was so excited that he didn't think of what he was asking of her and of her reputation in both her personal and professional life. He honestly expressed his thoughts of it being best to proceed calmly and not rush with it and if they found each other suitable, they could think about marriage, after all, they were at that age, came from good backgrounds, and had a mutual liking for each other. To his honest expression, she was pleasantly surprised and said she too felt the same way and also thought of many of her friends with broken marriages. Thinking she had said too much too soon, she hastily replied, "I must get back to my tacky office and interview some criminals. Some of them are really horrible and frightening. I am talking of women prisoners; you can't even guess that they would be capable of such crimes. Much worse than the men." She needed to slow down and take her time to really get to know this man. This passion was distracting, and she needed to focus.

He dropped her off at the police headquarters, with a flame of desire burning inside him, which she was quick to sense, and as she got off, she smiled, "You have my card. How about yours?" Without hesitation, he gave his card, which read - Vice-President, KBL Associates. Giving it a glance, she went upstairs. And as she sat down, she suddenly remembered that it was the same company that they were in serious investigation with, whose Managing Director, had almost been killed in a car crash and the driver of the van had been murdered in Ambala. Her investigative instincts kicked in immediately as she thought it to be a strange coincidence and promptly went to see Shanker and placed the card before him.

"Uh! Who is this person," asked a confused Shanker. "The man I introduced you to before lunch," said a very serious Shyamala.

"Oh, the boy whose father is a professor? He looks like a suitable match for you," Shanker declared.

"You have not seen the card properly," Shyamala replied with emphasis.

He looked again, eyes opening wide then frowning said, "What a coincidence that he works for KBL Associates. They have over 600 associates working for them. It doesn't mean anything, and he is possibly in middle management. In any case, to be on the safe side for your sake, I will check up on him." She felt reassured and was glad that she had put her cards on the table. She didn't think more about it until he telephoned the next day and said, he was speaking from Bangalore, where they had a large office and did the IT work for the southern states, particularly Kerala and Chennai.

"So, you have to travel a lot?" Shyamala wondered if he was involved in the case in any way.

"Yes and no, sometimes when we get a joint project, I am constantly visiting Cochin. I love the place, just outside the city are lovely resorts, you must visit some of them."

"Hmmm ..." she muttered.

"Yes, a lot of foreigners come for the famous Kerala oil massages and cures, overweight people from the gulf come to lose weight. I am coming back to Delhi on Sunday and will give you a call and maybe we can meet for lunch or dinner on Monday."

Shyamala reported briefly to Shanker about the conversation with Vikram. Shanker informed her that so far as his contacts had told him, the boy was alone abroad at the time of the accident and if his company's very senior executives were in any way involved, he would have nothing to do with it. He was good at his job and enjoyed a good reputation in the company.

"I don't think there is any conflict of interest here", Shanker commented.

Shyamala breathed a sigh of relief.

"If you like him very much, continue dating him. He is a good catch, like I said, someone like him can easily find a switch in another I.T. company." Changing the subject, he said, "Now, let's talk about his boss Mr. Ramesh Pratap. I have been busy with the investigation and Mr. Ramesh Pratap is not what he seems to be; a wheeler-dealer shall we say. He has made contacts with politicians and pays them handsomely for various deeds. He is close to the party in power in Karnataka, and as such, his company's position in Bangalore will become better. He is also a big womanizer and has a mistress in every part, as they say, and is having an affair with his secretary, who is a former model, and he makes no bones about it. He also has another beauty whom he has promoted to a high position, and she looks after the company's P.R. in Bangalore. In Cochin, he also has one to keep him company when he visits, which is quite often."

Chapter 4

Shanker telephoned Ramesh Pratap and inquired about his injury and health in general and asked if he was attending the office or working from home. He said he was working from his house till late hours in the evening, taking care of the employees. He had even arranged meals, tea, and snacks to be catered to them. Shanker indicated that he would come over for a few minutes.

Upon his arrival, Shanker was shown to Mr. Pratap's large office where he found the businessman busy at his desk. After greeting each other he showed Shanker how his leg was healing and asked Shanker if their investigations had provided any leads. Shanker then asked him if knew Navin Kochar. Ramesh hesitated for a moment and replied, "Uh … Yes. We have been dealing with him at RML Bank. He is a director now and has done well for himself. We were in the university at the same time and used to meet at the cafe and at mutual friends' parties. Why? Did you happen to meet him recently?"

"Yes", answered Shanker. "He came to meet me in the office. We still have a lot of common friends. In fact, his wife is from our community, and we have common relatives. But he came to discuss the contract with me and had nothing really to add, though he was involved with it. The decision was taken at a higher level. As there is a large public sector holding in it, he hinted that politicians and the concerned minister may have played a role in awarding the contract." Ramesh kept quiet, then said, "This is how things work in India. I would say it is now a worldwide phenomenon and we have to play the game to win. In some countries, the amounts are much larger, particularly in Eastern Europe."

At that moment, an attractive lady brought tea service and elegantly poured it into the cups. Shanker couldn't take his eyes off her, she was very attractive, and her face looked familiar. Tall and leggy like a model and had beautiful shiny hair with makeup that enhanced her natural beauty. Her office attire was not tight, but it fell softly against her body in an appealing way. When she left the room Shanker could not help but ask, "Mr. Ramesh, was she a model or an actress?"

"She was a model and worked for one of the leading advertising companies and used to model for soaps and shampoos. She was quite popular and did well for herself, but then, after a certain age, they retire you and find younger models. She bargained and got a good compensation, and then joined us. She is very well educated and comes from a decent middle-class family. Her father was with the Income Tax department and retired as the commissioner in Agra. She and her mother never shifted to Agra and kept their government accommodation, and later bought a flat near Chanakya Puri."

"Is she married?" Shanker enquired.

"No, I don't think so. I should know."

"Are you married, Mr. Shanker?"

"No, I had a long affair with a classmate, but she ditched me and went off with a friend and they settled in New Jersey."

"Oh, so you are eligible, you must be in your middle or late 40s."

"You are right", Shanker grinned.

"Why don't you go dating with Surya? She would be a suitable match for you. Should I help?"

"Yes, but would she be interested in a boring Assistant Police Commissioner," he laughed.

"I think you underestimate your charm, Mr. Shanker. You would be quite a catch and she is also getting along in age and is from a similar background."

Surya came to ask Shanker if he wanted another cup of tea. Ramesh hastily said, "I need to go to the house for something, she will look after you."

She smiled at him, "Is he trying to matchmake again?"

"Yes. Nothing wrong with it. He told me about your background, and, in some ways, we are similar. My girlfriend left me high and dry for another man. She is now married and in New York. Policemen, of course, are a boring lot, but if you are interested, we could meet for dinner on Saturday?"

"Oh well, there are some nice places in Select City Mall. We can meet at 7:30 p.m.," she replied.

He reached the mall a little earlier, dressed casually in khaki dress pants, loafers, and a dark green long-sleeved shirt. It not only complimented his complexion but also showed off his physique which remained mostly hidden under his uniform. Not wanting to look dowdy next to her, he ensured that his appearance was classy and casual. He had trimmed his moustache and shaved away any shadow of a beard. His accessories were a wristwatch and a very fine chain around his neck which was almost invisible. He waited for her near the entrance of the huge concrete and glass structure with its semi-dome-shaped pattern and its well-manicured garden-like appearance. He saw her alighting from an Uber and entered the mall with her without the formalities as the guards seemed to know him, they even saluted him.

"Huh? They are private guards and not from the police," she quizzed.

"Yes, but they know me as they saw me getting off a police vehicle."

"You came in a police vehicle?"

"Yes, I don't keep a personal car." He explained, "The official vehicle is not a jeep but a sedan, but with the official plate, and the personal security officers in the guise of drivers, they have to guard me also." She looked worried.

"Don't be worried. Nothing will happen to me, or you, when we are together."

They went to a nice Burmese restaurant of her choice, and they seated themselves. The restaurant was very cosy and comfortable. The walls on one side had flowers, fans, and other decorations engraved with a booth-like long chair that lined the wall. The other wall was accessories with a shelf displaying cultural clay figurines by the pairs and below, softly cushioned booth seating against the wall. There were tables down the middle with passages on both sides. The far back had a tea bar with high stool seating. The ceiling lighting was a golden glow blanked by wide framed basket-looking shades. She ordered unfamiliar dishes with names he had never heard before, which he picked on pretending to relish them. His facial expression, however, soon gave him away; either that or the embarrassing noises of his stomach which he wasn't sure she heard.

She looked at him and laughed, "I don't think you are enjoying this, are you?"

He sheepishly replied, "It's ok, but I am a typical Punjabi, my choice is tandoori food."

"So am I. Actually, my father as you know is a Punjabi and for his sake, my mother has become an expert tandoori chef."

He found himself staring at her from time to time and wanted to get to know her better. He commented, "You are very attractive. How is it that you haven't found a smart young man from a rich family?"

"At heart, I am very simple. I have been a model and met all the dandies, but I found them very superficial. I dated quite a few, but I don't think we clicked."

"Let's meet again, and get to know each other better," suggested Shanker.

She agreed, and they settled for their next date the following week at one of the farmhouse restaurants in Chhatarpur.

Shanker was waiting for Surya at a restaurant on MG Road, inside the complex of an exclusive hotel that was mainly used for marriages but was also part of a five-star international group. He still did not trust this lady; she could have well been planted by Ramesh as a spy. What had appeared to be strange was the easy manner in which she had agreed to date Shanker and even in the mall, her behaviour appeared so pretentious to him. He would have to be very careful as Ramesh and his group were under investigation and it was quite a coincidence that Shyamala had also been asked out on a date by Vikram and was under his spell. It was strange to Shanker, with his investigative skills, he would have to unravel what he thought maybe a plot conceived by Ramesh Pratap.

He turned to look at the door and saw the waiter usher in a stunning lady; all heads turned to watch her. She came and sat in the chair next to Shanker and apologized for the delay. "I just could not get an Uber. I had to request the manager of the office to help out and he arranged an office car for me."

Shanker knew that she was privileged, so it would not have been difficult for her to make such an arrangement. He could not take his eyes off her in her dress, which was quite revealing. The colours complimented her complexion as well as her figure. The deep V of her short blouse was covered by a thin shawl giving a tantalizing hint of the swell of her firm breasts. The shawl continued to her hips revealing her trim waist and flat stomach. There was a reflective stone in place at her belly button that glittered with her every stop; mesmerizing one with every step of her long, well-shaped, manicured feet in high-heeled transparent slippers. He woke up from his thoughts as she teased, "A penny for your thought," as she smiled.

"Oh, nothing much, what could I be thinking when I am sitting next to you? No compliment would do you justice, but we policemen do not know the meaning of romance and how to serenade a lady. In our line of profession, we meet all sorts of errant women. We know how to deal with them, but with you it is different. I will have to take a course on '*How to woo a lady*.'"

"You don't have to take a course. You are quite natural, that is your best asset. The other men play smart, but I can guess what is in their mind by one look."

"Oh, yes? Tell me, what is in their mind?" Shanker grinned with the hint of a mischievous glint in his eyes.

"You jolly well know it. They just want to add another feather to their cap to later boast about it."

"Is it that bad? I wouldn't have imagined it so."

"Can I call you Shanks?"

He laughed. 'My word', he thought, 'she is getting familiar now.'

"You know Shanks, God, if he makes you very attractive, he is doing you no favour. You must have read a lot about Hollywood beauties, most of them had difficult personal lives and divorce was common among them. Men do not like women who outshine them. It is the same in India."

"I don't know what to say, Surya, but I never thought along these lines, as I rarely date a woman like you, except on duty. I have met some beautiful women who were married to rich men just for their money. They cheated on them, even murdered them."

"Anyway, I am not dating for your money", she mused continuing "though some police officers do make a lot of money on the side. I liked you, the minute you came to meet Mr. Pratap, and then we are also from a similar background."

Shanker was so stunned by what she had been saying that he just smiled and said, "I am not a romantic, but I like you and I think we will get along well together."

They had a light dinner, and he ordered some red wine for her, which she had enjoyed drinking. He let her do the talking while he listened. He was fascinated by her but still could not get it out of his mind that she may have been planted.

After dinner, they walked in the beautiful adjoining garden, and he caught her hand but was hesitant to kiss her as there were other families walking in the garden. "Maybe next time, we can find a lonely spot," he whispered in her ear.

Chapter 5

Shanker called Shyamala and asked her if she met the young man Vikram Sharma again. "I know he dated you and I will not ask more, it is your personal life."

She blushed, "If you are asking if I slept with him, no, I haven't. I admit that I was tempted to, but we didn't reach that stage. We were both a little cautious, and yes, he did kiss me and all that, but nothing more."

Then she asked him, "You also dated the secretary of Mr. Pratap - Surya, a former model, a good looker. You must have been fascinated by her. I won't ask more because you are my boss."

"Well, I think we both didn't go beyond that point. What I wanted to discuss is that to me it looked very well planned, or do you think my mind is being over suspicious?" he asked.

Shyamala became thoughtful as she replied, "I was thinking the same before I came here. It looked too much like a coincidence."

Shanker and Shyamala looked at each other, and then Shanker declared, "He is playing on us?

If so, we will play along with him. I don't mind and neither do you, I suppose, as they are both attractive propositions."

Shyamala laughed and said, "I have never seen you so excited about someone."

"Don't tell me Shyamala, you have also fallen for Vikram. By the way, where is he?"

"I think he is in a resort near Cochin, but he should be back soon. I think he said he would be back by Sunday. He should have come back yesterday," she said.

"Don't worry. He will give you a call as soon as he is back. Just check your phone and see if there is a missed call." Shyamala doubted him but took out her phone and went to the missed calls, and sure enough, his call was there. "Oh, my goodness,' she gasped. "What are you? A voodoo man or something." "I told you", laughed Shanker, "that he would telephone you as soon as he gets back. In fact, he may have telephoned you from Cochin also, and probably due to some connection problem, he couldn't get through. He is not going to leave you Shyamala."

"You mean it is not put on, but for real?" she asked.

"I think so, to me it looks very possible, but I can't say, because young men these days date many girls before they decide and vice-versa. Marriage among a certain class is becoming old-fashioned, and I know some live-in couples, who are unmarried."

"What about Surya? She is getting on in the game and must be desperate to find someone suitable and who could be more suitable for her than you," she laughed.

They both laughed, and Shanker said, "Let us see what happens in the next few days, but don't get seduced so easily, as he may then use you and ditch you afterward."

Shyamala telephoned Vikram and apologised for not taking his call. Her phone was on silent as she was at one of those boring meetings, they regularly have to discuss the law-and-order situation in the capital, which was becoming more difficult every day.

He laughed, "I can understand, Shyamala. But you must get away from it and relax. How about having some wine with me at the *Yellow Brick*, in the hotel next to Khan Market? I am sure you know the place."

"Of course, I know it. 7:30 I'll be there. And ask them to cool some white wine or champagne for me," she said jokingly.

"Sure, I will be ready with a glass of cold champagne, when you arrive."

Shyamala deliberately arrived 15 minutes late and apologised, "I got caught by one of the seniors at the last minute. A murder case in Chandni Chowk."

Vikram didn't look disappointed and poured some cold champagne for Shyamala.

"I get tipsy on champagne, so don't try to seduce me and, if you do, I will put you in the lock up," she laughed.

"So, tell me, where did you go?"

"Oh, I went to Cochin and there is a company, part of a multinational, whom we deal with an overseas collaboration, even the IT work in Saudi and the UAE, is done by us. This company is not that large but is pretty successful."

"I had to put in long hours, of course, two assistants came from our Goa office to help me. This company makes major parts for our trawler, a lot of assembly work and machinery is imported from China, as usual."

"Then, I had a day off and I went to a resort called Pawar, not far from Cochin, and relaxed - got myself massaged - not from women, but mainly men as I have a slight back pain problem. So, these massages are pretty useful."

"I don't believe you, the girls at the resort must have given you the massage," she said and laughed. "I wish that were true, but Cochin is not Bangkok."

"So, what are your plans now," she asked, "Are you going to be in India or going abroad or something."

"I don't know," he said, "We have also to start the reorganization work of RMC and I am part of the team and leader of some of the teams, who are to be doing the work."

Then he looked at her suddenly very serious and said, "Shyamala, I know what you are thinking, and it is not the case. You know what I mean, and I don't have to explain it to you."

She said, "It certainly did evoke curiosity, which may be there could be a connection. However, I am glad that you have clarified it through your own initiative."

"Then let us enjoy our meal, drink good wine, and then, after a few good hugs and kisses, I will drop you home, or if you have a car then your driver can take you back. I am not the type who dates girls and then beds them and uses them," he explained.

"I know, don't forget that I am a policewoman and can read peoples' minds, we are taught that, particularly lecherous men's minds," she hinted pouting a little.

He laughed, and commented, "Shyamala you are very attractive, which man wouldn't like to take you to bed, many must have tried, I am sure."

This, she confirmed saying, "Yes, they are trying all the time, particularly some of our senior officers – Shanker ji excluded - he is a very decent person and treats me like a younger sister."

"So, I noticed," said Vikram. He took her hand as they went towards the entrance, where she had called the car.

"Next time I go to Cochin, I am going to persuade you to come with me. You will love the massages and other attractions as well."

"You are tempting me, Vikram. I may agree." As they passed one of the large pillars that cast a shadow and was a bit out of direct view, he gently pulled her behind it, giving her tempting mouth a long and passionate kiss to which she responded equally with passion as she ran her fingers through the hair at the nape of his neck deepening the kiss in the process. This caught him off guard as he desperately struggled to keep his passion in check. The fury of desire was threatening to break free as she hugged him strongly. Her soft tight body and the mere smell of her had him panting for control as he leaned into her warm body. 'Oh my god', he thought, 'help me to stay in control as she too mindless yearned for his touch; the feel of him pulsating into her as they revealed in the moment. Her soft skin felt so good under his touch as he ran his fingers along her arm, over her shoulder, and down her back settling at her waist. He circled her waist with his shaking hands to gently push her away, but they had a mind of their own; they drew her to him. 'Oh, wow', he thought 'she feels so good against his body.' She had a passion that totally blew his mind almost sending him over the edge of self-control. "Shy..." he purred as hot blood flowed through their veins and enjoyed it thoroughly until she heard the number of her vehicle being announced. 'Bit of an anti-climax,' she thought, but she loved it thoroughly.

He let go, with great reluctance, as it was not a place where there was privacy to continue. They slowly walked towards her car giggling like teenagers at this behaviour and him using her purse to cover the evidence of his desire as he willed himself fully under control.

When she reached home, she telephoned him expressing the pleasure of his company. "Vikram, it was one of the most enjoyable evenings I have had in a long time. We must complete what we left unfinished next time."

"Definitely Shyamala, you were really terrific. I couldn't even imagine that a policewoman could be like you, we all have a different view or idea of different women, but you are really amazing, I would say. I think we are going to have a serious affair and we will both enjoy it."

She gave him a noisy kiss on the phone. "Next time, we can do FaceTime, it would be fun." Then bid him good night.

There was a bit of a buzz in the office when Shyamala arrived and wondered what it was all about. She went and knocked on Shanker's door and then entered. He was busy dictating to the stenographer and motioned her to come later.

He called her on the intercom half an hour later and told her that they were having a meeting in the conference room. After half an hour, some evidence had emerged. Her mind was buzzing with various theories, but she couldn't come to any conclusion.

They met in the conference room, and the SHO of Saket was present; an officer specially deputed by the Ambala police was also present. The Saket SHO started by saying that the van and all its antecedents had been traced, but they were of no relevance as the driver Kurhu, had been set up by someone from any of the three organisations involved in the contract. It could be someone from RMC itself who did not want the study done, maybe because they were benefiting in some way with the present setup. Navin Kochar had hinted as such, but it was just a vague hint.

The other party, which was likely to win was Singhal & Co., who were competing for the tender. They certainly would have benefited financially from being awarded the tender. The sweet talk by Mr. Singhal was all put on and he appeared to be an expert at it. But there was nothing to indicate their involvement.

PBL Associates had won the contract. So it could be that there was someone within the organisation who wanted Ramesh Pratap out of the way, to take order himself and benefit from the kickbacks on the billings. This was normal. If they had a link with somebody in RMC, they could easily use overfilling or other such means to earn extra and split it between themselves.

The police officer from Ambala was listening, and when his team came, he told them that he had thoroughly investigated the background of Kurhu, and what he gathered was that he was from a village near Ambala, where his clan lived, they were relatively low-level people and not well educated, and are mainly engaged as drivers of trucks, buses, etc. and ran taxis and scooter rickshaws, etc. None of them had gone beyond 10th class or attended university. But they managed and earned enough to lead a lower middle-class type of life; some also joined the railways as signalmen or cleaners etc. They managed and helped each other.

Kurhu was well known to them. He became a driver at a young age, after completing class 8 at a government school. He was not married and was fond of drinking and eating good food. He lived in a quarter with colleagues from a similar background in Delhi, in a low-class type of building, slightly away from the slums. He was, to their knowledge, not criminal-minded, and had never been arrested for any offense.

They had not been able to find any clues as to who would have murdered him. It is obvious that he was killed because of some connection with the contract. But whoever organised it, or did it, they did not know. They had failed to find the culprit or the gang which may have organised it. There was some indication that it could be someone from Meerut, an area famous for crime and criminals.

It was populated by Muslims who had not migrated to Pakistan at the time of partition. They were originally from U.P. and settled there, and were mainly farmers, or engaged in animal husbandry, and most of the meat was butchered there and exported to the cities in U.P.

The meeting ended without any conclusions and Shanker, though disappointed, didn't show it and paid compliments to everyone for their hard work and hoped some clue would emerge about who hired the van driver and later had him killed. The two events were definitely linked, they all agreed.

Shaker got a telephone call from Surya, which he had been waiting for. He knew she would telephone over some excuse or the other. He acted pricey and told her that he was busy and would contact her after a few days and they could then meet. He was attracted to her but was not certain about her motives as she had emerged from nowhere after the case started. He was suspicious that she was planted by Ramesh. He was quite sure that she was a diversionary tactic planted by Ramesh. He wondered how Shyamala had been getting along with Vikram. He called her on the intercom and asked her to come inside. She came with a cup of tea in her hand and sat down in front of him, offering him a biscuit to eat. He took one from the packet and ate it, but it was no fun eating it without dipping it in a cup of tea.

"Surya telephoned and I told her we can meet after a day or two."

"She must have been disappointed, I am sure. She seems to be attracted to you, that is my impression."

"I am not too sure," said Shanker, "I still feel that she is playing games and the perpetrator is Ramesh."

"Tell me Shyamala, why would a lady like her take interest in a police officer?" Shanker sounded very suspicious. "She is used to a different kind of environment, isn't she?"

"I don't think so," replied Shyamala, "After all, she is the daughter of an IRS officer, which is quite similar to our lifestyles." "Agreed, she became a model and started leading a glamorous life, but that period is over, and she is back to her familiar life. She could have married a glamorous male model or an actor or someone in the film industry, but I think it didn't work out."

"But tell me", said Shanker, "How has she suddenly emerged from the woods and contacted me when the fruit of this case started ripening, in which no doubt her boss is involved?" "That is quite a surprise," said Shyamala, "But it would be the same for Vikram and me, how did he contact me in a similar manner?"

"I don't want to hide anything from you, but I met him very recently and we had dinner at a restaurant called *Yellow Brick*, near Khan market. He was very charming and fawning all over me. I found him very attractive and difficult to resist. After dinner, he took me to a quiet corner and almost made love to me. My car was announced, so we couldn't go further in our passion, but he was irresistible. I frankly don't know what to do, as I have 'fallen for him'. I don't know whether he will propose to me, but if he does, I will say yes."

Shanker heard Shyamala and was not surprised, as Vikram was an attractive boy and a good catch if there were no strings attached.

"I don't know what to say, Shyamala, except to be very sure that it is genuine and not a game being played, as the stakes are very high."

She left feeling relieved. Shyamala knew she could trust Shanker completely and his advice was generally right.

Surya telephoned Shanker and said that her drama society was putting up a play at the India Habitat Centre. She said she had a prominent role in it, and it was directed by a well-known director.

"I am inviting you and would very much like you to come." Shanker couldn't refuse and did not want to refuse; his heart wouldn't allow it.

"Sure, it will be my pleasure. I will come at 7 p.m. and hope to see you perform. I have seen this play before, performed by another group, but it is a very interesting play, and I wouldn't like to miss it, particularly as you are acting in it."

Shanker dressed casually and went to the Stein Auditorium at the Habitat Centre. He put another dollop of aftershave lotion, an expensive French one, which someone had gifted to him. He noticed that even since he shifted to the head office, he was getting presents from someone or the other every day.

He had been given tickets for the front row and he sat comfortably and, as soon as he sat down, a photographer clicked with the flashlight coming on his face, and another liveried waiter in white asked him if he would like to drink beer, wine, or whisky. First, he refused, then said, "Ok, I will have a small bottle of beer." The waiter brought a well-known foreign brand and poured it into his glass. He placed some peanuts and crisps on a plate with the beer.

Everyone was wondering who this VIP was, and why he was getting special treatment. He heard someone whisper, "He is a senior police officer. 'I have seen his photographs in the newspapers."

The play was a sort of musical with an orchestra and dancing, both Indian classical and filmy songs, with a love story woven into it, modified by a budding author, a young man in his 30s, who was introduced in the beginning.

Surya had a role in it as the sister of the heroine and he was impressed with her acting skills. She sang a filmy type of song melodiously. She looked more attractive on the stage as she was wearing fancy clothes and makeup.

He enjoyed the play and sat through a comedy quiz with funny parts. After it was over, he got up and went outside and saw Surya waiting for him. She had removed her makeup and was wearing a nice salwar kameez.

"So, did you like the play," she asked, "We have a theatre group and we put on a performance at least once a month. I enjoy acting very much and tried in Bollywood but failed. They have their cartels, and it is difficult to break in unless you are willing to - you know what with the producers and directors."

Shanker stated, "Yes. I have heard of these cartels; they are very strong and controlled by old and well-established families. It is difficult to break in unless, as you said, you play along with them the way they want to."

"It would have been difficult for you as you come from a different background."

He suggested that she join him for a snack or a bit at the Oberoi since it was just around the corner. She readily agreed but then her attention turned to the minibus waiting to drop her off at her flat. She thought of asking the driver to wait till she returned but Shanker told her to let the bus go and agreed to drop her home after coffee. She had a small flat of her own in the building which her father bought for her so she could have her independence.

As they stepped into the hotel, he heard whispers at the reception, and then, a smartly dressed young man ushered them into the coffee shop at a nice table on the side. Surya was surprised that he was well-known in this five-star hotel.

Noting her surprise, he related to her that he was involved in an investigation of a murder at this very hotel last year. He reminded that she might have read about it in the newspapers; the victim was a Russian lady and lamented that despite their efforts the killer had not been caught because he managed to take the next flight out of India.

They chatted and as they looked at each other, Shanker Dayal had so many thoughts running through his head. He really wanted to know if she was oblivious to the clandestine activities in the office or if she was a very good actress off stage as well. In his heart, he would love to believe that she was in no way involved in any of it. Her beauty was captivating as was her personality, so much so that it was becoming more difficult for him to ignore whom she worked for and where she worked. As they finished their snack Shanker probed, "What are your plans? You want to continue your job at KBL as Pratap's secretary and assistant?"

She replied, "He pays me very well, and he treats me with courtesy, but it can hardly be an ambition. But I am not qualified for any other job. I am not an engineer or administrator, haven't been to a business school, and barely passed my B.A. from Kamla Nehru in Pass Course. So, where can he place me?"

He smiled and commented, "At least you know your limitations, most women don't."

They got up and took a casual stroll around the swimming pool but felt uncomfortable as he knew someone was watching them. She sensed it and said, "I know what you are thinking, we are under observation."

He said, "Next time I will take you to a place, where I am unknown."

She smiled knowing well that that would be difficult.

Chapter 6

Shyamala was sitting on the sofa and having a cup of coffee; she liked coffee with milk or cream if she could get it, particularly in the morning. She switched on her phone, which she had switched off at night, as she did not want her sleep disturbed by some emergency call.

There were three missed calls from Vikram, and she wondered why. She decided to return a call to him.

"Where are you, as these calls are from outstation?"

"I am in Cochin and was hoping to persuade you to come for a few days if you can take leave."

She excitedly replied, "If Shanker agrees to give me three days off I will try and come. I have not seen that part of India."

She went to Shanker's office to ask him for three days' leave.

He looked at her and said, "Why do you want leave, any problem in Lucknow? Family, ok?"

She said "Yes, actually I want to go to Cochin. I have never seen that part of India. Kerala, I believe is very scenic."

"You aren't going there for scenery; Vikram must have telephoned you."

"How do you know Vikram had telephoned?"

"He called you at the office also. Your secretary told me. Shyamala doesn't make it easy for him. Play it cool, otherwise, he may use you and then dump you. Moreover, I think there is a motive behind his invitation. My intuition tells me Mr. Pratap may have set it up. He is an exceptionally shrewd man, after all, you don't become an MD in such a large company unless you are highly intelligent and shrewd and know how to play the game."

"My advice is, if you want to go, please go, but don't jump into bed with him. We have a very nice guest house there for senior officers. I know the superintendent well; I will book a nice room for you with a sea view."

"That would be great," she said, "Then I can go."

"Of course," he telephoned his assistant to book a ticket for her and said that she was going for police work, so please charge it to the office account.

She was quite surprised that when she boarded the flight, the air hostess upgraded her to business class, and she sat next to an elderly pleasant gentleman. His command of the English language was excellent as he told her that he was an executive with a large company in Kuwait and it was a very nice country to work in and they paid him well.

When she got off the plane, Vikram was at the terminal waving excitedly at her. She was pleased to see him too as he hugged her tightly, making her pleased and a trifle embarrassed too. She heard her name being announced, and there was someone with a placard waiting to receive her. She then informed Vikram about the accommodation arrangements Shanker had made for her stay at the VIP Police Guest House, and that there was someone here at the airport to receive her. Vikram, on the other hand was disappointed since he had booked a room adjacent to his with a connecting door in a five-star hotel, but he knew she had to follow protocol. Vikram promised to call Shyamala in the morning so they could make plans for her visit. She happily agreed as she was looking forward to that but was quick to add that her presence would be required at the guest house since it was her first night there and she believed that a few of the officers were looking forward to having dinner with her. These were her colleagues at the academy, particularly Somaya; they had become good friends over time. Somaya was now married and looking forward to having Shyamala not only to catch up with but also to have her over for lunch/dinner to meet her husband and two boys. Upon hearing his, Vikram was crestfallen but didn't show it. He had really wanted Shyamala all to himself.

The next morning, Somaya called her for breakfast, and she ate typical Chettinad cuisine with seafood thrown in. Oh, it smelt so good it made her mouth water. The scent of the spices and sun-dried meats played harmoniously on her tastebuds. Shyamala was particularly fond of seafood but not so much mutton or red meat. She inhaled the tantalizing chilies, peppercorns, cinnamon, and other spices as they beckoned her hungry tastebuds in attendance. They chatted as Shyamala savoured every bite. Somaya giggled, so happy that her friend was enjoying the meal as Shyamala munched in agreement with her happy tastebuds. As the salted vegetables smoothly found *that* spot of satisfaction in her digestive system, Shyamala realized that Somaya was talking. She was asking her what case, if any, she was engaged in. Shyamala explained it to her in detail but was not quite certain there would be any connection to it in Kerala, but all the same, they wanted to make sure.

She accompanied Somaya to her office where Somaya called the secretary and asked about the file of KBL Associates and RMC bank.

RMC bank, it appeared to Shyamala's surprise, was quite active in Kerala and had given loans to enterprises but appeared to be cautious as to who to lend money to, and therefore, Somaya checked and didn't find any serious debt replacement problem, except in 2 to 3 cases where money had been lent to companies dealing with companies or enterprises in the gulf countries, particularly Kuwait.

"Well," said Somaya, "You are bound to have some defaults, but they take adequate security to cover the loans in case of default. Of course, it doesn't always work that way, but banks are quite careful about whom they lend to."

"As far as KBL Associates is concerned, they have done consultancy work for mainly shipping companies and have a very strong and notorious agent called Ravi Mathew. He is some sort of a 'Don' here and has offices in Cochin and Trivandrum. They operate through him, and I believe he has a substantial shareholding in KBL Associates. He spends a lot of time in Kuwait where he has several businesses, again in the maritime area. He is a shareholder in a well-known shipping company belonging to the Royal family. He gets a commission from them for the business he gets for them. They have ships operating in Kerala and Chennai all year round."

"I think your friend, who is trying to woo you, must be working closely with him."

"We have been after Mr. Ravi Mathew for a long time, as we know that he is involved in the smuggling of expensive items like watches and even precious jewellery items. Please be careful, he is a dangerous man if you get on his wrong side."

"I think the first thing is that you should go along with Gopi Vijai, he will remain in the background to ensure your safety."

She met Vikram for lunch and demanded to be taken to a typical Cochin restaurant serving good local food, with authentic flavour, particularly seafood like prawns, lobsters, etc.

Vikram was a little surprised but took her near the docks to a small restaurant which was full up, but he seemed to know the manager, so he got a good table. He ordered one herbed prawn dish for her, which was their specialty. She enjoyed the buttery spicy taste and told him so.

"So, what are you doing here in Cochin, Vikram?"

"Well, we won a contract for consultancy with a company that makes maritime products for an associated company in Kuwait."

Shyamala was not surprised as Kerala exported the largest number of workers to the gulf countries, their remittances were a major source of income for many middle and lower-class families as well as manual workers, who lived in dormitories in the gulf countries, though they were clean and comfortable, and the workers were well looked after. Most of them were Christian and Muslim families.

"So, have you got an office here, or are you operating from the client's premises?" she inquired.

"No, we have a very influential agent here, who is also a shareholder in our company. We use his large office in one of the new office blocks which is very comfortable to work from there as its infrastructure is very good."

After lunch, Vikram took her there and she was impressed by the setup. He had three assistants, two young men, and a middle-aged woman.

They had a cup of coffee and Vikram then suggested going to the hotel and relaxing a little. Shyamala could hear Shanker's voice in her head saying, *"Shyamala don't make it easy for him. Play it cool, otherwise, he may use you and then dump you… don't jump into bed with him."* She didn't turn down his offer and they went to his hotel. When they reached the hotel, Shyamala headed towards a quiet, secluded place in the lounge and sat down. Vikram sat down but said nothing. A little later, a waiter came, and Shyamala ordered some green tea. "This is the only thing I can have after that heavy meal at the restaurant. Now, tell me, Vikram, why have you brought me here to the hotel? Were you planning to invite me to your room so that we could spend some amorous time together," she said, looking him straight in the face and he smiled.

"Shyamala, you know my feelings about you and, of course, I find you very attractive. So, obviously, I want to spend some time with you."

She glared at him. Was he saying that it as his intention … without even blinking and with that stupid smile on his face?

"Really! "Do you take me for a naive fool to jump into bed with you after meeting three times and hardly getting to know you? Do you think you are that attractive that I would do what you want? You are sadly mistaken. What is exactly in your mind, let me understand. After all, you emerged from nowhere after the contract was awarded to your company and started dating me and flirting with me. I don't understand what this is all about. Did Mr. Pratap instruct you to do this charade to keep me and Shanker in check as investigations are going on? Has your company done something criminal?"

Vikram's face became red, and he found it difficult to say anything at all. He gulped and slowly drew out his words, "Have your tea Shyamala, and then we can chat. Firstly, Mr. Pratap didn't set me up. He just encouraged me when he found out that I was interested in you and maybe he had a motive in all this. But Shyamala, let me tell you, I don't know anything about the contract at all. I am not connected with it, at the moment, maybe he has it in his mind to involve me, of that, I am sure. Otherwise, why would he send me here, as maritime work is included in the contract? So, I guessed, and I have worked on three contracts in Kerala previously, so I know the systems here and the people as well. When I saw you, I found you to be very pleasant, with a nice personality and was attracted to you. You are also the right age for me and from a similar intellectual background. I believe you are also from a family of academics and was told that your family was disappointed that you joined the police."

She laughed. "Vikram, you should have been in the police, you have done your homework. Yes, you are right. I am from a family of academicians, and we also run a coaching academy for aspiring IIT students, though the brightest as we know prefer to go to Kota, which has become the coaching capital of India."

"So, what are your plans for your stay in Cochin? I could take you to some nearby resorts. They are very good for Ayurvedic massages as people from the gulf countries, in particular, believe in their cures."

Shyamala noted that he had changed the subject quickly and she wasn't done with him as yet, she wanted to see this reaction to what she was about to say to him. "Well, if I have time for that I would like to go to one of them and get a back massage, as my back does give trouble. However, I would first like to meet your big boss in Cochin; Mr. Ravi Mathew." This got his attention.

"Who told you about him?" asked a stunned Vikram.

"Don't forget, I spent the morning with my batchmate Somaya, and she gave me all the information about the businesses he operates here and in the Gulf. You report to him in Cochin, don't you?" Shyamala mentally took in his desperate attempt to mask the shocked look as he willed himself to smile and remain calm.

"No, I report to Mr. Pratap. But I also have to deal with Mr. Ravi Mathew. He is a shareholder in our organisation and manages the business in Kerala and Chennai, where we also have contacts, thanks to him. He is not an easy person to deal with, but I have developed good relations with him. The others are quite scared of him and keep a distance from him. I have made two trips to Kuwait with him as well." Vikram really liked Shyamala and he didn't want her anywhere near Ravi Mathew. He was good enough to work with and a shrewd businessman who cared for little else other than money, but this woman was too beautiful to be around or anywhere near him. He used his influence to get and take what he wanted.

Shyamala shifted to the edge of the chair saying, "I better get back to the police guest house. We are having a special dinner, as some VIP bureaucrat from Delhi is coming. He is a high official in the Home Ministry." With this, she got up. Vikram caught her hand and tried to pull her towards him, which she resisted but eventually allowed him to hug her, and she allowed herself a minute to relax and enjoyed it as mild tension began to build. Gosh, this man smelled sooooo good … even on a humid day. She rained in her thoughts and calmed her emotions before they turned in a different direction. She patted his arm fondly as she drew herself away and stood up. "See you tomorrow," she said. Vikram just leaned down on one elbow in the chair gazing at her with a lost puppy kind of look pouting his darn sexy lips, drawing his brows together and pretending to cry as he stretched his other hand out to her. Shyamala erupted in girlish giggles as he sat up before anyone could see him. She waved goodbye and was lost from his line of sight. He relaxed in the chair all serious, now remembering that she wanted to meet his boss. If he didn't set up an appointment, it would seem as if he had something to hide.

He telephoned her the next morning and said, "I have taken an appointment with Ravi Mathew for

11:30. I will come to your guest house by 10:45, and then we can proceed. It will take half an hour or more to reach his office, which is on the other side and sometimes there is a traffic jam, as the road system is not very good." She agreed and thanked. She knew what she had to do.

She had her breakfast comfortably while chatting with Somaya. She told her the gist of their conversation and Somaya advised her to play it cool until she was sure about Vikram; that he was not a distraction or decoy as this will leave Shyamala in an embarrassing position and possibly a broken heart. They were sitting in the small lounge having coffee which is very popular in Cochin, and they make it properly unlike in North India, Somaya explained to her. He waved to her, and Shyamala beckoned him to come in and introduced him to Somaya. She teased, "Don't flirt with her though she is very attractive. She is married and has children."

Somaya laughed and said, "Shyamala Mishra, you underestimate yourself."

A seemingly embarrassed Vikram offered an excuse for not being able to spend more time since he come official car with a driver, and it was waiting. They said their goodbyes to Somaya and left. Vikram didn't talk too much in the presence of the driver, as he knew he would report it all to Mr. Ravi Mathew. Shyamala, on the other hand, misread this thinking that he was disappointed, so she remained fairly quiet and didn't speak about anything important.

Vikram took her upstairs via the lift to the ten-floor attractively designed building that had a mixed style with a Kerala touch. Mr. Ravi Mathew was waiting for them near the lift and greeted her by clasping his hands and a slight bow. He led them to his office, which was very large with a sea view and the harbour. Vikram introduced her as Shyamala Mishra, NCR Police, Assistant Superintendent from Delhi. Mr. Mathew looked at her slightly surprised and remarked, "You look too young for such an important position, and I thought from your name that you must be from Uttar Pradesh."

Shyamala proudly responded, "Yes, I am from Uttar Pradesh, and the only one from my father's family to join the police." As they got talking, she said, "My family is in the educational field. They have a coaching academy; a technical college and others are mainly schoolteachers or professors."

"So, I would have thought from your name and background." He commented and continued, "How is it that you joined the I.P.S. (Indian Police Service)?"

She explained that she was coached for the exam in the family's coaching academy and scored well, but couldn't manage I.A.S. (Indian Administrative Service) so she opted for I.P.S. Her mother was very happy as she was from a Sikh background and her family came to Lucknow after the partition. Her maternal grandfather was in the I.P.S, in Lahore, so when he came to Lucknow, they offered him an equivalent job in the U.P. police and he retired as No. 2 in the state cadre and was also posted for a while in the Intelligence Bureau in Delhi. Shyamala indicated that she liked Delhi so much that she thought she would take a job there studying in the I.P. College near their house in Civil Lines."

Ravi looked at her and smiled and said, "So you achieved your goal. Now, you are posted in the city of your choice, and where you attended your college. You must have a lot of friends in Delhi from your college days?"

To this question, Shyamala smiled and replied saying, "We meet regularly. I was very happy when I was posted to Delhi as I found Lucknow very provincial and stuffy, full of envious relatives always judging you and passing snide remarks. People are so provincial there, not like Delhi or Mumbai, where I attended the training course."

"So, what have you come to Cochin for, to spy on us?" he said jokingly.

She responded carefully to his joking remark which she knew was what he wanted to find out. "No, I wanted to come here, and then you know that we are investigating the KBL Associates matter, and the city is very much part of the investigations along with RML Bank, which is active in Cochin and Kerala. There is no specific issue, but we want to make sure that no one from Cochin is involved in any wrongful activity. As you know, already one person got murdered and there seems to be serious reluctance on the part of

RML Bank to co-operate. After the report from KBL Associates, there would likely be an audit from a large international audit firm like Grant Thornton, KPMG, etc." She paid keen attention to his facial expression which was deep in thought.

Ravi Mathew listened in silence, then said, "You can be assured that we will cooperate with you. I only hope there are no issues." While they were discussing this, Ravi Mathew's secretary came and whispered something in his ear. He got up and excused himself and went to the other room. When he came back, he told Vikram that RML was not allowing our consultants to enter the bank. Shyamala was surprised, but it was nothing to do with the police. It was between the parties of the contract to sort it out. Vikram then said to Shyamala, "I am sorry to disappoint you, but I will not be able to accompany you to the resort. One of our consultants, Vidya, will go with you."

Shyamala was disappointed but had no option but to go with Vidya. Vikram took her aside and said, "I will be in Delhi day after tomorrow and will contact you. I am quite unhappy with the turn of events, but what can I do?"

Shyamala went to the resort; the massage was very good, and she felt relaxed and the pain in her neck ebbed away. She spent the rest of the afternoon at the flat relaxing before packing for her flight.

She caught the evening flight to Mumbai and the connecting flight to Delhi and reached home at 11 p.m.

When she returned to work, Shanker found his way to her office before she could get to his, and almost startling her in the process. "So, Shyamala, I hope you enjoyed your trip to Cochin and had an enjoyable time with the young man Vikram," he said with a smile.

Shyamala looked at him shaking her head in amusement answered, "I did enjoy the trip but not with Vikram. Somaya, my batchmate whom you also know, guided me and told me the identity of one of the bosses of KBL Associates."

This got Shanker's full attention as he enquired if it were Mr. Ravi Mathew, who was the large shareholder in the company KBL Associates and somewhat of a 'Don' in the city. This Shyamala confirmed and related that she visited the large establishment and had tea with him, but then some incident happened that she knew nothing about but it required his and Vikram's attention so they excused themselves and left the building, leaving her in the capable hands of Vidya, an employee working under Vikram who took her to the resort.

"I didn't even get to say goodbye to him," she sighed.

"Oh, that is a pity, lamented Shanker giving her a cock-eyed look, before returning to his serious expression then stated, "Let me find out what the emergency was," and he telephoned a colleague who was a senior police officer in the city. After ending the call, Shanker said that one of the cranes had crashed and four persons were killed. This was at Mr. Mathew's establishment.

"They are investigating whether it was an accident or a well-planned move by some employees who are against his organisation, or it could have been labour trouble. He said that they would let him know as the investigation progresses."

"So, we are back to square one," remarked Shyamala. "We really don't know who is pulling the strings and creating problems. The incident in Cochin was deliberate, I don't think it was an accident. It was clearly an attempt at sabotage."

Later, Mr. Pratap telephoned Shyamala to inquire if she was all right and also to apologise to her having to leave due to the incident. He also extended an invitation to both Shanker and Shyamala for lunch the next day, if they were free, at his residence office. They accepted.

When they arrived at his home the following day, they were guided to a luxurious but small dining room within the main building of the home. There was a beautiful round table with six light brown leather upright dinner chairs around it. A tall vase with freshly cut lilies stood in the centre of the table. Above that was an antique chandelier light with five imitation candles hanging from a golden ball with crystal links connecting them all together. The walls were a light cream colour with neat white moulding trimmings at the edges. The curtains at the window were brown and white, matching the dining chairs in a diamond-cut design and on the opposite wall were French doors separating this small dining room from the rest of the house. The parallel walls had an electric fireplace at one end and a floor-to-ceiling China cabinet at the other end. To their surprise, Surya was standing with a big bouquet of flowers for Shanker and a gift for Shyamala, which she didn't open. She waited to open it at home. She looked beautiful in the traditional but formal elegant long kurta top with stylish straight pants and sensible pumps. Her beautiful hair was pulled back in a wavy ponytail at the back of her head. Her accessories were a simple long chain and matching earrings.

Mr. Pratap wore a readymade silk jacquard sherwani in beige. This short-collared neck and full sleeve attire was allured with buttons down the front with a white cotton churidar.

Anupama, Pratap's wife, joined them and acted as the hostess. She had on a beautiful casual green chikankari kurta from *Nakkashi* Lucknow accessorised with her diamond tear-drop earrings.

She said "Shyamala, it appears that your trip was somewhat muddied by the accident, they didn't tell you what happened, but quietly left. But I believe that you enjoyed the rest of the trip …, yes?". She continued without waiting for an answer. "It is a lovely city; I like visiting there and it has excellent resorts. I love the area with the Italian name and management and feel very relaxed." She paused and smiled, then said, "You know, they have very good arrangements, and the visitors are international, many from the gulf countries - oversized sheikhs trying to lose weight and they have other problems like high blood pressure, diabetes due to obesity. Europeans also come from Italy and France." Her eyes took on a far-off expression as she smiled as if reminiscing on past visits. She chatted on, "I have made a booking for next month, for a week, and I'm looking forward to it. I get a pain in the shoulder, so these massages really help, much better than taking pain killers."

"Don't tell me that, Anupama dear, you are a bit of a hypochondriac. If you get a headache, you think it is a brain tumour," her husband teased.

Shanker laughed enjoying the banter between them, "It is good to be a hypochondriac. My aunt was one and she gave my uncle a tough time but lived for 96 years." They all laughed at this point and got seated.

"Now, tell us, Mr. Dayal, have you managed to find any clue as to who would have liked to have murdered me, and who murdered the driver of the van?" asked a seemingly curious Mr. Pratap.

Shanker looked at him and Shyamala explained, "We have traced the driver to his family, outside Ambala, but they don't know why he did it, and he had been out of touch with them for more than three years. He had not visited their habitation on the outskirts of the Meerut region. They all do menial jobs like rickshaw drivers, truck drivers, signalmen on the railways, etc. None of them has ever been in any trouble and were surprised that Kurhu was involved and think that it could be only someone from the Meerut region, which is a semi-criminal area, to have done it. We are putting pressure on the Meerut police to actively investigate, but nothing has been found so far."

Mr. Pratap voiced his concerns and thoughts aloud saying, "So, we don't know who was involved, that is surprising and worrisome. I feel the incident in Cochin is somehow also linked to this contract. I know Ravi Mathew very well and he is also a large shareholder in our company and handles our business in South India. He has got us large consultancy assignments in the past and we made good profits from them. Whatever may have happened, he will be able to handle it one way or the other," he said and looked at Shanker and smiled.

All business aside, they had pleasant conversation over a very tasty and sumptuous meal and when it ended, they knew that they had both overeaten.

On the way out, Surya gave the flowers to Shanker and there was an envelope attached to it. Shyamala didn't notice, but Shanker quietly put it in his pocket. When he reached the office, he opened it and Surya had written:

My dear Shanker,

When are we meeting again? I am missing you. Please telephone me, we can talk.

Love, Surya.

Shanker smiled to himself. He was feeling quite nice about what Surya had written but decided to telephone her the next day.

The next day, Shanker was undecided whether he should or shouldn't telephone Surya. He was not sure, but he liked her, and instead of sitting at home, why not go out with her. 'It would be far more interesting,' he thought.

When the finally made up his mind and called, her voice sounded a little heavy causing him to become very concerned. He asked her what the matter and she was indicated that she had a bit of a bad throat, so was hesitant. He said, "Don't worry. We all sometimes get a bad throat, cough, cold. It is nothing to worry about. You don't have a fever do you," he asked.

"No, I don't think so. We can meet if you don't mind my hoarse voice and all that," she laughed.

They met at *The Yellow Brick* near Khan market. Both Shanker and Shyamala liked the restaurant because the food was mouth-wateringly good, and the smell greeted you with a warm embrace. The place was colourful as were the plates you ate on; the ambience was relaxing with bright yellow walls, green and yellow cane chairs with colourful cushions that made you so comfortable that you forgot it was wooden. The atmosphere was cosy, and the staff were always friendly and happy to serve you.

She ordered a vegetarian dish though she liked the chicken dishes, and he followed suit by ordering a vegetarian platter.

They chatted and Shanker told her about Shyamala's trip to Cochin, and the crane accident which killed 4 labourers.

"That's sad," she said. "It should not have happened. Was it an accident or something else?"

"Why do you say that, Surya?"

"Well, if you know Ravi Mathews, anything is possible with him. He is sort of a 'Don' in that area."

"How do you know?"

"Well, I work with Mr. Pratap and Mathews is an important shareholder, and I have met him on several occasions when he comes for meetings. I am scared of him. I find him intimidating and he doesn't treat the staff with dignity, particularly the females. You know what I mean."

"You mean it may not have been an accident, it could have been something else?"

"Yes, it could," she stated in a matter-of-fact tone.

"The police are investigating," Shanker indicated, "and we will have their report shortly."

"I wouldn't be too sure about the accuracy of their report, he has them all in his pockets; he has gotten away with having his way in the past."

Shanker felt embarrassed since he knew he and Shyamala were clean, but she spoke the truth.

Surya seemed to read his mind as she expressed looking him directly in the eye, "Not all police officials are like you and Shyamala. Even in Delhi, there are many police officers who are not above board."

"I know Surya. I won't deny it. Most countries have this problem except for a few."

In an attempt to lighten the atmosphere of the conversation, Surya suggested that they should talk about something more interesting. Shanker agreed, telling Surya that even though he was dull and serious police officer, and she was a very attractive and vibrant person, he thought that they could get along more than friends.

She laughed, looking him squarely in the eyes saying that was exactly what she was looking for. She confirmed this by putting her legs through his under the table, squeezing them in an exciting manner, which sparked a response from him that she could feel.

Shanker lowered his gaze thinking what a temptress she could be at times. He smiled retaining a calm composure, raised his eyes to her, and responded, "What you did just now was very nice and exciting, but a restaurant is not the place for such amorous moves," and then he kept quiet.

"We could meet at a quieter and more private place, there are many farmhouses where we could spend some time together."

That was an invitation that Shanker was expecting and waiting for. "You would know such places, Surya," he replied in a monotone with a hint of sarcasm.

'How dare he', she thought. She was a little ticked-off that he may be thinking ill of her, that she may be part of such behaviour. Well, let me tell him some of the duties which this *well-paying* job which she made look good and smiled sweetly even if her gums hurt and she absolutely hated some of the tasks because it made her feel sick to her stomach, so she laid it out for him; no sugar coating just blunt and to the point.

Sitting up straight in her chair and adjusting her posture, narrowed her eyes and said in the sweetest tone like the Madam from the *'Red Light District'* curling her sensual lips in a smile that didn't make its way to her eyes and declared, "Yes, *I* make arrangements for some of our V.I.P.s often, particularly those who come from abroad. They love this type of arrangement and Delhi is full of women who, for a price, can be part of the rendezvous at these places. Of course, we pay the bill and sometimes get the contracts, and many times we don't. There are other companies who do it the same way, so there is an element of competition in all this." As she continued, her neck did a snake-like dance to give emphasis to her words.

"In business, there is a price to be paid if you want to get clients, particularly overseas clients. Those affluent, well-loaded fat cats from the gulf countries are a lot choosier, and more used to being pampered and want luxury." Shanker realized that she was annoyed by his mental assumption of her. It had hit a nerve.

"In addition to this, they are also fussier about the food and like women who are well endowed and fair in complexion. They prefer Muslim women, which is not a problem, as they are more easily available for such work. We have very good contacts with certain farmhouses and guesthouses, who are able to arrange the facilities for them." She narrowed her eyes again as she continued. "It all costs money, but then that's the price that we have to pay to get jobs, and our business works like this." She eased back in her seat and tried to calm herself as she fussed with the purse which only indicated the end of the evening. She had said enough and made her point; let him absorb it now.

Shanker was amazed at what Surya had told him. He suspected it but was not aware of the extent to which it reached, particularly the hosting of foreign clients was surprising, but he was aware of it as it is so in their own countries as well. He knew what he was told about her and Mr. Pratap, but to judge her solely on that bit of information and his tone implied that because she is beautiful that she indulged in certain activities with overseas clients or VIPs. He felt like a heel and did not know what to say. He felt embarrassed, stunned, and that he had judged without knowing the full story.

Shanker got up and said, "Let me drop you home, and see a doctor if it becomes worse, and we will get together when you are feeling better."

Chapter 7

Shanker called Ramesh Pratap and asked him a series of questions as he tried to follow up on further development with regard to the contract, if any. He wanted to know if the RML Bank cooperating as the consultancy was for them, if any obstacles had been put in their way again? What about the crane accident, if a report had come, or were the police taking it easy on the investigation?

Ramesh answered saying that he had not heard anything more about the accident. He added that he didn't think any investigation report had been prepared. He said that he, knowing Ravi Mathews and his influence, didn't expect any further developments to emerge. He believed that Mr. Mathew was very resourceful and knew how to operate.

Shanker still encouraged him to let him know if anything came out of it since it appeared that everything was somehow linked.

Shanker then called Shyamala and asked her to sit down and tell him if she had heard from her boyfriend, Vikram, about the ongoing events in Cochin.

Her face became red with embarrassment. He was quick to realise it and asked her what he should call him.

She managed a smile and told him that she herself didn't know after what happened in Cochin. She wasn't sure and was disappointed as she thought differently that it had nothing to do with the contract and that he was genuinely interested in her as a girlfriend, as it could be termed.

Shanker looked at her and smiled encouraging her by saying that maybe things will work out the way she expected them to, or maybe Vikram was doing it as part of his job and his boss has told him to get close to her so that he could report to him about what was happening in the investigation.

He asked Shyamala whether she thought Vikram had put on an act or was serious in trying to woo her. He added, "Of course, as a young man, maybe he wanted to have a sexual relationship with you because you told me how he behaved in the hotel lobby." Shyamala just kept quiet and looked disappointed.

The next day Vikram telephoned Shyamala and said that he was back in Delhi and would like to meet her. "Now, Shyamala, don't get me wrong. I know what you are thinking. Let me explain it to you. Will you meet me for tea this evening at your favourite restaurant?"

Shyamala tried hard but couldn't find the courage to refuse him and she needed information. She said, "Ok, I will meet you there around 5:30 p.m." She got there five minutes before him and sat down and ordered a cup of black coffee. She had a lot on her mind and when espresso was brought, she returned it and opted for a large cup of cappuccino and one of the walnut cake pieces too, considering she was a little hungry."

Before the waiter could return with her coffee and cake, she saw him enter carrying a large present, beautifully wrapped in expensive cloth. It was shining.

He went around her chair and gave her a peck on her cheek and said, "Shyamala, I have brought you a present as compensation for ditching you in Cochin." She looked at him as he continued.

"I felt so bad about it and was looking forward to taking you to the resort, where I had made all the arrangements. You must have been disappointed that instead of me Vidya took you," he said and smiled.

Shyamala kept a calm face, but excitement bubbled as she questioned, "Why don't you sit down, and what is in this exotic wrapper? It is some sort of present, but you don't want to tell me." He only smiled. "It is a surprise, which I will be revealed when I open it at home?" she laughed.

"Vikram, I underestimated you. You are very good at charming ladies. I suppose you have done it so often before that it comes naturally to you."

He smiled and said, "You overestimate me. I am not a ladies' man like you presume, I don't know which word to use, but you bowled me over."

"So, what happened in Cochin, after I left?"

"Oh, we went to the site and there had been a nasty accident and four labourers died, when the large crane fell. The concerned police department is investigating whether it was something to do with union rivalry, which is rampant in Kerala as the unions are controlled by communist parties.

We will be made aware of it unless the government scotches the report and does not make it public. There are two unions in that area, and they are always at each other's throat."

He changed the subject enquiring if she had done anything exciting while he was away. She said she had been occupied with work and then rather bluntly asked him if she meant something special to him or was just a part of his work. She waited for a truthful answer.

He looked at her, and admitted that it had started as work, but now it had developed into something more and that in all honesty he had her in his thoughts all the time. With that, he held her hand under the table and put his fingers through hers squeezing them. She looked at him wondering if he was toying with her and her feelings. She withdrew her hand sighed and told him quite honestly that he would have to work harder if he wanted to win her over as she was not convinced.

She then informed him that she has to go to an official function. Shanker had gotten information from the government intelligence wing that KBL Associates were not the favourite of the concerned ministry, and RML Bank had indulged in many irregularities and had given loans to the best of politicians and ministers, which may emerge from the consultancy report, though it was not in the form of an audit. The audit of the bank was given to a mid-sized firm, who were amenable to political pressure and had not strongly written about these transgressions by the directors under political pressure. She then got up and left.

The senior person told Shanker that they would approach Mr. Pratap who was amenable, and they had dealt in other consultancy work undertaken by KBL with him and he had covered up to please the relevant authority. This was the reason KBL was their first choice; they knew the weaknesses of Mr. Pratap and had no problem dealing with him.

What Surya had told Shanker looked truer than ever, and what she didn't mention was that he also used the facilities they offered to foreign customers.

It was not a problem, and the hotels would not charge him as he gave them regular business.

So, was the offer of Surya meant for him also? It wouldn't surprise him that they would have hidden cameras and use them if required for blackmail. It would be too dangerous in the case of foreign customers as they were very shrewd and would make sure that their company is not compromised, and if they did try to pressure them, they would be boycotted internationally. The word would quickly spread through the grapevine, and they could even sue the party concerned in their own country. The damage would be very high, particularly because the American courts gave very large compensation figures with costs.

He telephoned Surya and asked her if she was free for dinner at one of the rendezvous places where they entertained their foreign customers. She sounded very surprised by his request, especially after their last conversation but asked if she could ring him back after one hour.

He said, "Ok, I will wait for your call."

About 45 minutes later she called Shanker back stating that could meet him near the Chhatarpur temple and they could proceed from there; he agreed.

The tall, majestic temple stood as bold as a palace in all its splendour, emanating peace into the atmosphere. The rich ancient architectural design was intriguing from the ceiling to the floor, but the walls were worthy of admiration with its intricate depiction of the gods and their power. The vast space of the surrounding garden beckoned devotees all the more.

Shanker reached the temple half an hour earlier and went inside for darshan and to listen to the lovely songs sung daily by chosen singers. It was very melodious, casting a peaceful ambience over the temple and he loved it. He always loved visiting the temple and it was very pleasing from the inside. The only problem was it was very popular and there was always a large number of devotees who wanted to enter and offer their prayers in the main hall.

He flashed his badge, and the usher took him straight to the *panditji* - Ram Gopal, whom he had somewhat befriended. Panditji gave him his blessing and put a tilak on his forehead and also gave him a box of special *ladoos* and a big box of sweets for his family. He always sent it to his aunt who was a great devotee of the temple and worshipped there whenever she got a chance. 'Shanti aunty would be very happy,' he thought.

As he came out, he saw Surya standing and waiting for him. He took the *ladoo* out and broke it into half and gave her the other half and ate his half. She was reluctant, but he said that it was made of pure ghee, and with the blessings of the *panditji*. He put it in her mouth, and she smiled and said that it was delicious. "I have never tasted such a delicious *ladoo*."

"Do you ever visit this temple? It is one of the finest new temples in New Delhi. What about your parents?"

"Oh, we are *Arya Samajis*, and our temples are very simple with just a *havan kund*. We believe in the Bhagavad Gita; it is our Bible."

He commented, "I know. Many Punjabis are from the *Arya Samaji* community and visit Sikh gurudwaras as well."

"Yes, my mother goes regularly to the gurudwara near Connaught Place. Her mother was from a Sikh family. I like the serenity of the Sikh gurudwara and feel more comfortable in it, so I accompany her."

"So, where are you taking me for dinner," he asked jokingly, with his tilak on the forehead and hands full of coloured ghee. She giggled at the sight of him.

"I will take you to a nearby farmhouse which has very good food and atmosphere, and also has music, and a good band with an outstanding singer. It is not the type of place for foreign customers, but I know for sure you will enjoy the lovely tandoori food."

So off they went to the farmhouse, with its lovely trees and foliage, rows and rows of a wide variety of flowers, filling the air with its natural perfumes, and a particularly very attractive rose garden with chairs and tables and a small podium where a band was playing the latest Hindi songs.

Shanker was very impressed and felt comfortable with the environment. As she knew the management, they got V.I.P. treatment and very comfortable chairs.

Before he could even sit down, the waiter had brought a very expensive bottle of scotch whisky with soda and water along with a bucket of ice. He came back and poured Shanker some scotch. She told him to give him only a small peg as he was not much of a drinker, and he had it with a platter of kebabs, both vegetarian and non-vegetarian.

As his eyes wandered, he noticed a large mansion on the side, which possibly had rooms for guests.

"So, this is the place you bring your special guests to," he asked.

"Just one of the places, most of them are not first timers and have their preferences. This is good for a nice dinner and a drink, and for listening to lovely music, which is good and sometimes outstanding, and could be Indian, Western, Korean, or Japanese style. They are very well organized and can get you the music you want for a price."

He found the music very nice, "It is semi-classical Indian music which I love, and also the old film songs of Lata, Kishore etc. I still watch on Netflix or Prime Video those old movies I am very fond of. Maybe I am living a little in the past, but we all do. I used to go with my mother to watch these movies at the Odeon, Rivoli Plaza etc. Now the world has changed and so have the stories and themes and some of the new productions are very nice and contemporary, and the actors and actresses are more attractive. I like foreign movies too. Hollywood and the French and Spanish serials are also very interesting, though I have to watch them with subtitles. I still enjoy watching them. The other day I watched a very interesting Israeli movie with subtitles.

"Now to come to the point, what way are we heading in the investigation, Surya? Have you been put on me, to find out what is going on? Like I said before, you are an attractive lady, and I am just a boring police officer. Of course, I am likely to have a good future ahead and can become, at some stage, also a commissioner. But I will still be a policeman."

She laughed, "You underestimate yourself, Shanker, all my girlfriends always ask me about you and would give anything to go on a date with you."

"You still have not answered my question," he stressed.

"Let me give you the latest. The confidential report from Cochin has come, and they have concluded that it was an accident and have given very lengthy reasons for reaching their conclusion." She put her hand in her bag and said, "Here is a summary of the report. It's ten pages long; you can read it in your office." "Yes, I will," he said. "I don't want to spoil our dinner by reading it now, and then discussing it with you."

There was a sprightly tune being played and everybody started dancing. She got up and caught his hand and said, "Let's dance. It is supposed to be a fun evening." He got up to join and the music changed to something soft and romantic. She put her cheek against him and kissed him lightly on his lips. He responded and caught her tightly pulling her towards him and rubbing against her as they danced. She didn't pull away but responded as her soft curves moulded well to his body as they both reeled in an exciting experience of controlled sensuous deep-rooted emotional arousal and intimacy. She appeared to be enjoying it more or was pretending to, he was not sure. The music stopped and they returned to their seats as the spell was broken. The food came which distracted them somewhat and gave them a chance to return to reality. It was a wonderful spread and they both ate relishing the flavours that tantalized their tastebuds causing a sweet symphony of satisfaction as the food made its way to their happy stomachs.

"I forgot to tell you something, Shanker. Mr. Pratap, after reading the report, tore it up and threw it into the wastepaper basket. Of course, it was only a copy," Shyamala commented as they eased into comfortable conversation.

"Why did he do that?"

"He said that this report is all rubbish and Ravi had got it manipulated, he knows how it is done. But I can't do anything about it. He has all the connections in the city."

Shanker was surprised. "Are any important politicians involved," he asked.

"You think Ravi Mathew is running his business without their help? He has several companies and relatives of politicians are shareholders or partners in his companies. Oh, you don't know how powerful he is," she affirmed.

He looked at her and said, "Surya, what is that big manor type house there?"

"Oh, it has V.I.P rooms for guests. Do you want me to show you around? I will be quite happy to do so."

He looked at her hesitantly and replied, "Surya, let us not rush things. Let us be sure about each other, then when we reach that stage, we will visit those V.I.P rooms," and saying so, he squeezed her hand quite tightly, making her wince. They had finished the meal and were completely filled.

"Let's go," he suggested, and they got up. As they walked out, he hugged her tightly and led her towards his car. It was a wonderful evening and he thought it should end on a pleasant note.

The next day, he was sitting in his office chair and doodling. He was making strange figures when Shyamala entered. She knew his habits and so said nothing. She watched him doodle and knew he was sunk in his thoughts and so she walked out until he called her from the intercom. Shanker apologised saying "Sorry, I was in deep thought. May I ask you if you are thinking along the same lines as I am, what are your conclusions?"

"I am not sure, because I am more vulnerable than you, but I somewhat feel that we have been very clearly set up, but I cannot understand the reason for it."

Shanker looked at her and said, "I agree with you. It also appears to me that we have been set up. The reason is that, in my opinion, they don't want us to come into the picture at all and are trying to distract our attention. It is the old game they all play, but these people are somewhat smarter."

"If the police start serious investigations in the murder of the van driver or the workers killed by the crane, maybe it would create problems and questions for them to answer. After all, I have confidential information that the contract was given to them to shield some politicians who had taken loans or benefits from the RML Bank."

"I have gone through the audit report, and it shows a large number of unpaid advances but doesn't give the name of the parties. This, we could of course easily verify by calling their senior partner and asking him to give a complete list. I am surprised the CAG's office didn't comment on this."

Shanker telephoned the audit company as per their report and spoke to their senior partner, Mr. Rajan, who had several qualifications to his name, and asked him to come in for a meeting with him the following day.

Mr. Rajan seemed a little surprised and rang back to ask what information they wanted so that he could come prepared.

Shanker updated him and Rajan asked for a day to tabulate the information from the audit file and bring it along with him. Shanker agreed.

Mr. Rajan came the next day with the complete audit file and all the audit statements which were of no interest to Shanker. He straight away asked him for the audit file and from the index located the pages concerning loans given to parties.

He was shocked as he ran his eyes through it, almost half of the advances were to parties connected to politicians and many to bureaucrats through their companies - genuine or paper companies. It was a large amount.

Shanker then went to the pages relating to loans and advances in arrears and they showed a similar picture. Most of them appeared to be shell companies floated by influential people in power from all parties, the ruling and opposition. The maximum was from the state of Kerala, Tamil Nadu, and Andhra. No wonder, the bank was on the brink and suffering losses due to bad loans and advances that they would never be able to collect.

The government had to order a consultancy sop to show that they were taking action by appointing a well-known and reputed firm of consultants, who they knew would be able to cover up the several fraudulent dealings. Most likely, none of the shell companies were in operation and making money, it was just a cover-up.

What could Shanker and Shyamala do? Shyamala's face turned red when she saw the relevant pages and she was absolutely shocked. She started breathing heavily.

Shanker thought the best starting point would be to meet Ramesh Pratap again and bring to his attention what he, of course, already knew though he may not have gone into the details of the audit report. He most likely had skimped through it and asked one of his junior fellow directors to scrutinise and let him have his comments.

Who was the fellow director who had done the scrutinising and given a report to Ramesh Pratap?

Did Ramesh Pratap know the details and then brushed them aside? All this needed to be seriously investigated.

The next day, Shanker and Shyamala were in Ramesh Pratap's office and had coffee with him at 11 a.m. Shanker asked Ramesh whether he had gone through the audit report in detail, particularly the important parts regarding loans, advances, and those in arrears which were substantial for a relatively small bank, and if that was the reason the bank was not making profits which it should have. Shanker also asked him who had done the scrutinising of the document.

Ramesh was quite surprised that Shanker had done all his homework on this case.

He told Shanker that Hari Mohan, his fellow director who looked after the audit details, had studied the report and had given a go-ahead for the consultancy job. It was based on Mr. Mohan's recommendation that they bid and worked hard to get the consultancy contract. There had been a lot of counterarguments and some directors had opposed it, but Hari Mohan had the full support of Ravi Mathew, who was an important director and shareholder in the company and was resourceful as well. He explained that they had relied on him in the past to bail the company out of difficult situations.

Mr. Shanker Dayal then told Mr. Pratap that he had gotten a call a few days ago from someone in the Intelligence Bureau who indicated that the Finance

Ministry was very concerned about another bank going under, in which the government had fairly large holdings and that the bank had given loans and advances to politicians or their kin, which were not recoverable, and it would be embarrassing if matters reached the court, for recovery. Also, he, Mr. Pratap was selected because he was known to play along.

Ramesh Pratap fidgeted in his chair becoming red in the face, and stammered, "I delegated the matter to Hari Mohan, and he gave a totally different report to what you are mentioning, it is most surprising. I will have to talk to him again."

Shanker said, "We would like to be present when you talk to him. You can call him tomorrow at teatime. We will be present." That being said, they excused themselves and left.

As fixed, Shanker and Shyamala were at Ramesh's office at 4 p.m. Shyamala did not telephone Ramesh to confirm, taking the time they had decided on, for granted.

However, when they arrived at his office, Surya met them and asked them to sit down and apologised that Ramesh was not there but would be back shortly.

After about ten minutes, Surya came into the room explaining that Mr. Ramesh had telephoned and said that he was at the hospital in Saket and was not well and had to be hospitalised. Shanker and Shyamala realised that this was a convenient excuse as Ramesh didn't want them to meet Hari Mohan. Before they left,

Shanker took Surya aside and asked her quietly what the real problem was.

Surya looked and felt embarrassed and said that she honestly didn't know as she was not that important to be kept in the loop but would find out and call him when she did.

In the morning, soon after Shanker reached the office, his secretary told him that a lady called Surya had telephoned and wanted to talk to him. Shanker called her on her mobile phone, and she picked it up immediately and promised to call him in half an hour.

He was in suspense and could hardly drink his morning coffee. She eventually called him 45 minutes later informing him that matters had taken a different turn. Mr. Hari Mohan was indeed in hospital because he had had a heart attack. She added that the company was arranging for him to have the heart operation at a private hospital in London. So, he would be leaving by the night flight with his wife, daughter, and an executive from the company.

Shanker was surprised and telephoned the hospital in Saket where he knew a very senior doctor. He wanted to verify this information and get to the facts. The doctor looked up the records and assured him that it was not a major surgical issue but a bypass that they perform on patients on a regular basis, but the company had decided to take him to London instead, leaving the doctor to assume the company could afford it.

In the morning when Shanker reached his office, he saw Kochar, the Director of RML Bank at the reception and sensed that he was waiting to meet him. He deliberately let him wait for 20 minutes before seeing him. Shanker asked whether he would have tea or coffee and inquired how he could assist him. Navin Kochar gave his preference for coffee in the morning, preferably black, and without sugar.

Shanker asked him whether he had a problem with sugar. He explained that he preferred it without sugar but sometimes used sugar-free pills.

"Now, Navin, you haven't come for a social chat. What is troubling you?"

Navin sat up straight in the chair, "You know what is troubling me, Shanker, I am the director of the bank, but with virtually no power," he complained. "The power is with the Chairman and the Managing Director and two government nominees who sit on the board and keep on changing." He continued, "You know the system Shanker, in such organisations, particularly banks - RML is no exception. Though the government has a minority stake of less than 40 percent, they call the shots as the banks need funding from the RBI and the other organisations and that's how they exercise their will and interfere in the running of the bank."

Navin's facial expression was not that of a happy person at all. He looked fed up and disgusted as he continued to speak, "As you must be aware, the loans were given to the kith and kin of politicians who made fancy project reports from consultants including KBL, Singhal, etc. But those projects were seldom executed, and the money was siphoned off; maybe used for political purposes, bribery, and corruption. How do we recover that money?" He looked tired and aged. "The auditors were also those with close connections to the political class and we never got any audit report giving the details which should have been mentioned." He continued to express his concerns as it worried him deeply and needed to talk about the injustice of it.

"Shanker, you know by now the reason KBL was appointed for the consultancy. Shanker, I am thinking of resigning and joining a Japanese bank, which had made me an offer for their main branch in Mumbai. Of course, I want to be a director, but they are giving me a senior position with a high salary and many perks." He raised his eyes with worried brows looking honestly at Shanker as he declared, "Most probably, I will accept the offer and my wife Rajni would be happy as her family and relatives still reside in Mumbai. They have a flat in Bandra. Once I go to Mumbai, please come there and I will brief you about RML Bank and its twisted affairs. Mumbai is their biggest business area in terms of loans and banking services, including a large section dealing with share market, advisory services, where we have a research team."

Shanker was impressed, and said, "Best of luck, Navin. I think you have made the right choice; you will be much more comfortable working for an international Japanese bank and maybe even get a posting overseas."

Mr. Kochar's face brightened at Shanker's comment and he admitted he was hoping for an overseas posting, maybe Mumbai or Bahrain.

After Navin's departure from his office, Shanker was a little baffled by what Navin had told him. He, of course, had been given a tip off about it but he and Shyamala would have to tread very carefully as politicians were involved and they could be quite vindictive.

Shyamala came in and Shanker briefed her about his meeting with Navin Kochar. She smiled and said, "He is running away. I hope he is not involved in any manner."

Shanker said, "I don't think so. The Japanese are very thorough and must have made the offer only after they were satisfied with him."

Just then, the operator indicated that there was an urgent call on his telephone line. He asked the operator to put it through. It was the secretary of Mr. Ramesh Pratap who broke the news, "Mr. Shanker, Mr. Pratap asked me to give you the sad news that Mr. Hari Mohan died on the operating table in a London hospital at Harley Street."

Shanker and Shyamala were taken aback but not surprised. Shanker had expected that they would do something to him. He had to be disposed of.

Chapter 8

Shanker could not sleep that night. He was amazed at the murder of Hari Mohan. Murder sure it was! The London police were investigating the complaint made by his wife who had a long discussion with the concerned officer from Scotland Yard. She spilled everything she knew, which appeared to be quite substantial.

The operation was conducted at a private, small hospital in London at Harley Street, which is where the medical profession operates from in London, and the doctors there are world-renowned, and patients come from all over the world for their treatment.

Later, Shanker telephoned a friend at the High Commission, who told him that he was aware of the case and Hari Mohan's wife had come to the High Commission, who was also from Kerala and was known to her family. Shanker was sure that Ravi Matthew was somehow involved when he heard that the heart surgeon was also of Indian descent and had settled in London after his medical studies. The case was now out-of-reach for Shanker. He could only coordinate with his friend in the High Commission, who was middle-level officer from the Indian Foreign Service and was his contemporary from the academy.

He telephoned Shanker and told him that he would keep him informed, but he had his limitations. Scotland Yard was a highly efficient police force and was world renowned, and if they decided to investigate, he was sure there would be no compromise.

He and Shyamala could do nothing but hold on to their patience and await the investigation results.

In addition to this, Uday Kumar from the High Commission telephoned Shanker to inform him that a certain Mr. Ravi Mathew, a big businessman from Cochin, had come and met the High Commissioner and it was rumoured that he had good contacts with some Harley Street specialists, as he recommended patients to them. This changed the complexity of the case as Ravi Mathew, as suspected by Shanker, was a key player in KBL Associates and had a large stake in it as well. Also, the consultancy was mainly being handled by him, particularly in the southern states where the RML bank had given loans and Ravi Mathew was the intermediary with the politicians. It was now a wait-and-watch game.

In the meantime, Shanker telephoned Surya and invited her for dinner at the *Yellow Brick* restaurant. He dressed in his usual casual attire which he knew made women especially give a second glance. A blue round-necked polo shirt, khaki-coloured corduroy pants, and black loafers with a black leather blazer.

Surya was looking lovely as well with her wavy hair cascading over her shoulders. She wore a bright yellow kameez with embroidered flowers down the front on the left side and a yellow and white salwar. Her shapely feet were clad in yellow wedge-heeled sandals. The accessories were simple as she was already beautiful and breath-taking in whatever she wore; one yellow band on her left wrist and a white beaded one on her right. She was a vision of a sweet summer breeze.

"So, what is going on," he jokingly asked her, after planting a kiss on her cheek and brushing against her lips. She was surprised but didn't show it. She enjoyed it, but it was too public a place for a more aggressive move on his part.

"What do you mean, what is going on," she asked. "We have more than 25-30 major consultancies in hand, and we are working very hard at them, at least 10 are with customers in Saudi Arabia and the gulf."

"I am not talking about them," said Shanker, "only about the RML bank job. Your director, who gave a clean chit of sorts to the audit report, Mr. Hari Mohan, and absolved the auditor of negligence in not reporting about the bad debts or accounts of loans to politicians' kin, died on the operating table in London, in the Harley Street medical establishment, a world-renowned medical centre."

Surya kept quiet for a while and then said, "People do die on the operating table, particularly during heart operations, which are the most vulnerable."

"Yes, I know that," said Shanker, "but isn't it a coincidence."

"It is evident," Surya muttered. "Anyway, let's wait for the police report. In the meantime, let's enjoy our dinner and ask him to get me another glass of wine so that I can get tipsy, and then you can give me a big hug and a kiss to top off the evening."

Shanker laughed and asked the waiter to bring a bottle of wine, then teasingly said "Let's finish it."

Vikram telephoned Shyamala and said softly, "We haven't met for some time. I am missing you." Shyamala was quite surprised but reacted as nicely as she could and said, "Hi, Vikram. Haven't heard from you for a while, where were you?"

He replied, "I had gone to Cyprus for a small consultancy project on the Greek side of the island. It is a very beautiful place. You must visit it, absolutely enchanting."

"Were you alone or with some co-workers," she enquired teasingly.

"No, I was with another consultant from our head associates. He was a Greek called Antonio. He lives in Cyprus. Anyway, we managed to complete the small project in less than a week and went on a motorcycle around parts of the island. Very enchanting, particularly the small towns near the sea. It has very beautiful resorts for tourists and all the hotels are filled during the season.

"Shyamala, I would love to take you out for dinner to a restaurant at the Imperial. It has the best pan-Asian food in the NCR. Are you free tomorrow, we can meet at 8 pm? I can pick you up and drop you back if you like."

She thought about it for a moment then replied, "Vikram, I can make it to the hotel, but you can drop me back." She was willing to risk all those gossiping neighbours of hers, females who had nothing else to do. Some of them were very nice, but gossip was a kind of infection they were plagued with, and one couldn't blame them. Their husbands worked long hours, sometimes on overnight police duty. She even played rummy with them on low stakes, but mostly lost as she was not very good at it."

The following evening, Vikram took a seat near the window as it overlooked the well-lit gardens and Shyamala, despite her reservations, was happy to see him. She found him to be very charming, dreamt about him, sometimes erotic dreams that left her yearning, and she awoke all aroused, breathless, and with beads of perspiration on the face but didn't have the courage to move to that point in their relationship. She was still not sure about his intentions. She had worn a simple bottle green and rust brown salwar kameez with a rust brown scarf over her shoulders, and low-heeled rust brown pumps and a matching purse.

When she arrived, he took her hand, kissed her on both cheeks rather lovingly, and ushered her to her seat.

"So, what have you been up to," asked Vikram.

"Nothing, just normal police work."

"Oh, come on Shyamala, you can tell me more than that. I know about Hari Mohan and his unfortunate death on the operation table in London. I was quite surprised as it was not a very complicated procedure, and that too in a Harley Street clinic, which specialises in such operations and does hundreds of them every year. It is very popular with Middle East patients, particularly from Saudi Arabia."

Shyamala looked at him and said, "Let's wait for the report from Scotland Yard. They are among the best police forces in the world. I went on a training course 50 miles outside London, near Brighton, the famous sea resort."

"I don't know what to say, Shyamala. Sometimes, I feel I am not cut out to work for a company like KBL Associates. I come from a simple background of academics. Maybe I should immigrate to Canada and do some further studies and join a firm of consultants there." His expression looked a bit distant, but she didn't know if it was an act or whether it was genuine. He continued, "Two of my classmates are working for companies in Toronto and are quite happy with the working conditions there, and the salary is also good."

Shyamala was taken aback at what Vikram said, and it was apparent that he knew a lot more about the KBL Associates and their style of working and was not apparently happy with it and may have already applied for an immigration visa for Canada.

She asked him straight, "Are you planning to immigrate to Canada, Vikram?"

He looked at her and said, "To be truthful, I have, and have been offered admission to one of their universities to do my Ph.D. in Engineering and a scholarship to go with it."

'Oh, wow!' thought Shyamala. "So, when are you planning to leave," she asked calmly.

"When all the formalities are completed, maybe in three months' time. After all, I have to give KBL resignation notice also, that will be for three months."

Shyamala's heart sank as she kept her head down, avoiding his eyes, unable to hide her disappointment; she didn't want to cry, at least not in front of him. She longed to get back home and be all by herself with her sadness; she finished her food quickly and asked Vikram to drop her back.

Shyamala came home nursing a sense of rejection. She had viewed him as a suitable match for herself, their family backgrounds were similar too. 'Anyway, now there was no need to even think of it as he would probably leave for Toronto after a few months. He had relatives and friends there and has also got admission in a university to pursue his Ph.D. course, after which he will take a job there or in the US and find a mate for himself', she thought to herself.

Shanker sensed that something was troubling her and asked her about it. She was a bit hesitant at first but on his insistence, she soon came out with her whole story.

His face became a little serious and he also responded by saying that he too was disappointed even though he suspected that Vikram was putting an act for Ramesh and his company.

"I must admit that he is a nice young man and would have suited you."

"Anyway, I must admit his honesty in putting all his cards on the table."

"Being a little bastardly, we could now grill him, and he may tell us a lot more than he has done so far."

Shyamala didn't reply and kept quiet. After a while, she snapped, "You do the grilling. I won't be part of it."

The next day, Shyamala telephoned him at his house and his mother answered. She spoke with the stern politeness of a schoolteacher, "He was expecting you to telephone. He told me to give you the message that he has left the country last night for London where one of the senior executives had died - Mr. Hari Mohan, and after that he will be going to Toronto to complete his admission process. I guess he didn't tell you but his visa for Canada had come last week." She continued, "I will be missing him the most. He is my eldest son, and I am very fond of him as his mother. He has asked me to come and help him settle down." She added, "It is disappointing that nothing worked out between you and him as you would have made a fine couple. On the other hand, he was sure that you would not leave the police force, where you have a bright future, to go to Canada and be a housewife or work in an office."

Shyamala kept quiet and then said, "He was right. I would never leave the police until my retirement, so it would not have worked out between us. But I will miss him because I did become very fond of him." The mother replied, "He was equally fond of you and was in tears when he boarded the flight. I will let you know his telephone number when he sends it to me from London; at least you can keep in touch with him."

Shyamala, when she reached the office the next day, went straight to Shanker's office and sat down in front of him, and told him about her conversation with Vikram's mother.

"She appears to be a very decent and well-educated person, I must admit. But now we won't be able to grill him as I said yesterday."

"Ramesh must have got a whiff of it, that is why he sent him immediately to London."

The next morning, Shanker telephoned Surya and asked if Mr. Ramesh Pratap was in Delhi as he would like to discuss some matters with him.

Surya replied that he had gone to London but would be back the next night, after the cremation and other ceremonies. Hari Mohan had relatives in London and many friends from his community who were looking after his family. They followed certain rituals which were being executed, as all facilities were available in London, which had a large Indian diaspora.

Then she suddenly asked, "What is it you want to discuss with Mr. Pratap, you can surely tell me."

"Well, Shyamala, as you know, was dating Vikram from your company and he has also been called to London for assistance and then is going to Toronto and has got his visa."

"Yes," said Surya. "I know all about it. The matter was discussed with him by Mr. Pratap a few days ago. But why the sudden trip to London and no resignation notice, was he relieved immediately?"

"I don't know the answer to that, Surya. I am not senior enough for them to confide in me about such matters to."

"But your guess is as good as mine, and you are an intelligent police officer." She said it with a slight mirth in her voice.

"Yes, Surya, I can guess but that doesn't get me closer to my investigation."

"Well, they are not at all happy that you are investigating and have been consulting lawyers in this regard, as to why the police are harassing the company through their investigations. They may go to court, but I think that would just be a threat, as you have every right to investigate."

"By the way, the preliminary report by Scotland Yard has been sent to the company, the hospital, and the medical association. I haven't read it, but it clearly states that the doctor was negligent and didn't follow all the required medical procedures, and it was for the hospital or the medical association or whatever their body is called to take action after the following due process."

After his call with Surya, Shanker telephoned his friend in the High Commission and requested to obtain a copy and send it to him.

Shanker was sitting in his office when his secretary brought the email received from his London friend. His friend had been quite prompt.

It was along similar lines and the police had rightly delegated any further action to be taken against Dr. Ajit Kumar Hegde, who was from Mysore city originally, by the medical association which was highly regarded all over the world and it was a great honour for a doctor to be on its board.

The hint he had gotten from one of the doctors was that most likely he would not be found to be negligent as many people die during surgery on the operation table and it was difficult to prove negligence. This doctor was in fact known to him as the High Commissioner referred senior officials and ministers to him and his associates. There was always a difference in the view of the police authorities and the medical fraternity. "Ajit Kumar had performed several operations that day successfully. Only this one was not successful. It happens all the time," his friend said.

"What about Mr. Ravi Mathew, did you get a chance to meet him?"

"No," he replied.

"However, he came to meet the Deputy High Commissioner, whom he evidently knew quite well, and he invited him to his house for dinner the following night."

Shanker was totally baffled by the turn of events and the tremendous leverage that KBL Associates had, which stretched up to London. Their contacts were amazing.

"Did you by any chance meet any executive called Vikram Bajaj? I think he left for London the night before last."

"No, I haven't met him, but will most probably meet him for tea at Mr. Ravi Mathew's house in St. Johns Wood, the day after. I will keep you informed."

"So, Mr. Ravi Matthew has a house in London also. He does have a business office there as well," he asked.

"Yes, didn't you know? He has a medium-sized office and is an important shareholder in two British companies that own cargo ships. These cargo ships, besides taking deliveries to the gulf countries and

North Africa, also deliver the cargo from India, mainly from the west coast including Kerala. Oh, Mr. Mathew is a very big businessman and very rich, nobody knows the extent of his true wealth, but it is enormous. He plays low key and does not show off much. He has attractive secretaries in each location, and I am sure he takes full advantage of them."

"I will telephone you. After you have met the young man Vikram, please telephone me," he said.

'Now what do we do,' he wondered. It was becoming more and more difficult, and their investigation was leading nowhere. From a small accident and murder, it had now developed into an international conspiracy. He was sure that Hari Mohan was murdered because they were worried that he may spill the beans after interrogation. It would be very embarrassing for them, and if the media got hold of it, there would be no limit to the embarrassing publicity. There could be a further inquiry and the contract could even be cancelled.

He called Shyamala, and she came sneezing and had likely caught a cold. She was looking a little pulled down and answering in monosyllables.

Shanker briefed her and also told her that Vikram was in London, and he had asked his friend from the High Commission to contact him. "Maybe he could, if he wanted to, give us some information of value. It is quite evident that the doctor will get away, as negligence would be difficult to prove to the medical counsel, whatever the police may assert. They defend their kind and, in cases of negligence, the financial penalty the hospital would have to bear would be substantial. What do you think," he asked Shyamala.

"I would like a word with Vikram if you could get me his London telephone number."

She was still angry with him and needed to let him know exactly how she felt. He had put an international number sim card in his mobile phone. He answered her call immediately.

"You have to apologise to me. You never told me about your plans to immigrate to Canada and led me on. I expected more honesty from you. I am disappointed."

He sighed then replied, "Shyamala, I certainly owe you an apology, but I was so infatuated with you, that I wanted our relationship to continue. You don't know how miserable I am feeling about the whole thing, and I am missing you for sure. I dream about you at night, and sometimes," he laughed on the phone sounding husky, "the dreams are wild. We never reached that stage, but I can fantasize about it."

Shyamala felt hurt, torn, deceived, and mad at herself for still having feelings for him in spite of everything. She even asked herself, 'why was he laughing … was this a joke to him?

"Come on, you can't be serious Vikram. We have to forget each other as you are going to be at the other end of the world and will find plenty of interesting girls to date. You should have no problem with that score." Before disconnecting, she added, "Best of luck and stay in touch." She sobbed after that as she missed him and would have loved to continue their relationship.

'Well, he will find someone, and maybe I will also find another who will sweep me off my feet. I should seriously start looking around.' She went home and put on some calming jazz music, took an Alprax 0.25 tablet, and went to sleep.

The next day she was woken up by the noise of the vibrating mobile phone. Squinting from the sunlight coming through the curtains, she felt for the phone and sleepily answered it.

"Do you know what time it is?" asked Shanker's secretary.

She peeped at her watch with now wide eyes. It was 10:30 a.m.

"There is a meeting at 11.30 a.m. Please try and come on time," she said.

"Oh, my goodness, please send a car for me ... thanks." She dropped the phone and was off the bed like a shot. She was in and out of the bath and changed with two minutes to spear before the police car that came to fetch her. Shyamala reached the office in a record time- 11:29 a.m.

"What is this meeting about," she asked Shanker's secretary. "I haven't received any agenda."

She was handed one and glanced through it as she went into the empty boardroom where she quickly tried to fix her not-so-neat hair before anyone came.

Shanker came, glanced at her, and smiled. "Did you have a good sleep? It looks like you are still yawning. Don't take sleeping pills. They are dangerous and forget Vikram. I know it won't be easy for you, but in a few days' time, he will be in Toronto and onto another life and will forget you when he meets his friends and makes new friends, both men and women. That's the reality, Shyamala. I am feeling very bad talking like this, but you have to get out of this and face the reality. Don't feel bad, slowly you will forget him and find someone else."

'Darn… how can he read me so well and know that I even took a sleeping pill,' she wondered as she finished smoothing her hair and pinned it neatly in a bun then took her seat. She knew he was right with what he had just said. Looking at the agenda again, she mentally pulled herself together and prepared for the meeting as the others entered the room and seated themselves.

Shanker presided and updated the officers on the KBL Associates contract, and the death of Mr. Hari Mohan on the operating table. They all said it looked fishy, particularly Shyamala's colleague, the Asst. Commissioner, but Shanker told them that they could not do anything about it, as it had happened overseas.

He also told them that Vikram had caught the last flight the following night to Toronto, two days before his planned departure as he was afraid that he could be targeted as he knew too much. This shocked Shyamala, she sat there feeling numb and cold on the inside. "He is lucky that he got away as my friend in the High Commission told me that he was targeted through a local gang, and they came to know somehow, and his friend arranged for him to leave that night. He sent his High Commission car to drop him at the airport." Shanker said, "I told him that this scenario was possible, and he should help out."

"Vikram was lucky, otherwise Ravi Mathew would have made the arrangements to eliminate him."

Shyamala was totally shocked and asked, "How do you know that Ravi Mathew had arranged it?"

"Well, he is sort of a 'Don', and people in Cochin openly talk about it."

"So, we can't proceed further in the investigation as we have no information to proceed with. Scotland Yard, even if my friend makes a complaint, has nothing to proceed on with, as Vikram got away, and is safe in Toronto, and I don't think Ravi Mathew would be interested in pursuing him further as he is now out of the way. They will send his dues to the bankers in Toronto and that will be the end of the matter. Vikram is too intelligent to pursue the matter further and will concentrate on his Ph.D., studies."

"Since, we have nothing else to go on with, let's end the meeting."

"I am waiting for Mr. Ramesh Pratap to return from London with Hari Mohan's wife and his ashes."

"I will meet Ramesh Pratap when he arrives and question him but I don't think he will jeopardise KBL Associates by talking and I doubt Hari Mohan's wife will have the courage to open her mouth. Ravi Mathew must have given her appropriate financial compensation after consulting Ramesh Pratap."

Shanker sat in Ramesh Pratap's office and waited for him to call him. He was busy with another gentleman, who looked like a senior advocate, and Shanker thought that his face was familiar but couldn't place him."

He came out and went up to Shanker's sofa, and said, "How are you, Mr. Dayal? Police work must be tiring these days." Shanker recognised him; he was a partner in a leading law firm with branches in Mumbai and Bangalore.

"I am fine Mr. Tambowalla. I thought you were practicing from the Mumbai office."

"Oh, I am, but the Supreme Court is in Delhi, so I have to make several trips if required, though we have a large office in Delhi, Mumbai, clients want us to appear as they are familiar with us. Call me if you visit Mumbai, we can have lunch together."

Ramesh came out of his office and took Shanker to his cabin and they sat at the conference table.

"A lot is happening in your company," said Shanker, with a smile. "Five murders and the death on the operating table of a senior executive looking after the financial matters. It is getting more and more complicated every day."

"Well, the persons who got killed in the crane accident had no connection with KBL Associates. They were employees of a company managed by Mr. Ravi Mathews."

"I know what you are going to say, that Mr. Ravi Mathews is a major shareholder in our company, but that company was managed by him, he was the main shareholder in it. He is a very big businessman and mainly involved in the marine sector."

"What is it that you want to know now, Mr. Shanker. You seem to have all the details."

Sighing, Shanker probed, "I wanted to know why a reputable company like yours took on this assignment. I know the substantial fee was a major factor, but there could have been other factors like political pressure. I went through the auditor's report and met their senior partner, and it was very apparent that most of the loans and advances were given to politicians' kin, and it would be very difficult for RML to recover more than one-third of it. Am I right, Mr. Ramesh?"

He took his time answering as tiny beads of perspiration began to appear, and then said, "We went by Hari Mohan's report."

"You knew that the report was doctored and not factual as per the audit reports for the last three years. So, you forced Hari Mohan to give you a doctored report, and when we found out about this manipulated report and wanted to question him, you took him away to London for heart surgery."

"We have checked with his heart surgeon at the hospital at Saket and he confirmed that his condition was not serious, and the operation could have been done here. This hospital does dozens of such operations every month and he fully trusted his doctor and wanted to have the operation in Delhi, but you persuaded him that London would be better, and he agreed. Who would not agree to a Harley Street surgeon performing an operation? His wife also agreed, and you gave permission for her to accompany him at company expense.

Then what happens… he dies on the operating table. The operation is performed by an experienced Indian doctor, but something goes wrong. Scotland Yard finds the hospital guilty of negligence, but the medical counsel, who always defends its colleagues, exonerates him."

"What are you getting at, Mr. Shanker, I want to know." He was fighting to remain calm as he continued in an accusing voice. "You are just groping in the dark and have no proof to support your statements."

"It would be a heyday for the media if they get hold of the names of the politicians to whom loans and advances were made, and those who had not paid a single rupee back." Shanker Dayal was annoyed at the gall of Ramesh; the man was lying through his teeth, and there was not a thing that the police could do to prove it. These fat calves lived a fancy life while corruption was under every step that they took. Even as an officer of the law, Shanker had to be careful how he investigated this case.

Ramesh continued his eyes wide and defensive as he continued talking, "All the loans were made after the act of diligence I suppose. Well, why have we been appointed? We will give a fair report and not hide any facts."

"You better not," said Shanker, "otherwise you will be exposed as you have many rivals, and they know more than you think." He continued leaning forward to the edge of the chair, "But we still don't know why you took this assignment, most likely under Mr. Ravi Mathew's pressure, and who are the powerful politicians who forced you to take it?" With that, Shanker got up and left and met Surya on the way out.

"You didn't call me again; I was waiting for your call." She looked him in the eyes with a smile.

"I would like you to take you out again," he said, "I will telephone you."

Shanker met Surya at the *Yellow Brick* at teatime, after her working hours. She was looking very attractive as always and Shanker could not help himself nor take his eyes off her.

She asked what he was staring at? He said, "You, of course. Who else can I stare at when a pretty young lady is sitting in front of me?"

"You are surprisingly romantic for a policeman," she smiled.

"Why?" "Are policemen not supposed to be romantic," he asked, "Have you dated any policeman before," he asked.

"No never, never even thought about it," she said pouting her sweet, heart-shaped lips.

He laughed, "What made you change your mind then?"

"Well, when you came to Ramesh sir's office, and I met you, I changed my mind. You underestimate yourself, Shanker. I am sure many women would be attracted to you, and don't tell me you haven't had girlfriends before."

"Yes, I have, but of a different sort. Mainly teachers and family friends' daughters, they are quite different. My aunt, who is always matchmaking, used to get after me to meet girls for marriage, always suggesting someone."

Surya said, "This is not the right place for flirting, for that, we would have to go to the farmhouse at Chhatarpur again. It was a fabulous place, wasn't it, and such nice music."

He smiled and said, "You are right, Surya, maybe next week." He still wondered about her being genuinely into him or if she just playing him for her boss. It bothered him because she was such a beautiful woman whom he really liked. He could easily get lost in her and the sensual madness of desire and bliss. Then… there was the ever-eventful case they were trying to investigate.

"Now tell me, what is troubling you, Shanker?"

"Well, the sudden turn of events, Mr. Hari Mohan's fatality on the operation table, and the Scotland Yard report, of which I had a copy."

"Well, in operations you can't tell, Shanker, a small slip of a knife and you are dead," she made a sound.

"It sounds too obvious," said Shanker. "So, tell me what has been happening in the office. Anything new? Who is now going to lead the consultancy assignment?"

"Well, different executives have been assigned in concerned states, most of the business, besides the NCR, is in Kerala and Tamil Nadu, particularly Chennai."

"Who is going to replace Vikram in Goa, now that he has left the company and gone to Toronto?"

Surya laughed, "Well, your assistant, Shyamala, I believe is very upset about him pushing off when things were developing between them. I think Vikram was very fond of her and not just flirting to pass the time and she also liked him." He noted that she was being evasive again; she knew something.

She shrugged her shoulders and said, "Such is life. I suppose they will find new partners again; both are young and attractive."

Shanker nodded and said, "But Surya you are being very cagey today and haven't told me anything interesting."

"Well, you know that Mr. Ramesh is quite a womaniser and has several liaisons."

"I believe after the funeral in London, he went to Scotland – Edinburgh, where he has a woman friend called Angela Scott. She is a divorcee, and he has known her since they were at the university together. I believe he spent 4 days with her, and they went to scenic spots near the city and stayed at the hotel together."

"Who gave you the information, Surya," asked Shanker.

"Oh, I have my sources. I sometimes pick up the extension phone, without him knowing, so that is how ... I have also seen her photographs in an album in his office, which he hides behind some books, I know where it is."

"You would make a good spy, Surya. Interested in joining the intelligence bureau," he asked teasingly. Somehow, he got the feeling this bothered her. Shanker paid close attention.

She laughed. "Just curious. It is not my profession."

"Yes, I know, but you can always change professions. Many people do it, even ones older than you. I can find out what the procedure is."

"Ok, I have no objection." She smiled and then looked away.

They got up and the manager followed Shanker to the car. Shanker was surprised that Surya had ordered an Uber. The manager told Shanker that he would have arranged for Surya to be dropped at her office in the hotel cab.

Shanker was disappointed as he didn't get a chance to hug and smack Surya, which he was looking forward to, and having dreams about it. 'Maybe next time at the farmhouse,' he thought, maybe they could spend some time together in one of the suites, which would be more interesting.

Chhatarpur temple was another attraction for him. He would like to visit it again for darshan.

Shanker and Shyamala were sitting and discussing strategy in the office and how to proceed. They didn't have much to go on except that RML was in dire financial straits due to bad loans to politicians and their kin, but this was a matter for the consultants to highlight by scrutinising the auditors' reports and requesting a forensic audit by one of the large international audit firms.

Navin Kochar telephoned from Mumbai and asked Shanker if he had made any progress. He said, "I forgot to tell you that the biggest culprit is a big co-operative in Maharashtra and one in Kerala. Both are linked to one of the most prominent politicians in these regions. They are extremely successful co-operatives, but they deliberately show poor results on the excuse that farmers are not paying them, so they can take advantage of the banks and financial institutions and tell them that they are not in a position to pay back the loans and to decrease their rate of interest. It was one big fraud."

"How am I to investigate this?" said Shanker.

"You could pressurise RML to give you the details of the outstanding through their auditors, who are already familiar with it."

Shanker called the senior partner of the audit firm and asked him if he could come to the office.

The partner said that it would be preferable if he could come to their office for obvious reasons, as all the files and papers were there. Shanker understood and fixed a time with him and requested CAG's office if they could spare one of their executives to help out.

They concurred, and Shanker fixed a time with the audit firm for the afternoon, two days hence.

He met the middle-aged executive from the audit and accounts department, and they proceeded to examine the books.

Shanker talked to the senior partner and let Krishan from the audit office do his work. He very meticulously and carefully went through the files and made extensive notes.

He emerged in the evening after a snack and went to Shanker's office.

"Mr. Dayal, it is an enormous fraud, and I don't know how they have gotten away with it. This co-operative that I am checking is their biggest borrower and they are large with huge collections, but they clearly rearranged their accounts to show poor financial results and blame the poor farmer, whilst the money is funnelled out by the big boys, the relatives of the politicians who use it for fighting elections and also for buying expensive bungalows, even sending it abroad by hawala.

They are the largest creditors of the bank and owe crores in interest and repayments.

It is absolutely shocking. RML must have been put under pressure to give them loans. It appears that a big businessman by the name of Mr. Ravi Mathew is the main actor in this drama along with Maharashtrian politicians who are in league with him. It is now in the hands of the KBL Associates to expose all this, which they won't as Mr. Ravi Mathew is one of their biggest shareholders."

Shanker thanked Mr. Krishan profusely and had a cup of tea and guffawed. Shyamala upon hearing it came into his room and was shocked to see him laugh so loudly.

Chapter 9

Vikram telephoned Shyamala to inform her that he had reached Toronto safely. He told her that he had been lucky to get away that night, otherwise fate may have taken a different turn. Ravi Mathew had made arrangements, but with the help of an officer in the High Commission, he managed to catch the last flight coming from Delhi, and with a halt in London, proceeded to Toronto. It left at almost 4 a.m. although they had boarded at 3.15 a.m. They were sitting in the plane for almost an hour before it took off. He was now safely in Canada and was staying with a cousin-his father's elder brother's son who was a professor at the university. He added that he would take a job with a consultancy company and also study further with the help of his cousin and do his Master's degree in Canada as the Indian degrees did not have the same value as the British and the US degrees.

"There is no doubt that Ravi Mathew was involved in the death of Hari Mohan, as he knew too much and if he had started to spill the beans to the local authorities, Ravi Mathews, who also has business interests in the U.K. and is a shareholder in their cargo shipping companies, might have been put in a difficult situation. In England, they don't spare anyone, however big or powerful he may be, and they are known for their honesty. Anyway, now Ramesh and Ravi Mathews must be quite happy that Hari Mohan is out of the way. I do not know whom they will delegate for the inquiry, they have many consultants working for them, but I don't know whom they can trust."

Shyamala kept quiet and at first hesitated to inform him about the audit check by the government audit officer who was quite amazed by the loans given to the co-operatives concerned; Krishnan had given Shanker the details.

She asked Vikram if he knew anything about the loans given to the co-operatives in Maharashtra and Kerala, where Ravi Mathew was a large player in the management body or whatever they called it. She told him the preliminary findings were that there were powerful politicians who were involved through their relatives and had taken loans which were not re-paid by them, including interest, and the bank would have to write them off.

Vikram was a little hesitant, but then told Shyamala that she was right- the loans were extended on the advice of Mr. Ravi Mathews, who, through political pressure, persuaded RML bank to give these loans. "They did so, I must admit, most reluctantly, and soon afterwards the Managing Director of RML was asked to look for another job. He left the country and took a job in Australia. I believe he is now working for a bank in Canada, I will try to find out, and meet him if possible. I am missing you Shyamala," he said, "why don't you at least come for a holiday? I will show you around this vast and beautiful country. I would love to meet you again. Of course, I will also be visiting Delhi, maybe after two years, after finishing my degree. I want to meet my parents. I know my mother is missing me and telephones daily to find out how I am. You know how Indian mothers are."

Shyamala said, "I can understand well. My parents also telephone me more than once daily and are always worried as police jobs can be dangerous. Vikram I will plan, maybe I can come for a holiday if I can afford it on my government salary," she laughed.

"Well, you just have to pay for the fare, I will look after the rest."

She put down the telephone and was in tears. She was missing him and thought it was so thoughtful of him to have telephoned as soon as he had reached Toronto.

"I will try to go next year, even if I have to borrow from my father who will never refuse me."

Shanker was sitting in his office and was being disturbed frequently as there had been some serious accidents, burglaries, and a murder or two. In a large city, it was not at all surprising, he would have to delegate to the officer concerned and had to listen to the umpteen complaints about harassment, etc.

He got totally fed up and was thinking of Surya. He picked up his mobile phone and dialled her number. He got a recorded message that she is busy and will call back. He waited for her call, strumming his fingers on his desk, trying to play a tune unsuccessfully.

Surya telephoned after about an hour and said that she was busy attending a meeting that had been called by Ramesh Pratap along with some consultants. She couldn't hear very well as the doors were closed but caught a whiff that it was about RML consultancy.

When they came out, she heard them say that Ajit Kumar would now replace Vikram and be posted accordingly and would have to relocate to Cochin in their office in the building owned by Ravi Mathews. He was older than Vikram, was married and had one daughter. She didn't know his plan about the relocation of his family as his daughter was studying in a leading nursery school in East Kailash, where his wife was also a nursery teacher.

Most likely, his family would not be joining him, but he could visit Delhi regularly and he had an apartment in Defence Colony, not far from the school.

Shanker wasn't really interested in the details about Ajit Kumar, he was interested in Surya and told her he wanted to visit the Chhatarpur temple for darshan and asked if she would like to come with him.

She laughed and said, "Shanker, I know what you have in mind. You want to spend a romantic evening with me at the farmhouse which I took you to, don't you?"

He laughed and said, "You are more intelligent than I thought."

"Oh, come on Shanker, it doesn't take much intelligence to guess what is on your mind."

"Alright, can we go on Friday night, you can meet me at the same spot at 8 p.m."

Surya hesitated, then said, "It is okay with me, but we may have to return earlier as we have some guests staying with us."

"That is alright with me," said Shanker.

He had two difficult days as he was constantly thinking of her and having fantasies about her in his sleep; upon awakening, an unsatisfied pulsation in his groin that left in beads of perspiration, with steamy frustration of unfulfilled blazing desire, and in hope of some sort of fulfilment which would not break his heart or jeopardize his career. His days were filled with him holding on this his temper and meagre self-control where Surya was concerned. God help him! How could a woman have so much power over his sexual behaviour was amazing and simply beyond his understanding. He needed blessings from the temple to guide him and keep him out of trouble.

On Friday, he went to the temple and did the *darshan*. The assistant of the priest took him to a side room so he could take the blessings of one of the senior pandits, who was attired like a sadhu and had his eyes closed. He opened them for a minute and put his hand on his shoulders and blessed him with a prayer in Sanskrit which he had heard before but didn't know the meaning of. He would find out from the other priests whom he knew quite well.

He was happy with the blessings and the smile of the senior pandit who looked old and wise.

He met Surya outside the temple; she was waiting for him, and he caught her hand and took her across the road where the car was parked. He had not brought the driver and drove himself, which he seemed to enjoy. Surya was visibly impressed with his driving skills.

He explained that in his younger days he even competed in rallies. However, he hadn't won any but came third in one of them. He found them very interesting and a colleague of his, Vijay, who was now posted in Pondicherry as the Assistant Commissioner of Police, had been his co-driver.

They drove to the plush farmhouse, where they had dinner last time and enjoyed the music.

When they sat down, he asked Surya what had been happening in the office of late and wanted to know if Mr. Ramesh was back in action and if the consultancy work was proceeding smoothly even though they were a bit behind schedule. Shanker indicated that he believed one Ajit Kumar had replaced Vikram, who had left London for Toronto. He asked her if she knew what had happened, and she nodded her head. He didn't believe her and still didn't trust her. He continued talking and observing her.

"Vikram was the next target after Hari Mohan, but with the help of an officer in the High Commission, he managed to catch the last flight to Toronto by Emirates from the London airport."

Surya remained quiet and kept on listening most intently. Shanker was not sure if she knew everything or was only pretending.

He looked at her and she smiled saying, "I thought we had come here to spend a romantic evening."

"Of course, that was the idea, Surya, I have been missing you and remembering your lovely smile. Then let's dance and order food… the music is so nice, let's get on the floor, and ask the band to play some romantic, English songs and tunes."

"He plays the piano very well," said Surya. "I will ask him to play a romantic tune."

They both got up and went on the floor and Shanker held Surya tightly and danced cheek to cheek with her. He was confident about this self-control even though her body felt so good next to his… it fitted like … as if they were meant to be but could he trust her?

She took the initiative and kissed him on his lips but he was not sure whether it was a good idea with so many people watching and he wasn't sure if any of Ramesh's spies were taking photographs. He still didn't trust Surya and had a nagging suspicion that she was a plant by Ramesh. These people were extra clever.

They sat down and by that time the food had come along with some red wine.

His stomach was empty, and he took a sip. There was a hint of something, but he couldn't put his finger on it, so he poured it into his glass and ate some starters in a salad with herbed lemon-flavoured fish, buttery crispy prawns dusted in a seasoned thin batter, seasoned cabbage pakoda and masala vada (lentil fritters). Then felt like going to the toilet which was just a short distance away.

After relieving himself, he felt slightly light in the head, like he had never felt before. He used to drink wine, but this reaction was different. He felt as if someone had drugged the wine. Hmmm… maybe this was the taste he had gotten when he had taken a sip. He couldn't get up without her help. His mind worked very fast because he knew he needed to get help before things got worse. He went to the side and telephoned his driver, whom he had told to wait near the temple, to come immediately. Surya was unaware of this, thinking all along he was without a driver that night, driving himself.

He sat down and felt better but was still quite tipsy.

"I thought we would spend some time in one of the suites after dinner, but now it doesn't seem possible."

She made a face and said, "I was also looking forward to it. Maybe next time, we will go to some other more luxurious place."

He then guessed that she had arranged it all, as she didn't want to spend an intimate evening with him in one of the suites. It was all a drama, probably orchestrated by Ramesh Pratap, to trap him. If a video was taken, he would be put in a very difficult situation and subject to blackmail.

Then he caught the sight, when he looked around, of the other assistant from the office hovering around and who would have put the pill in the wine. By then, his driver with the car had come.

Surya was left surprised. He hissed, "Don't forget I am a seasoned detective."

Shanker was sitting in his office in deep thought, he was wondering whom he could trust, certainly not anyone from the KBL. They were too sly and overly clever for him and would do anything to not involve the concerned politicians in their report. Ravi Mathew, it appeared, was getting concerned that he may not be able to pull it off without any fingers being pointed at KBL associates. It would be difficult for him, as the media had got suspicious and started writing about it in Tamil newspapers, and also on the internet.

Shyamala came and smiled at him, "So, how did it go with the lovely smiling Surya last evening."

Shanker threw an inkpot at her which just missed her and smashed against the wall, spilling some ink.

She laughed and said, "So, it was all a charade, tell me sir, what happened!"

He told Shyamala that she should know as she was assisting him in the case. He didn't hold anything back, except his intentions to seduce Surya in one of the suites, but Shyamala must have guessed his plan to some extent. She knew that he was smitten by her and was longing to take her out for a quiet meal and, thereafter, if he got a chance to seduce her in the hotel.

"But Mr. Shanker, it may be that Surya was not part of the plan and Ramesh may have recorded your conversation through a link or a tap to her phone and sent this assistant to trap you. I think you should give Surya the benefit of doubt; she would be miserable if she didn't know the plot.

Give her a ring and see her reaction. Call her to *Yellow Brick* for lunch and chat with her without giving out anything; play innocent. It may work, she may spill the beans."

Shanker thought it was a good idea and called Surya and apologised for his unbecoming behaviour and hasty departure. He called her for lunch at the *Yellow Brick*, to which she immediately agreed.

He reached 15 minutes late deliberately and saw her sitting at their favourite table, sipping a non-alcoholic lemon drink and strumming the table with her fingers.

He sat down and gave her one of his most amiable smiles. "How long have you been waiting? I am sorry to be late, but you know in our office how things are.

So, tell me Surya, I don't remember clearly what happened that night, the wine had a strange reaction on me, and I felt slightly giddy. Either it was a bad bottle, or someone had added something to the wine. I don't know, maybe you saw something as you are more observant."

She kept quiet for a while, and then said, "You may not believe me, but I myself was surprised to see Manoj, whom I recognised as he works in our main office and comes to give papers, etc. to Pratap. I didn't plan it and was looking forward to a different type of ending than what took place."

"But tell me Surya, how is it that Ramesh knew that you were meeting me at the farmhouse. Did you tell him?"

"No, I didn't, and I spoke to you on my mobile phone, not on the landline."

"Who has given you the mobile phone?"

"Ramesh gave it to me and two others in the office."

"That means, he has connected the mobile phone he gave you to his connection, which is very easy to do with a little help from the phone company and he can hear your conversations. Just show me your phone".

She handed it to him, and glancing at the screen he saw a tiny display indicating there was a connection. Using his mobile phone, Shanker telephoned his friend and asked him to check if this phone was interconnected and, if it was, then with which company.

Their meal came and while he was gorging on his masala pasta, the call came, and he noted down the mobile phone number that was interconnected to the phone.

She immediately commented that it was one of the mobile phones which Ramesh used; he had three connections.

Shanker suggested that she purchase another mobile phone and get a new connection from another company and not inform them. This way, she could make all her private calls from it. And if she didn't, she could land up in serious trouble one day, because they could be tapping her private calls to all her family and friends. It was the 'Big Brother Syndrome'. They knew each and every movement she made. He advised her not to disconnect that particular line as they may get suspicious, but only use it for business calls and also, she should check if her parents' phones are being tapped. He gave her one number to call, state his reference and she would be told how to go about it.

Surya was in anxious, worried, and flustered, close-to-fainting mode, which was apparent to him, but he reassured her that there was no cause to worry. She could have said something sensitive to her friends or family and advised her to be more discrete in future. She understood what he meant, and Surya had tears in her eyes as she got up and left for work, while he was still on his ice cream.

When he returned to the office, he went to Shyamala indicating she was right about giving Surya the benefit of doubt. He told her how Ramesh was keeping a tab on Surya and monitored every mover of hers. An amazed Shyamala in turn told him how Ramesh Pratap had planned to dope Shanker by sending Manoj from the office, and how a clever Shanker had outsmarted them.

Shyamala continued, "He was quite sure that you would ask Surya to one of the fancy rooms and try your luck. I am not so sure if Surya would have so easily relented, but if she did, then probably taken a video to honeytrap you. I hope you were seated on the other side of the table at the restaurant. But maybe Manoj could have taken your video of you dancing with her."

"I didn't see him while dancing, it was later. He was quite clandestine."

"Now, how do we proceed? 5-6 are dead, which includes those in the crane accident, if it really was an accident. This will be very difficult for us unless one of the family members comes forward to lodge a police complaint, but that may not be possible with the threat of Ravi Mathew and his henchmen hovering over them."

Shanker, with furred brows drawn together, eyes narrowed, toying with the edge of his moustache, he thought hard … then looking at Shyamala in the eyes requested, "Could you ask your friend Somaya to help?

She may be able to trace the families and persuade them to talk. You said she was quite fearless."

Shyamala agreed, "That is a very good suggestion, we may get some important leads from her. I am sure the Cochin police have got their spies on Ravi Mathew, though he is too clever for them." The way he had managed to get the incident buried so quickly, sans allegations, as a pure and simple accident, was really remarkable."

"The main thing is to get our hooks, as Navin Kochar hinted, on the politicians who took heavy loans and have not paid them back."

KBL Associates had been hired for this reason. Ravi Mathews was s a major shareholder in it and was also involved with politicians who were given the loans. It was not known how they were going to cover it up in the report, or if they would keep delaying it until the government changed after the next election.

With respect to the relationship between Ravi Mathew and Ramesh Pratap, sooner or later, they were bound to have differences, and most likely, Ramesh Pratap would be shunted out and Ravi Mathew would put somebody else to his liking in his place. Not that they didn't get along, but Ramesh was not that comfortable dealing with Mathews.

"Mr. Pratap would never have agreed to take Hari Mohan to the U.K. for the operation, but Ravi Mathews more or less forced him, for obvious reasons. I will go and meet Ramesh tomorrow," declared Shanker to Shyamala.

He telephoned Surya and fixed an appointment with Ramesh, who insisted that Shanker stayed on for lunch as well.

Shanker arrived about ten minutes late and acted very formally with Surya, and then before going into Ramesh's office, winked at her. He saw a smile on the side of her face, hardly noticeable as the peon was also standing there.

He went and shook hands most cordially and sat on the sofa opposite him.

"So, Mr. Ramesh, how is your consultancy proceeding now that Vikram has jumped ship and is in Toronto with aim to join his family profession of academics?"

"Oh, we have Ajit Kumar, who is quite competent and has relocated without his family to Cochin."

"You now have six deaths on your hands. Doesn't it sound strange for a consultancy," he laughed.

"It is most unusual I must admit," he answered.

"As long as you are connected with Mr. Mathews, nobody can predict what may happen next," commented Shanker.

Ramesh kept quiet.

"I would suggest you find a more acceptable person in place of Mr. Mathews, or you will end up destroying the image of KBL Associates. I don't know if it is possible as he is a fairly large shareholder. You could consider tying up with a large international consultancy firm like Deloitte, KPMG or Grant Thornton. They have a great international reputation and can easily swallow Mr. Mathews. It would enhance your image also."

"We had thought of it, but Mr. Ravi Mathews will never agree, that is the problem."

In the meantime, lunch came in.

"So right now, you have nothing to tell me. Am I right in my assumption?"

"But he is careful in dealing with me and Shyamala, we are very seasoned detectives," Shanker hissed.

Shyamala got a call from Vikram, and after exchanging pleasantries, he said, "Someone in Canada, from a neighbouring city, telephoned me and said that I should refrain from mentioning anything about the consultancy of KBL, my previous employers, as it would be dangerous as they were a ruthless lot and Ravi Mathews was nothing short of a mafia don."

He said that he had introduced himself as Prabhat Roy and was previously the managing director of RML Bank but was forced to resign under political pressure.

Vikram told him that he had heard about him from colleagues, particularly executives of RML Bank, and knew that Navin Kochar, who was also his friend, knew him quite well. "He didn't have your telephone number or new email, otherwise he would have given it to me."

Prabhat wished to meet Vikram in person. He was living on the outskirts of Toronto, a twenty-five minutes' drive from a mall, so he suggested they meet over lunch.

"I met him in the mall. Grey haired and balding, and a Bengali accent which had not changed in Canada, he told me that Ramesh Pratap was not a strong leader and worked under the influence of Ravi Mathews, who manipulated him and did his bidding. In return, he let Ramesh put his hand in the till whenever he got a chance, and he also supplied him with young girls whenever he visited Cochin or London. Ramesh's marriage was a farce. They were together because of their daughter doing her Ph.D. in London, and their son, who was in a top school in Delhi. He thought that the trust of Ravi Mathew paid for the expensive education of his daughter."

"So, I shall be meeting him again when he probably tells me some more; he is like that, it was just a starter, the main meal will come a little later when he develops trust in me. He is scared of Ravi Mathews, as his relatives live in Delhi and Calcutta."

Shyamala went to Shanker's room the next day cooing, "Guess who telephoned me."

"Someone from Canada, isn't it?" he grinned.

"Yes."

"Then I must order some coffee, it must be interesting."

She had cleverly recorded the conversation on her mobile phone and played it back to Shanker.

"This is very interesting. I must say," he said listening intently. "I had misjudged Vikram. I thought he was an actor like Ramesh Pratap, though at a lower level. But it seems he is quite sincere, and his reason for leaving KBL seems just. I think you should keep in touch with him, and if you get a chance, go to Toronto next summer. I believe it was very beautiful at that time. I wonder if I could arrange for you to attend one of the police meetings of the Commonwealth Association at office expense. I attended one of them in Nairobi, Kenya, many years ago. It was very useful."

Shanker was still in touch with Mr. and Mrs. Shah, a Gujarati couple whom he had met there and become good friends. They came every alternative year to meet their relatives in Surat, and then, for a few days, they came to Delhi and stayed with him.

Coming back to square one and thinking about how to proceed, she called Somaya, who answered immediately, "Shyamala please give one or two days more, I am on it and have some information, but not enough."

Shanker's secretary came into the room, and said, "Mr. Ram Mohan Thakur, the Managing Director of RML bank wanted to talk to you. I told him you are very busy and will telephone him in the afternoon."

'This was a new development,' thought Shanker. They had so far evaded any direct contact with RML bank for obvious reasons.

Shanker telephoned him and invited him for a cup of tea at his office the next morning. Their main office was near Parliament Street, in the connecting lane, not far from the police station, a decent-sized building with an impressive façade.

Chapter 10

Shanker went to his office to meet Mr. Thakur at 10:30 a.m. for a cup of coffee.

Mr. Thakur was not too tall, maybe around 5′6″, but was very impressively and immaculately dressed. He invited Mr. Shanker to sit down and cordially asked what he could offer him to drink.

Shanker opted for black coffee without sugar, then changed his mind and put two spoons of brown sugar.

Mr. Thakur started the dialogue by saying that he was not clear about what the police were investigating. Mr. Shanker Dayal explained that the investigation was because of the six murders on record, in which KBL Associates were directly or indirectly involved.

"You need not explain," Mr. Thakur said, "I know all the details as we are in daily touch with them, two of their consultants come to our office here about three or four times a week. We have earmarked a cabin on the floor below where they sit and do their work."

"That's interesting," said Shanker, "though not surprising as they must have been given an agenda by Ramesh Pratap's office and a deadline, and their highly researched manual on the procedure to follow for the consultancy. It is a painstaking job, and I am sure your staff is fully cooperating."

"Yes," responded Mr. Thakur, "they are, but you must be knowing a lot more why this consultancy was necessary. Well, the audit and accounts office of the government was concerned about the bad debts of the bank and losses on account of them, as they are also large shareholders in the bank. The banking division has been calling for it for a long time."

"But as auditors, why did they not give a proper report and do a proper job?" enquired Shanker.

"They are a medium-sized firm and not very efficient. The senior partner is a close relative of one of the senior bureaucrats in the Finance Ministry. If it had been given to a big firm like Grant Thornton or KPMG, then we would have received a proper report."

"Well, the police are not interested in the accounts, audit, or profit and loss, it is not our agenda. We are investigating if any criminal dealings were involved in the murders. We were informed that most of the bad loans were those given to the relatives of the politicians, and of course, they could not have used them for running businesses. They have no training or acumen for it, so how are they going to repay you? They must have used them for buying assets or for political campaigning."

"You are right, Mr. Shanker, that is the case, Mr. Roy, my predecessor, tried his best to run it as a commercial organisation, but the politicians over-ruled him at every stage and gave these loans under pressure to co-operatives in western India and Kerala."

"I believe the common link is Mr. Ravi Mathew of Cochin."

"You are right, Mr. Shanker. It is Ravi Mathew, a very powerful businessman, with strong political links. But not only is he a large shareholder in our bank, relatively small, but also has immense influence, because of his political connections and his widespread marine empire, particularly in the gulf countries and part of Europe."

"So, how do you plan to clean up the bank, otherwise you will have no choice but to merge with one of the large public-sector banks and play second fiddle to them," Shanker pointed out.

"Well, it depends on the report of KBL Associates."

"The government may not accept their report."

"Well, we will have to wait and see, Mr. Shanker."

"I will be meeting you again, Mr. Thakur, if required."

Shyamala asked a concerned looking and silent Shanker, "So, now where are we heading?" Eventually, he mumbled, "I don't know, any ideas?"

"Can't think. I haven't even heard from Somaya. Maybe she is not in a position to tell us anything now, after all Ravi Mathew is an extremely shrewd operator."

"I wonder how the replacement for Vikram, Ajit Kumar is faring. Maybe Somaya will know. I will call her tomorrow."

That night, Somaya telephoned Shyamala and told her that they had reopened the case of the death of the supervisor and three workers in the marine workshop owned by Ravi Mathew.

"How did you manage that," asked and amazed Shyamala.

"I was suspicious after reading the report, and went to meet my boss, who is the number two in the chain of command. After a lot of arguments, I persuaded him to re-open the case. He was very hesitant, and I don't blame him as Ravi Mathew is a powerful 'Don' and even the police want to keep away from him."

"For a moment, I thought maybe he was on the payroll of Mathew, but my suspicion was wrong as he is an honest officer with a good reputation and is angling for a post in Delhi in either CBI or IB as deputy director. He has been trying very hard and is a persistent person, so I think sooner or later he will get an assignment in Delhi."

"Anyway, he has now made me in charge of the re-investigation which will be approved at the next meeting. Fortunately, this will not require any nod from the political bosses."

"Shyamala, I will keep you duly informed."

The next day Shyamala repeated her telephone conversation with Somaya to Shanker.

"Let me not rely too much on Somaya. I know she is a competent lady, but there are powerful people involved who may try to scuttle things or arrange a cover-up."

"As far as Mr. Ajit Kumar is concerned, he is working very hard, but under the sharp eyes of big brother Mr. Mathew. I am sure he must have bugged his room and his telephone landline, besides keeping a sharp eye on him."

"He will write whatever Ravi Mathew tells him to, which will suit Ramesh Pratap also, as he does not want to cross swords with Ravi Mathew."

"We have to find the weak spot of Ravi Mathew, but I don't know how to," said Shanker. "Maybe my friend in the I.B. can help me. I will go and meet him tomorrow."

Shanker made an appointment with his batch mate, Bharat Shah in the Intelligence Bureau, he was now one of the deputy directors. Bharat was very forthcoming. They had become friendly in the academy, and he kept in touch with him in Delhi, also having a drink in the Services Club now and then. He was from the Gujarat cadre but had spent most of the time in Delhi on one or another assignment.

"So, what is it this time" he asked Shanker.

"Oh, nothing concerning the IB, but we are doing some investigation into murders connected with

KBL Associates, who are doing a comprehensive consultancy on a bank called RML, which is running into losses due to loans given to the kins of politicians in western India, mainly co-operatives in Maharashtra and Kerala. The trouble spot is Kerala.

"One of the large shareholders of KBL is a powerful businessman called Ravi Mathew, based in Cochin. He has large interests in the marine business in India and abroad. He is also very close to relatives of politicians in that region and had influenced the bank to give them loans, which are not paid back and not likely to be paid back."

Without hesitation, Bharat said, "We have several files on Ravi Mathew, but have not been able to nail him down. He is very shrewd and has very strong political connections.

"One investigation we had to stop as he brought strong political influence on us, and our director agreed to put a hold on it. We have not written it off but are not proceeding with the investigation.

You can go through the files if you like, but they are not of much help."

"Yes, I have read several files on him," said Shanker, "but it did not lead me anywhere."

"KBL associates' Managing Director, Mr. Ramesh Pratap is subservient to him, as he is a large shareholder in KBL, and it is a clear conflict of interest that the consultancy was given to them."

"These things happen," said Bharat, "in India all the time, in every state. Politicians interfere and don't let the investigators do their jobs."

"Alright," said Shanker, "So, we don't have much to go on. But the murders are connected to KBL associates, four in the workshop of Ravi Mathew, a driver connected with the KBL, and their Finance Manager who died on the operating table in a private hospital in London."

"Surely, Scotland Yard must have done their investigation," he asked

"Yes, they did point fingers at the hospital, but said it was a case of negligence, and the medical association sided with the hospital and its doctors."

"So, how can you call it murder?"

Shanker gave him the details about Hari Mohan and how he was forcefully taken to London. Bharat remarked that it would be very difficult to prove since the death happened in London. It would be impossible for them to even point a finger at the investigation. Added to the fact that the last word remains with the medical association which no one would question. Shanker commented that they were back to square one and asked Bharat for advice on how to proceed. Bharat told Shanker that regarding the financial aspect, the Intelligence Bureau could not investigate since it was not their job to do so, however, they could involve the audit and the accounts office of the government to be a part of the investigation.

Bharat doubted if the government would agree as KBL had been appointed as the consultant and sighed that they would just have to await the report since there didn't seem to be any other way.

Shanker was a little disappointed as he left the meeting. He thought of meeting Surya again, and this time without any slip-ups. So, he telephoned her, but she was busy and said she would return a call to him later. She didn't telephone him that evening, and he was disappointed and thought that maybe she didn't want to meet him anymore.

To his surprise, she called him the following day, speaking in a whispering tone she promised to call him from her landline at home, which she did later, all the while very suspicious that they were possibly recording her conversations on the mobile phone, and hoped her landline was not tapped as well, she had plans to apply for another landline from a different telephone company. Shanker revealed his desire in seeing her again but at someplace else as he believed there were informers at the farmhouses and hotels in that area. He knew of an old and beautiful haveli in the Chandni Chowk area, where they could never be traced. It was practically unused as the owners - old aristocrats of Delhi for the last six generations, due to family squabbles, had abandoned the place for another house in the posh localities of New Delhi. But the family did rent it out for parties, wedding, and other functions. The furniture was at least 100 years old but in immaculate condition.

Shanker was as excited about an evening out there, as much as Surya for it sounded interesting. He made plans for a cab to have her picked up and he would get there in a different cab.

Surya got home rummaging through her wardrobe, deciding what to wear and settled on an elegant pink saree in cotton.

The taxi came at 7.00 p.m. and reached the place in an hour, weaving its way through the traffic.

Clad in a handloom kurta pyjama, he was waiting for her at the stairs near the entrance dressed in a kurta pyjama. She was left visibly impressed at the architecture, the beautiful carvings, marble façade and exquisite period furniture, it was like a sultan's palace.

He took her around and showed the beautiful, faded wall paintings which had been touched up but appeared to have been neglected lately. The family may have not wanted to spend more money, or there might have been a lack of cooperation between them. He took her into a special room full of mirrors and silver or metal candle stands and old-fashioned sofas with fading upholstery, maybe cleaned up for them. She sat down on a green coloured sofa, and he came and sat down on a chair close to her. They had to be careful as there were servants around, dressed in old-fashioned and outdated dresses. One of the better dressed waiters came, he must have been head of the coterie and put delicacies in front of them.

She had never seen this old-fashioned variety of food, almost from a different era, the cuisine of the old Delhi nawabs and rich families The savouries tasted awesome, and the sweets were out of this world, nothing like the ones you'd see at the restaurants and hotels in New Delhi.

She looked up and put her hands on her head- the huge chandelier was hanging so low. It was just a few feet above her, the lights had not been put on as it would have made the room very bright.

Shanker saw her predicament and started laughing. "Don't worry Surya, it won't fall," he said and cupped her face with his hands in reassurance.

"This is the old world, which we have probably never seen. It doesn't exist anymore. This haveli is an exception, maybe there are three or four more like this, but the charm of these havelis is matchless."

Then the Manager came and whispered something in Shanker's ear, and he nodded. Five minutes later, a three-piece old-fashioned band came one musician with a flute, the other with a *tabla*, and the third with a type of harmonium. They started playing old romantic songs of the 60s and the 70s. Shanker and Surya also hummed along softly and were familiar with some of the lyrics.

She said, "My father and uncle are fond of these old songs and play them all the time or listen to them on some T.V. channel or the other. My mother prefers instrumental music and used to play the sitar before they got married, and even continued until a few years ago, but rarely ever plays now. Even the sitar is gathering dust."

They enjoyed the music till the dinner was served ornate thalis and bowls and they relished it to the core, enjoying the aroma and savouring every bite with music to soothe away the tension of the present-day activities and worries. The servings were generous, and the service was regal, true aristocratic class!

After dinner, Shanker took her upstairs to show her the magnificent bedrooms with multi-coloured furniture and antique lamps on the side tables and carvings of all sorts that cast an enchanting and romantic atmosphere in the rooms.

She was tempted to try the bed but he sensing her mood checked her just in time, the management would object as they did not like it to be made into a brothel of sorts and may have cameras positioned strategically. One of his colleagues had made that faux pas in another similar haveli, with the wife of a friend, He was trapped that way and had to compromise on a serious offence against the lady's husband. Shanker and Surya just had to find another place. "We have to find a safer venue and your farmhouses are certainly not safe. You blackmail people by taking their videos there, I myself have seen them. Your boss might also have instructed you to go to the farmhouse with me, but the attempt failed."

Surya went quite red in the face. "It will never happen again, Shanker." She had tears in her eyes, "believe me, I have had many affairs, but with you, I feel differently."

Shanker smiled at her and said, "We better go." He took her to a corner behind the curtain and gave her a very passionate kiss. She wouldn't let him go and kept kissing him with all the sincerity and passion she had in her.

The next day back at the office, Shanker told all about his date to Shyamala and not having obtained any new information. "Back to square one," Shyamala commented, as she smiled at Shanker in the office. "What is the agenda now?"

"I don't know," mumbled Shanker. "You are the clever one, and the younger one with good ideas. Have you heard from Vikram lately?" She said no. "I suppose he must be busy or has found a new girlfriend. He wouldn't have a problem; with his charm, they would swarm all over him."

"Don't feel jealous, Shyamala. He asked you to come, but you refused. But in the summer, you should visit him if he offers to send you a ticket."

"I don't mind buying a ticket. I would love to see North America, particularly New York and Washington. I have relatives living in New Jersey."

"Well, let's discuss how we are going to proceed further."

"Shyamala, have you heard from Somaya, your friend in Cochin?"

"Not yet. She has not got back to me, with any further news. I will try after two or three days. Maybe she is busy with another assignment."

Just then by chance, the call came from Somaya.

"We were just thinking of you, Somaya, what a coincidence. Do you have any news for us or not?" she asked.

"Yes, I called Ajit Kumar, the replacement of Vikram, to my office yesterday. He came, but I could make out he was talking in monosyllables, and just had two or three sips of coffee, and got up to leave. I was very surprised by his behaviour; it looked as if some serious matter was bothering him. I stopped him from leaving and smiled at him and asked him if his wife and children were not missing him too much and if he was worried about them. He cooled down a bit and said that he was missing them very badly and that he talked to his daughter and son for half an hour every night. He really wondered why he had agreed to take that assignment, even though they were paying substantial extra allowances, but all the time he was worried about his family who was living in a good apartment in one of the better colonies, Gulmohar Park, where they had, against his wishes, posted two guards 24 X 7 for the safety of his wife and children. They are no ordinary guards. They are trained spies and send information to Mr. Ramesh's assistant every day, giving details about who came, and who left."

"How do you know?" I asked him.

"Don't forget, I also have friends and associates, and one of the female secretary's son's studies in the school where my wife teaches. She is friendly with us and tells my wife everything. In return, my wife takes good care of her son in the school."

"Why this snooping? I don't understand. Even here in Cochin, I am constantly spied upon, my phone is tapped. I don't know how they manage that with mobile phones. I am sure Mr. Mathew must have arranged that, and my small apartment is under constant surveillance. I can see cameras hidden near the top ventilator."

"I dare not protest, otherwise they will get suspicious."

"What a life, Ms. Somaya," he said.

"I said you can call me Som for short, everyone does.

He smiled and said, "Okay."

"But you haven't told me anything about your work as a consultant. What are your findings, etc.? After all, you are a consultant and are supposed to make a comprehensive report? RML bank is paying you for it, am I right?"

"You are right, and I had that intention when I arrived to do my homework. I wanted to prepare a fair and reasonable report, and give it to my boss, Mr. Ramesh Pratap. I wanted him to read it and then make a decision, based on facts, of what he would like me to include. But I have not been given such a chance, they pressured and force me to make a report which would suit their purpose and include facts which don't exist and are untrue."

"Every evening, my notes are sent to Mr. Ravi Mathew, who scrutinises them and alters them to what he would like me to include. Under these circumstances, it is impossible for me to work."

"So, what do you want to do?" I asked.

He got up and said, "Let me think. I will get back to you."

Shanker was not at all surprised with what Ajit Kumar had told Somaya or Som as she wanted to be called. Anyone decent and cultured would be hopping mad if his privacy was intruded upon.

"Did you by any chance record what Som told you" he asked Shyamala. She looked at him and said, "Of course, I did. Do you want me to play it back?"

"He took out his earphones and re-heard the conversation word for word.

"We might have to record this on our mini-recorder and play it to Ramesh and ask for his comments if the chance arises, or the necessity."

"That is not a bad idea. It will put him in a spot, and his reaction would be worth hearing and the expression on his face worth seeing."

"Well done, Shyamala, let us go and meet Mr. Ramesh."

"I don't think it is such a good idea and poor Ajit Kumar might lose his job," said Shyamala.

"Well, then what other option do we have? We have to confront him. Maybe we can use the recording as a last resort."

"We have to confront Mr. Ramesh sometime, why not tomorrow?"

"Oh, I will telephone his secretary and see his response."

The secretary telephoned back and said, "Mr. Ramesh can meet you for coffee at 11:30 a.m. tomorrow if it is suitable." Shyamala confirmed it.

Shanker made notes on what he would like to ask Ramesh Pratap. Whether he would respond or not was a different issue.

Chapter 11

As expected, Mr. Ramesh was waiting for them. He was dressed in a three-piece suit, probably stitched in London on his last trip, with a matching tie. 'Probably going to a lunch reception,' he thought.

Shanker and Shyamala sat down on the sofa, opposite his large comfortable chair. After ordering coffee and snacks, he said, "Mr. Shanker, you seem to have become a regular visitor here, am I using the right word!"

"Yes and no," said Shyamala. "You can call it whatever you like, but the polite word would be … well it is not coming to my mind right now."

"Mr. Ramesh, we wanted to inquire, how is the consultancy in Cochin proceeding with Mr. Ajit Kumar, because if I am not mistaken, Kerala and Maharashtra are the two states where these loans were disbursed by RML, to co-operatives with political connections."

Ramesh was taken aback by Shanker's question, but kept his cool and said, "I am sure that it is proceeding well. Mr. Ajit Kumar is an experienced consultant."

"But I hope Mr. Ravi Mathew is not interfering with his work. He is used to dictating to everyone. He is overbearing and dominating, according to what I hear."

"No, I am sure, he is not interfering. He probably doesn't have the time for it," replied Ramesh shifting a bit in his chair and his chin tilted a bit in a defensive manner nonetheless he remained polite.

"Well, our information is that he is virtually dictating what Ajit Kumar should write."

"Well, I think you have been misinformed, Mr. Shanker. I am sure that Mr. Mathew would let him do his work."

Shyamala took out her recorder and started playing the recording. Mr. Pratap listened to it intently and his face became red like a red plum as he swallowed several times.

"I am shocked Mr. Shanker. I never knew, as he had never complained to me."

"I will call him back to our Delhi office. I would not like to lose him as he is a very hardworking and competent executive."

"Whoever you said will not give you the correct information, with Ravi Mathew's overpowering presence. He will make sure that he gives the report to his liking."

"I agree with you, Mr. Shanker. Let me consult other directors and then decide how to handle the situation." Shanker said, "If you need help from us, please let us know."

On the way out, he saw Surya sitting in a corner and typing something on the computer. She waved to him and continued typing.

He was pleased that she didn't show any familiarity as he noticed a camera on the left-hand side of the room, placed strategically on top.

It would record anyone entering or leaving.

They were a little disappointed from the response by Mr. Ramesh, and expected him to be more forthcoming, though it would have been difficult for him.

Shanker sat in the car and doodled, wondering what to do next. He wasn't sure how to proceed, as their job was the criminal investigation and not the consultancy review in any manner.

The information Som had given was for the benefit of KBL Associates and not their investigation. They had no role to play in the consultancy, though in his view, the criminal element was interfering with a fair report which was expected from KBL.

In his view, it is not possible to prepare a fair report, with the criminality involved, particularly on the part of Mr. Ravi Mathew. Their job was to find out if the bank was influenced to give loans and whether the politicians indulged in corrupt or criminal tactics to get the loans.

Ravi Mathew was certainly involved in Hari Mohan's death on the operating table, but it was not possible for them to do anything about it, as the medical association in London had given the hospital a clean chit, despite the reservations of Scotland Yard. It would be impossible to open that investigation again.

It was doubtful if Som and her colleagues would be able to find any malefice in the death of the supervisor and three workers at the workshop who were killed by the crane. The local investigation had said that it was an accident.

Shanker again thought, 'What would be the connection of the supervisor and the three workers, that they would be targets? What were they involved in the KBL Associates report, as they were only workers? There must have been a good reason to suspect malefice, and they had so far not found one, neither the police nor anyone else.'

If Som came up with something, then they could point fingers at KBL and Mathew.

He contacted Hari Mohan's wife not only to pay his respect but to see what if any information could be had. She lived in Safdarjung Enclave on the 2nd floor of a decently constructed house. He took off his shoes as was customary in their community in Karnataka. She indicated that it was not necessary, but he insisted, which pleased her.

"How are you faring?" he asked.

"Oh, I have no option but to carry on with my life. They have given me generous compensation and are paying for the education of my son in an engineering college in South India and my daughter's schooling in a good school in Delhi."

"What else can I expect from them?"

"No, I think they have treated you well, certainly. But it was very sudden that your husband had to be rushed to London for an operation which could easily have been done here."

"Yes, you are right, Mr. Shanker. There was no need at all to take him to London. His doctor at his hospital, who was treating him, could have easily done it, and most likely he would have survived."

"The flight to London and all the tension certainly aggravated his condition, which was unnecessary, but who was I to argue with them and even Hari Mohan told them so, but they insisted and said that London was the best place for the operation and doctors there were world class, and the hospitals were well equipped."

"Whatever happened, Mr. Shanker, it was God's will."

"Was it Mr. Hari Mohan?" he asked.

"I don't have an answer to that as the medical council gave a clean chit."

Shanker got up and said, "Thank you for meeting me. If you need any help, anytime, please contact me," and he gave his card and left.

Vikram telephoned Shyamala; she was quite surprised to receive his call. She asked him jokingly, "Do you still miss me, haven't you found a girlfriend yet?"

"Oh, there are plenty of girls available for dating and going out with, but they are very different, and I have not been able to adjust myself to the culture here. It will take some time for that. I have yet to dig in my foundation. Though I attend classes at the university, I have also joined a medium-sized consultancy firm and they pay me quite well, so I have shifted out of my brother's flat, and gotten a small apartment for myself. It is quite comfortable, but I am quite lonely, as I don't know many people and don't have any friends here. I suppose I shall make friends eventually, as I have joined the tennis club and gym, and there are quite a lot of Indian members there, particularly Sardarjis, and some are quite friendly, and I speak fluent Punjabi as my mother's family is Punjabi Sikh."

"They dragged me to the local gurudwara. It was quite impressive and very clean, and I had a good Punjabi meal after a long time. The Gyani was very nice to me and said that I could drop in for a meal anytime. He claimed to be a distant cousin of my mother's family, but I could not connect as I am pretty bad at these relationship connections. Anyway, having him as a friend is very useful to me as he has good local connections and he invited me to his house as well."

"The local Canadians are a little reserved and don't mix much with us. Though they are helpful, and I get along very well with my tutors at the university."

Shyamala kept on listening, and then asked him, "When are you planning to visit India, surely you want to meet your family."

"Most probably in winter as the university is closed, and I can take leave from my employers, and it gets miserably cold here, I am told, so I will come in December, most likely, three months from now."

"Have you received any calls from KBL Associates?"

"Yes, I have. Mr. Pratap telephoned me and asked me when I was coming to Delhi as there were one or two matters for which he wanted my assistance on a voluntary basis, in case I was prepared to do so."

"What did you tell him?" asked Shyamala. Then she added, "I suggest you keep away from them. I don't know what they have in their mind. I would not trust them after the way they behaved with you."

"You are right, Shyamala. I have to be careful. I will not tell them when I am coming and telephone them when I arrive at my convenience. If I go to their office in Delhi, particularly to meet Ramesh Pratap, it is quite safe."

"Have you met them again?" he asked.

"Yes, Shanker and I went to meet Mr. Pratap, but nothing new emerged except," and she repeated what Som had told her, "And he said that Ajit Kumar would be recalled, and they will send someone else."

"I am not at all surprised," said Vikram, "Mathew will not let anyone work independently. He wants to dictate what he thinks is his strategy. I could not figure out as he was always going round in circles with me, and I got totally fed up and told Mr. Ramesh. I don't think Ramesh can do very much; Mathew is very powerful."

Shyamala listened and then asked him, "Now that you are out of it, maybe you can guide us on how we should proceed, as at present we are getting nowhere."

"It is difficult to answer Shyamala, but let me make some notes, and I will send them by email, on your computer."

"Look after yourself, Vikram. I am missing you," she said.

He responded, "I am also missing you and will see you in winter."

Shyamala told Shanker about the conversation with Vikram, and also that he will be making notes, and sending them to her as guidance. "I told him we are not quite confident of the proceeding."

Somaya telephoned Shyamala and told her that she called Ajit Kumar on the landline to be on the safe side and one of the girls called Shanti picked up the phone and told her that he is not available. Somaya related that she told Shanti who she was and that his family wanted to get in touch with him but couldn't, so they telephoned the police office. She related that Shanti got very worried and said she will telephone her from a secure line.

Fifteen minutes later Shanti called again saying that Mr. Kumar had been taken to one of the Ayurveda clinics for treatment as he was suffering from depression. It was twenty kilometres from Cochin.

"What are they up to?" Shyamala asked Somaya. "It sounds very fishy to me, as Pratap told me that he was calling him back to Delhi and was sending a replacement." She continued, "I think you better send somebody to that Ayurvedic Treatment Centre, to make sure that he is okay."

Somaya agreed and said that she will send some trusted person, preferably a male of junior rank.

The following morning Somaya called Shyamala indicating that the junior officer, Shashi had gone to that Ayurvedic Treatment Centre. The Centre could not make any excuses to the officer, and he was directed to Mr. Kumar's room where he was lying in bed sedated and wrapped in sheets. The officer reported that Mr. Kumar didn't look too good, so he telephoned this to Somaya, who told him not to leave Mr. Kumar alone and that she would send an ambulance to bring him to the hospital where she knew the doctors well, the manager was a relative of hers.

Mr. Kumar arrived three hours later and was admitted to the hospital. It was related that his condition was so bad that they had to shift him to the Intensive Care Unit immediately. Somaya then Shanti that she had better come to the hospital, or she would have her arrested. A scared Shanti caught a taxi and was at the hospital within 40 minutes. Somaya terrified Shanti by putting her under arrest by two female policewomen. She was so frightened that she asked her if she was under arrest and was told yes, for attempting to murder Mr. Ajit Kumar.

Shanti was so terrified that she broke out in cold sweats as she repeatedly denied her involvement in what had happened to Mr. Kumar. She told them that it was Mr. Mathew's secretary who had arranged to send Ajit Kumar to the Ayurvedic Treatment Centre for recuperation, as he had complained that he was not feeling well.

Somaya then telephoned the director of the Ayurvedic Treatment Centre, who told her that when Mr. Ajit Kumar came, he was in a bad state and in his view, had been injected with some substance, which they were still trying to analyse from blood samples taken upon arrival. It looked like a dangerous drug. The Director of the Centre thanked Somaya and others for getting Mr. Kumar out of the centre to a proper hospital, as they were not a hospital and didn't have the required facilities to deal with such illness.

Somaya asked the director where he had sent the blood samples for analysis and he gave her the name of a well-known clinic, called SRL, which has many branches in Kerala. He also told her that someone from Mr. Kumar's office had telephoned and taken the address of the clinic. At this point, Somaya was shaken up that she rushed in her car to the clinic, but it was too late. The report had been collected by

Mr. Kumar's office; however, he said that if she could wait for 15 mins, he would make a duplicate copy of their findings. This was received which showed that he had been injected with a dangerous drug and if they had not sent the ambulance, he would have gone into a coma, and maybe something worse.

Somaya went back to the hospital and was relieved to learn that Mr. Kumar was recovering and would be shifted out of the I.C.U the next day. Not wanting to take any chances, Somaya kept a police constable to guard him just in case anyone attempted anything.

Shanker telephoned Ajit Kumar's wife the next morning asking her if her husband had come back to Delhi. She was quite surprised to receive a call from a senior police officer of Delhi and answered matter of fact, that he was in Goa on an assignment, but he had not telephoned for two days, though his office kept saying that he was very busy and would make contact when possible.

Shanker told her to stay at home and to take leave, not to attend school. He advised that Shyamala, his assistant, would come before lunch and meet her. This caught Mr. Kumar's wife by surprise prompting her to ask if everything was okay now sounding extremely worried.

He assured her that she could send the children to school because they should not miss their classes. She informed him that the school bus had already picked them up and they should be at school soon.

Shyamala reached her house in Gulmohar Park by around 11 a.m. and felt sorry for the worried look on her face. Mrs. Kumar was so desperate for answers that she grabbed Shyamala by the hand asking her what it was that she was hiding. Shyamala slowly told her everything and assured her that her friend Somaya had a police constable guarding him. She then telephoned the guarding officer and introduced herself. He was polite and reported that Mr. Ajit Kumar was feeling better and was awake; he would give his phone to him so that he could talk to his wife.

She went into the other room and talked to him for almost 20 minutes. Eventually, he became tired and couldn't talk more. The doctor had given him a sedative, so he was drooling and couldn't talk that clearly.

His wife told Somaya that her husband's condition sounded worse than what she told her. She further asked whether she should go to Cochin and bring her husband back. She even suggested leaving the children with her mother who is very fond of them or their granny, who is equally fond of them. Shyamala explained that she would speak to her boss, Shanker, and also my colleague Som about what they advised.

They both advised said that she could travel the following day and they could catch a flight back to Delhi. Somaya could send a nurse with them out of abundant caution. Ajit Kumar's wife, Rani agreed and Shanker telephoned Ramesh Pratap's office, but as he was not available, Shanker talked to his secretary and explained that he should make urgent arrangements to bring him back.

Ramesh telephoned in the evening, just before Shanker left his office, sounding very perturbed to say that KBL will make all the arrangements and ensure that Ajit Kumar is safely brought back.

Shanker listened to him then advised him in a very stern tone, "You go ahead and come and meet me in my office tomorrow at 11:30 a.m."

Shanker could hear the heavy breathing of Mr. Ramesh Pratap as he paused before saying, "Yes, I will be there, Mr. Shanker."

He came to meet Shanker at 11:30 a.m. along with his legal assistant. They were shown to his office and seated. Shanker was in no mood for pleasantries since Ramesh kept being evasive when he knew exactly what was going on and failed to 'grow a spine and put his house in order'. Shanker spoke in his most professional, stern and penetrating tone as he said, "Mr. Pratap, you know what happened to Mr. Ajit Kumar, he almost died. If the Cochin police had not acted in time and brought him from the Ayurvedic Treatment Centre to the hospital in time, he would not have survived." "They are putting all the pieces together and will criminally charge all those concerned in your office, and in case you and Mr. Mathew are involved, then it is up to them to frame the appropriate charges."

"Is this how you treat your consultants?"

"I would not advise Mr. Ajit Kumar to continue working for you, but that is between you and him."

"Vikram was lucky he left in time and is now peacefully settled in Canada."

"If the press gets a hold of what is happening in your consultancy, there may be questions raised in the parliament."

"I suggest you put your house in order Mr. Pratap, things are getting out of hand, with six deaths and this might have been the seventh. The newspapers and T.V. channels will make hay while the sun shines, as the saying goes."

"You should settle matters with Mr. Mathew, and if you cannot, it may be better if you find another solution. That is up to you to decide, but things cannot continue the way they are right now."

Mr. Ramesh Pratap and his assistant both remained silent and then got up and left.

Shyamala telephoned Som and appraised her of the meeting and asked her how her investigation had been proceeding. She told her that it would take time as obstacles were being put in their way.

Shyamala went the following day to meet Rani in Gulmohar Park; they had come back the night before, by the last flight via Mumbai. He looked better and half an hour later, Shanker joined them. He was sitting propped up by the cushions on the sofa chair and was drinking a glass of lassi.

Rani appeared to have made a jugful of lassi and offered it to Shyamala and Shanker.

"Is it sweet," Shyamala asked.

"No, it is bland. I put syrup in it if he wants sweet, otherwise some salt and pepper. I generally drink it with a little salt and a dash of garam masala."

"I wouldn't mind a glass of that," said Shyamala and Shanker said that he would prefer the sweet concoction.

They sat quietly drinking the lassi until Ajit broke the silence. He started by telling them about constant interference and how they were dictating to him what to write. They tore his notes and threw them in the wastepaper basket and gave him a typed sheet and ordered him to write along those lines. They were very aggressive, and he could not refuse.

He related that the next day, he wrote the preliminary report and wanted to see some files which he thought were necessary for him to go through to proceed further. They refused and said that they could not trace those files. They must be with Mr. Mathew or Mr. Pratap.

He continued that he told them that he could not proceed further without the required information because he could not write without any links with the file concerned. He mentioned that the senior clerk, Mr. John was quite upset and said he will have to check with Mr. Mathew. Those files were related to loans given to the relatives of politicians and the co-operatives. They were closely guarded, and he thinks Mr. Mathew kept them securely in his office, and no one had any access to them, not even his private secretary, John.

So, he didn't say anything else and when Mr. Mathew called him to find out how he was proceeding and to show him the file with the notes, Ajit told him that he had not completed the notes as he had not been able to get the required information.

At this point, Mr. Mathew shrugged him aside and asked what was so important about the files that he couldn't make his report without them. He even suggested that *"John will tell you whatever you want to know, he has a very good memory and so does Rosie Lashkari. She is very good, and between them, they can answer all your queries."*

Ajit continued that he told Mr. Mathew that he would like to double check himself, as he didn't want to slip up on anything.

Mr. Mathew was notably quiet for a few minutes as he observed Mr. Ajit Kumar and then he slowly said, *"You sound tired. Why don't you go to the Ayurvedic Treatment Centre for recuperation? It is just 2 hours' drive from here, the driver will take you comfortably and Rosie can accompany you. After all their Ayurveda baths and massages, you will feel like a new man. They are famous for that, patients come from abroad for their treatment."*

Mr. Kumar mentioned that he was utterly disgusted and agreed, as it would give him a break from the office which he felt he badly needed. So, he related that he went the next day in their Mercedes car. The dwelling was very comfortably, and was put up in a nice cottage, well-furnished with an adjoining room for Rosie on the same floor, but a little distance from my room designed for treatment of patients with all the attendant gadgets. He said that the food was nice, and he relaxed and took a small nap. Later, a doctor and nurse came and took his temperature, blood pressure, etc. and then went away. They came back after two hours and gave him some ayurvedic medicine to drink. At least he thought it was an ayurvedic medicine, but he did not know much about those medicines. It made him feel very sleepy and he fell into a deep sleep. However, he did feel them giving him an injection and the needle did pain even though he could not make out what was happening. He added that a few hours later, he got up and was in great pain over his entire body. He was sweating and had difficulty breathing; he thought he would die.

That was when he saw a hospital ambulance and they put him in it and took him to the hospital in Cochin where the doctors saved his life. He concluded that if he had not been taken to the hospital, he most likely would have died in the cottage. Mr. Kumar remarked that by now the hospital must have detected what injection they had given him.

He was told that the lab has not been able to conclusively come to a definite finding as to what treatment was given to him. They said it was very difficult, but they do have a good idea. It is a drug that revives or puts you in a coma and can even lead to death, depending on how it works on you.

"You are very lucky, Mr. Ajit Kumar, that you are alive," he remarked. He could see the tears in Rani's eyes.

Chapter 12

Shanker telephoned Ramesh Pratap and said that he had met Ajit Kumar and recorded whatever he told him which is absolutely shocking. It appears that Mathew's assistant wanted to kill him, and if Somaya had not sent the ambulance from the hospital and had him taken to the hospital, he most probably would have died.

Shanker continued in a serious tone, "I don't understand why he was treated in this fashion, after all, he was just writing a report and should have been shown files he wanted to see. What was so confidential in the files that you didn't want him to see?" There was no response, all was quiet.

"We will have to send someone from the state audit department, but of course, Mr. Mathew must have removed them by now." In a crisp and business-like tone, he continued as if a teacher was scolding naughty students; respectful but serious.

"Mr. Pratap, I am still bewildered as to why you bid for this consultancy, as it may ruin the reputation of your firm if an investigation is ordered, which it will be."

"The Cochin police have ordered an inquiry into the incident at the Ayurvedic Treatment Centre with Mr. Ajit Kumar, so let's wait for their report."

"What do you want to do with Ajit Kumar, are you asking him to leave your company or giving him a routine consultancy assignment? He is a good man, and I would try to retain experienced consultants, they are not easy to find."

Mr. Ramesh Pratap didn't answer and then slowly told Shanker, "I think this matter will be discussed by the board of directors. I will put it before them and let them decide."

"But Mr. Mathew is also a director, so how will it be decided without his consent? He is also a large shareholder. Nothing can be done without his nod."

"That is right, Mr. Shanker, but I have no choice in this matter. I have to do what the directors decide."

He telephoned Mr. Ajit Kumar and asked him how he was feeling both mentally and physically.

Mr. Ajit Kumar said that physically he was feeling better but mentally he was very confused and didn't know what to do.

He said he would go and meet Mr. Pratap and take his advice. He had helped him in the past also, and maybe he could talk to someone in another consultancy firm about an assignment for him.

"That appears to be a good idea, Mr. Ajit Kumar if he could introduce you to another firm. I am sure with his recommendations you would get another job. It would not be advisable to work for KBL."

Shanker was surprised to see his old friend and college mate Navin Kochar, who had left RML bank and joined an international consultancy firm owned by a Japanese business house but was based in Singapore.

They didn't try to dominate the consultancy as long as they followed the rules laid down, which were sometimes quite strict. They had offices in several countries and were associated with a Japanese multinational finance house, with investments, particularly in Asia, including India.

Indian companies wanting investments from Japanese financial firms would approach this consultancy firm as it would ensure Japanese investors that they were investing in a reliable company or bank. They preferred investing in large companies and big Indian private banks.

Navin Kochar was in Delhi, enroute to Mumbai, to assess companies that had approached for investment.

"So, what are you here for?" said Shanker.

"Oh, on a routine visit. One company in Delhi and three in Mumbai have been following up with us for investing in their ventures."

"Any progress on the KBL-RML front, I believe there are serious hurdles in proceeding further due to non-cooperation. I don't know who is putting the obstacles. It appears that KBL is putting obstacles in the way of their own consultants, making it difficult for them to do their consultancy."

"Who told you this Navin, you appear to be very well informed?"

He replied saying, "I had my sources of information at one time. I was the senior executive in charge of disbursing loans by RML and these loans, I was literally forced to disburse, to co-operatives managed by relatives of politicians and businessmen like Ravi Mathew, who is also connected closely with RML bank and is a shareholder as well."

"Wouldn't that be a conflict of interest as he is a large shareholder in KBL consultants as well?"

"He is a very clever shareholder, through the Benami route, which is not easy to trace but cleverly exercises his powers individually and so no one can raise a finger at him."

"The auditors have not mentioned anything like this in their report," said Shanker, "surely, they must know."

"They probably have some knowledge about it but have cleverly or under pressure not mentioned it in their report."

"I am not surprised at all, after all, they want to retain this audit, it is probably their biggest audit, as they are a medium-sized firm, and I don't think they have many qualified accountants on their payroll, probably cannot afford them."

"Now, the situation is," Shanker continued, "that KBL is stuck because of Mr. Ravi Mathew, and I had advised Mr. Ramesh Pratap to request that the consultancy be given to another firm, as they might end up losing their credibility."

"They would never give up this assignment, Mr. Ravi Mathew would never allow it and, moreover, it is a prestigious job for them, so why would they give it up?"

Shanker told him about the incident with Mr. Ajit Kumar, and Navin was shocked.

"It is obvious that Mr. Ravi Mathew has a lot to hide, and is under pressure from powerful politicians, whose relatives we gave loans to knowing fully well, that the recovery rate would not exceed thirty-three percent. I had calculated that we would have to write off sixty-six percent of the loans disbursed. It is in my memo, which I marked to the senior director at that time, you can see it in the files. In fact, one of the politician's nephews, whom we gave a loan, invited me for an evening party at his house, near Nasik."

"I was shocked at the opulence and the grand bungalow he had built, obviously they are not going to pay back the loan."

"Can't the bungalow be auctioned to recover the money?"

"Yes, it can, but they will go to court, hire the top lawyers, and the case will drag on and on for years, with appeals to the high court and then the supreme court."

"Yes, I understand," said Shanker.

"Anyway, I have to catch a flight to Mumbai," said Navin and left.

Shanker was pleased to meet his old friend Navin Kocher but disappointed that he didn't give him the type of information he wanted. He was being over cautious, maybe he was involved in some manner or the other, as he was disbursing the loans. It could be that he also gained in the process, no one is that innocent and Navin was quite sharp, and if he got a chance, he wouldn't miss it.

It suddenly came to Shanker's mind, how was it that he purchased a house in Defence Colony in a 400 sq. yards plot as with his salary he could surely not afford it. It would cost quite a few crores and his wife was also from a middle-class family. Her father had been in the government and retired as an additional secretary.

He must have obliged, whoever it was, and taken compensation and with that, he was able to buy a house in Defence Colony. Navin was no saint; he had known him since his college days.

He would grill him next time and maybe get more information from him than he had in the past.

Shyamala came into the room and sat down opposite Shanker.

"Any news Shyamala?" asked Shanker.

"Not anything of importance, but they did grill the Ayurvedic Treatment Centre's doctor about the treatment he gave to Ajit Kumar, which triggered a serious reaction on him, and Somaya had him transferred to the hospital, otherwise he may have died."

"The ayurvedic doctor said that this treatment was common, and they gave it to most patients but always checked if they had an allergy to it, which in the case of Ajit Kumar, they did not do, because he was middle-aged and not old, so they presumed that could go ahead and treat him." "That is a serious lapse on the part of the doctor."

"Yes, they have suspended him for the time being, until the two seniors give their report."

"Ajit Kumar was the first patient who reacted adversely, and they cannot understand why?"

"They are also checking if, in between, someone came into the room, and gave him a lethal injection, as at the hospital they did detect, in his blood, some substance which should not have been there but were unable to identify it."

Shanker looked at Shyamala and said, "It was certainly an attempt at murder. I am sure, and Som acted swiftly, otherwise, he may have died."

"Has Ravi Mathew any connection with this Ayurvedic Treatment Centre, is he a shareholder in the company that owns it? This is something we have to find out."

"I will ask Som to check it up, shouldn't be difficult. The records will be there in the office of the registrar of companies."

"Do you think that is all Shyamala because just an allergy would not give such a strong reaction, in between a nurse had come, maybe she gave him an injection of I am not sure what, but Ajit Kumar does remember that the nurse came. She was a senior nurse, and he felt a slight prick even in his condition."

"You could pass on this information to Som, maybe she could check with the hospital. I am not how sure we would be able to establish anything but give it a try. If we can trace the nurse, who most probably has disappeared by now, and was most likely a plant and not a regular of the Ayurvedic Treatment Centre, that would help. We could have photographs of some of the senior nurses and maybe Ajit Kumar could identify them. He says it all started after the nurse left, and he did feel a slight prick."

Shyamala telephoned Som in the afternoon and told her what Shanker had suggested based on Ajit Kumar's narrative. Som was not surprised as an allergic reaction could not cause such a serious effect, particularly from ayurvedic medicine. Even the hospital doctor was surprised, but they couldn't do a full check-up as Ajit Kumar caught the flight to Delhi.

Shyamala wondered why someone would go to such lengths to murder Ajit Kumar. What was the purpose, what had he found out that Ravi Mathew's associates or executives found so dangerous? 'Was Ajit Kumar hiding something from them,' wondered Shyamala.

The next day, Shyamala telephoned Rani and told her that she would like to talk to Ajit Kumar and that it was important. Rani told her to come around teatime and have a snack with her. He was most stable at that time, though out of danger, he still had a bad cough, and sometimes spat out blood.

When Ajit Kumar got out of bed, he found Rani and Shyamala having tea. Shyamala could spot blood on his teeth and Rani asked him to gargle.

"Are you seeing a doctor for this cough as blood is dangerous with a cough," said Shyamala.

"Yes, I am taking medicines, but the cough will take time to stop, it has become a lot less."

"What did the doctor say it is due to?"

"He gave it a technical term, but basically it is due to some substance which had gone into my lungs, so it will take time for it to empty out. Otherwise, they will have to do a procedure, which they feel at present is not necessary. They have pumped most of the fluid out, but not all. I have to go for an examination in two days. The blood in the cough has become less and I am on strong drugs."

"You told Som that a nurse came in-between, and you felt a prick which could have been an injection?"

"Yes, I told Som and the doctor in the hospital, but he said that we would have to do a series of tests, you know how doctors are."

"Yes, I can understand his problem. Also, to get a correct diagnosis these tests would be required."

Shyamala told Rani to get in touch with her after his next appointment.

Shanker was looking at photographs when Shyamala entered and he smiled at her, "They are just nurses at the Ayurvedic Treatment Centre. Som has sent photographs of them."

"Please take them and ask Rani to show them to Ajit Kumar, and let's hope he can identify the nurse who came."

"But what surprises me is why were they so concerned about the report he was going to write, had he found something which he is not disclosing to us. You better question him, maybe he is afraid of disclosing it."

"I am meeting him after two days, I will ask him," said Shyamala and took the photos from him.

Shyamala went to meet Ajit Kumar and was having tea, sitting with Rani, when he entered the sitting room. Shyamala told Ajit that there must have been something that he had found that created anxiety for Ravi Mathew's associate or senior executive that he went to the trouble of trying to eliminate him. "Nobody does it for nothing. It is a very serious matter. You better tell us everything after seeing the photographs."

Rani sat down next to him and took the photographs out of the folder and started to show them to her husband, who scanned them very slowly and thoroughly. After he had seen some, he kept on looking at an old nurse, who had white hair coming out of her cap and said that it looked like the nurse who came and took his temperature and put a bandage on his wrist when he felt a pinprick, hardly painful very expertly done as if it was a part of the bandage procedure. It was a pin attached to the end of the bandage, he said.

At least he had now identified the nurse and the photograph which was numbered would be communicated to Somaya through Shyamala.

"Now tell me, Ajit, what was it you found that terrified the associate, Louis?"

"You know when I was trying to find the relevant files, I came across a file, at the back, cleverly hidden, most likely by Vikram, in which I found many names of loan receivers and the amount written against them. It appears that Vikram cleverly made a summary as he could not take the files or photocopies."

"This small-sized file, I hid it in my briefcase and took it to my hotel room. I didn't know where to hide it, so I went downstairs and asked for a locker and put it in the locker. If we are lucky, it may still be there as I paid the rent for a month and the key is with me. The locker no is 208, you could ask your friend to go to the hotel and get the locker opened and, if we are lucky, the file will be there.

They searched my room thoroughly but could not find anything of importance. They probably don't know about the existence of this file and may have thought that Vikram put it on his iPad and forwarded it to some unknown site under a different name. The iPad I am sure is still with Vikram. You could check with him. Even though he didn't put the information there, they thought he had put it somewhere. He may have forwarded it to Mr. Ramesh Pratap, most likely."

Shyamala said she will check with him, and also asked to open the locker and give her the number of the nurse in the photo. She telephoned Vikram at night; of course, it was afternoon in Toronto.

Vikram was surprised to receive her call and after flirting with him on the telephone, she asked him about the details he collected and sent from his iPhone to Mr. Ramesh.

He said, "You are very clever, of course, detection is your profession." He told her he had made a small file with the relevant names of the customers, mainly the kith and kin of politicians to whom loans were disbursed, and then took photographs from his iPad and forwarded them to Mr. Ramesh."

The file that he left was hidden behind one of the shelves and was surprised that Ajit Kumar had located it.

"What about the iPad, do you still have it?"

"No, Ramesh Pratap said it was the company's property and took it back from me in front of his secretary and gave me a receipt for the same."

"I felt cheated, however, I told him that I would like to delete all personal data, which he allowed me to do."

"Very clever of him," said Shyamala. After a little sweet talk, she ended the call and put the phone down.

They must have been suspicious that he knew too much and may have printed out the contents from a printer, which he failed to do.

He was lucky to catch the last flight out of London, or they would have most likely gotten him shot by paying a professional. London has no shortage of them.

The next morning, Shyamala telephoned Som and told her to check the contents. "A small file in the hotel locker no 208 and find the old nurse at Ayurvedic Treatment Centre if she is still around."

Chapter 13

Shanker and Shyamala were sitting in the office discussing a case when Somaya telephoned. She talked to Shyamala who listened intently. Nodding her head, a smile to herself now and then.

"What did she say?" asked Shanker eagerly after the call ended.

"Well, she said that the nurse we had identified was a temporary duty nurse and she left soon afterward and was to their knowledge working in another city, they did not know where. Maybe someone whom she was close to would know, they were trying their best to trace her. So far, with little success."

"As far as the locker was concerned, they had telephoned Ajit's office to come and take the contents as he had mistakenly left them behind. So, no luck said Som, we will have to start all over again."

Shyamala went to meet Ajit Kumar at his residence after contacting Rani.

She told Ajit, who looked quite disturbed and worried, particularly about the small file he forgot to take from the locker in all the confusion, but now Ravi Mathew's associate would be quite suspicious about him, but Shyamala assured him that they would not dare try anything in Delhi, and if he was badly worried, she could post a policeman outside his premises.

Rani didn't think it was a good idea, as it would raise their suspicions, and asked Ajit if by any chance he had taken pictures with his mobile phone of the contents in the file.

Ajit was confused and said that he was in the process, when, in the office, he was interrupted. He said his mobile phone was in the bedroom drawer.

Rani went upstairs and fetched the mobile phone, which was a Samsung smartphone.

She scrolled through it and went to the photos app which showed almost 156 photos. She went through the photos, and to her surprise, at the end, there were four photos with names and figures, which Ajit managed to take from the file. About 15 names with amounts against them.

Ajit had a look, and said, "Yes, I remember, I was in the process of taking the contents which were more than 25 pages but was interrupted. My plan was to take the photos and leave the file behind, but that didn't work, so I managed only the first 5-6 pages, but they were the main borrowers as the list in the file was from top to bottom."

"The important and big loans were disbursed in that order."

Shyamala transferred the photos to her mobile phone and said, "At least, we have something now to go on."

Shanker thought it was time to meet Ramesh Pratap, so he called him and fixed an appointment for the following day, around teatime 4 p.m. at his office.

Shyamala and he went to Mr. Pratap's office, which by now, was very familiar to them, including the seating arrangements. They sat as they normally did and were served tea in a silver service with assorted pakoras and pastries.

"Well, what is it this time, Mr. Shanker, that you wanted to discuss?"

"Yes," said Shanker, we wanted to discuss Mr. Ajit Kumar and his dreadful experience in Cochin.

"Well, he was almost murdered in the Ayurvedic Treatment Centre," and Shanker narrated the whole episode about how he was injected by a nurse who disappeared and if Somaya had not shifted him into the hospital, he most likely may have died.

Ramesh Pratap's face became crimson red, and he could hardly speak. "It was all engineered because he found a small file with the names of the loaners, to whom sums had been advanced, mainly the kin of politicians."

"That file he left in the hotel because of all the panic, and it was retrieved by the associate of Mr. Mathew from the locker, it had all the details. It was originally found by Vikram when he was on the assignment, but he hid it and couldn't bring it back, but he must have read the details or may have taken pictures of them on his mobile phone - I can't confirm it."

"That is why Mr. Mathew's men were after him in London and had taken a contract on him, but he was lucky, he caught the last flight to Toronto." Ramesh swallowed as he listened.

"Mr. Ramesh Pratap, you are in serious trouble, and we are consulting our lawyers in this regard. The charges against you will be very serious. First, Mr. Hari Mohan, which fortunately we can't do very much about as the hospital got the clean chit from the medical council. His wife is, of course, very upset that you took him to London, when the operation could have been done in Delhi.

In fact, it is the same Indian doctors who operate in London. The medical profession, particularly of surgery, is to some extent dominated by Indian doctors in both England and the USA."

Ramesh Pratap was absolutely silent and didn't say a word only breathing heavily. He eventually said, "I will have to consult my company's lawyer and follow their advice."

Shanker and Shyamala got up and left. On the way out he met Surya, who gave him a knowing smile. Shyamala proceeded towards the gate, whilst Shanker whispered to Surya and made a sign on his ear, meaning he would telephone her, anything else would have been misunderstood as there was staff present.

He reached his office pretty late and telephoned her.

She responded and said that she was missing him and wanted to meet him and will telephone him when she got back home, from another line which was safe, she was sure this one was tapped. It was quite a chance she took if this line was tapped.

'Women can sometimes be impulsive,' thought Shanker.

When he reached home, she telephoned him from her landline and told him that they could meet at the farmhouse on Saturday. She would confirm the details.

Shanker, as usual, went to the Chhatarpur temple and met his Guruji who was available that evening and sat with him, and made polite conversation as other important persons were present. It was not crowded but also not empty. He had no particular questions for Guruji, so he sat in his place, on a mat, and listened to the questions asked by the others.

He took his blessings and left for the farmhouse hotel and restaurant. He saw Surya sitting there on a side table on a comfortable chair and went and sat down opposite her. She was quite simply dressed but looked pretty as usual, without any makeup. She had probably done it deliberately so that she wouldn't be noticed.

He ordered a Campari with tonic water, and she had a non-alcoholic cocktail and ordered some snacks to go with it- pakoras and salted peanuts.

"So, what is new?" he asked. "Come on," she chided him, "say something nice and romantic, instead of asking about the politics of KBL. You policemen lack a sense of romance, I don't blame you, your work is such and the whole day you are soaked with criminals, etc, that your orientation changes."

"You are right, Surya, but you are looking very nice, and a simple dress suits you, they bring out your true self."

"Now tell me, Surya. what is it" And he smiled, "that you called me for? It was not for a musical evening. Though the music is nice, and I suppose after a while the Latin American band will take the stage."

Shanker was not sure if Surya was recording everything from her mobile phone in her large ladies' purse, or if someone was photographing them on the camera or through a smartphone. He decided to be cautious.

"So, what has happened since we last met?" asked Surya.

"Well, we saved Ajit Kumar's life, and also Vikram was lucky he caught the last flight to Toronto that night, or he may have met with a bad accident."

"Why are the KBL so afraid that they don't want the consultancy to be executed in a professional manner and are always trying to hide the facts. Even if it means harming people, six have already died, another one died on an operation table in London, but the medical council gave the hospital a clean chit. Hari Mohan's wife is very upset that he was taken to London for the operation when his own doctor could have easily operated on him in Saket."

Surya nodded her head and didn't speak a word. He understood.

"Ajit Kumar was lucky Somaya shifted him to the hospital as he had got a lethal injection in the Ardhyashala. So was Vikram, who with the help of his friend in the High Commission, managed to catch the last flight to Toronto."

He picked up Surya's purse and opened it, she did not object, and saw the mobile phone, which was switched off.

"You must trust me," Surya said. "You thought I was recording everything."

Shanker smiled a little embarrassed and apologized.

"I don't know what they are up to," she said, "they don't confide in me and even Mr. Pratap's secretary hardly communicates with me. I am looking after the hospitality only and they are quite happy with me on that count."

The Latin band came and played some romantic tunes, and they danced cheek to cheek, but Shanker was not sure if someone with a mobile phone was recording their romantic tryst. He looked around but couldn't see anyone suspicious.

He knew that Surya had nothing much to gain from him, after all she was no fool, and knew that he would not marry her, but her loyalties to KBL were very strong, and he was sure she was being well compensated. It was certainly a set-up, his intuition which was very strong told him so.

After having a nice dinner with wine, they parted. She had a KBL car waiting for her, which deepened suspicions more.

"We will meet again, Surya, after you have finalised your purpose and plans."

Shyamala telephoned Vikram in Toronto and he was surprised and pleased to hear from her, he wanted to know all the latest gossip, but she was not sure, if she knew enough about KBL's misadventures, but told him the details about Ajit Kumar."

He admitted that he had found the small file and hidden it, but Mr Ravi Mathew may have suspected him that he may have made copies or something and that he knew too much and would expose him. But he could not take the file out, and take it to his lodgings, but had taken photos of about 10 pages on his mobile phone, and then transferred them to his computer, and deleted them before handing over the mobile phone to Mr. Ramesh Pratap, who must have gone through it very thoroughly.

The computer was lying in his room at his residence in his parents' house, and he had told his mother not to tamper with it as there was some important information stored in it.

"She understood and locked it in my Godrej steel almirah. When I come to Delhi, I can open it and forward them to you."

"Vikram you could also instruct your mother to give me the computer and let me have the password and I can access those pages, they are important for us as so many lives have now been lost, and you were very lucky to have escaped that night."

"Let me think about it," said Vikram, "as I don't want to put my family at risk."

"Yes, I understand," said Shyamala. "I know the site, let me know if I can access it from one of our superior computers here. We have some computer wizards in our laboratory. Let me see if it is possible because I noted down the password, it is in my diary. I didn't risk putting them in my new mobile phone, which I bought at the London airport."

"Thanks, Shyamala, for remembering me, keeping in touch, maybe we will meet next year when I come to Delhi. Bye for now."

Well, she was happy to talk to Vikram, but his attitude appeared to have changed, which it was bound to, as he was living at the other end of the world and must have met some interesting young ladies in the university and at parties, etc. He was quite a sociable person.

She went to Shanker's room and told him about her conversation with Vikram. He was happy that she was still in touch with him but was not so sure how he would access the information from his computer in Delhi. "I suppose he may find a way, by asking his mother to switch it on, then with the password, to go to the site and transfer the data to his computer in Toronto." Then it was a matter of just forwarding it to Shyamala's computer or mobile phone. His mother as a teacher was quite familiar with computers, so Shanker was looking forward to receiving some information from Vikram.

A few days later, Shyamala got a telephone call from Vikram. She was not surprised, but at the same time, was quite pleased that he had remembered her and also responded to her request.

"Shyamala, I have managed to get those 9 plus pages, photocopies of some of them are not that clear, but legible, my mother, with the help of the computer teacher, was able to access the site with passwords forwarded by me and sent the data to my computer here, I asked them to delete it from my Delhi computer.

There are about 9 and a half pages, with details of loans to about 25 parties. It would be one-third of the information that was on the file. The total may be 50-60 parties. But there were important and larger loans

I think, as far as I can recollect. I will forward it to your computer if you can send me the relevant details, but please don't let anyone know that I sent them, I don't want any harm being done to my family. If you can promise me that then only will I send. They, of course, will come from a totally untraceable source, one of the computers in our laboratory, and no one will be able to trace anything, including the country they came from, except the country where the computer is manufactured, in this case that would be China. So, it would be impossible to trace."

"The Chinese keep a track of what is happening in all the important areas in India, their network is way ahead of the U.S. or Britain. Nobody can match them.

So, in the next two or three days, you will get the information. If you want me to send it to one of your office computers, I can do so, it will be safer, how many do you have?"

"About twenty in the main office. Then it will be better if I send it to a designated one in the office, which can't be traced to you also."

"Fine," said Shyamala, "I will send you the relevant details."

Two days later, Shyamala got a message from Vikram- Proceed.

She went to an obscure computer which was hardly used in the office on the ground floor, it was mainly used to track the punctuality of the arrival and departure of junior officers.

She sat on the chair in front of the computer to the surprise of the telephone operator and accessed the pages sent by Vikram, printing them out on the small printer, and then deleting everything including the printer access.

There was a total of 10 papers, and some were not very legible, but the police had a system of identification which was on a big screen, so Shyamala used it to overwrite the names and amounts of those that were not clear.

She made a file copy and locked it in her drawer.

Then she went to Shanker and gave him the file and also briefed him on the cautions Vikram had explained.

"Vikram has been very clever and cautious, and I don't think anyone will suspect anything, as the information has come from an intelligence source in Shanghai, China."

"We all know the Chinese are keeping a tab on us, on most matters, concerning their security and also other issues which may or may not be of importance to us. In fact, our intelligence agencies now and then coordinate with them, and they can be if they want to be, quite helpful."

"We can proceed and surprise Mr. Ramesh Pratap, he is not what he seems to be. In my opinion, he is totally mixed up with Ravi Mathew."

"These details and those that Ajit gave us from his mobile phone would be very helpful. I think now we can contact the audit and accounts department and take their advice."

Now that Ajit Kumar was feeling better, Shyamala called him to her office and asked him to bring the printouts of the pages he had managed to take photographs of from his camera.

Ajit came quite punctually, and Shyamala asked him what his plans were, was he going to continue with KBL or join some other consultancy firm.

Ajit first gave the print outs of the snapshots and then deleted it from his mobile phone along with all the other items compromising his position. Others, he transferred to his new mobile phone he had purchased with a different operator.

He said he will go in a day or two and return the mobile phone to Mr Ramesh Pratap.

His view was also that Mr. Ramesh Pratap was not the real boss, he was taking orders from Ravi Mathew who was the real kingpin of the organisation as nothing was moved without his consent, and Mathew was a real 'Don', in the true sense of the word, and would stoop to any level to attain his goals.

He had made arrangements in case he had to leave India; he could take residency in any one of the countries which for a price would welcome you. Dubai is a favoured destination as well as Qatar. He had excellent contacts in the UAE and owned properties there as well. Another advantage was that Dubai had many workers from Kerala working there and many businessmen as well from the state, who had developed good relations with local traders.

Mr Ajit Kumar had applied to various companies including in Saudi Arabia and Kuwait and was hopeful of getting a job in Kuwait, as his wife could accompany him and get a job as a teacher in an Indian school for expatriates. There was always demand for a science teacher, it was a favoured subject.

Shyamala was quite impressed with Ajit Kumar and wished him the best.

She took out the printouts of Vikram and compared the sheets. Only two of Ajit Kumar's sheets matched those sent by Vikram, which meant that now they had 7-8 sheets with different names and amounts against them.

How to trace these borrowers? She would need the help of the Central Govt Audit and Accounts division, and she telephoned their contact there, Mr. Kathpalia, and made an appointment for Shanker.

Shanker knew Kathpalia quite well and had played tennis with him in the club. Kathpalia was a good player and generally won.

Shanker gave him the papers and said, "They had come from a source in China which the markings showed." However, Kathpalia smiled and said, "Everything now comes from China, as the computers are based there." Shanker smiled but kept quiet.

"It is my duty to help the police and expose people who have taken loans and not repaid them, making it difficult for RML bank to function. After all, the government has a large shareholding in the bank."

"I will put one of my assistants on this job and ask him to get as much information as possible on these borrowers and where has the money gone, which, of course, won't be easy, but we will try. They must have spent it on buying land and fancy apartments and houses or used it for their kin's political campaigns.

I don't think RML will be able to recover much of the money and eventually, the bank will be merged with one of the large public sector banks as its subsidiary is under its control.

The bad debts will have to be written off and eventually the taxpayer will foot the bill.

What a pity," said Kathpalia.

Chapter 14

Surya telephoned Shanker. He was quite surprised to hear her voice. He politely asked her where she was speaking from and she replied that she was speaking from the theatre at the IHC, where her group was rehearsing for a musical. She was one of the directors, and they had managed to get a good group of artists and singers.

"I was going to ask you to come and see the rehearsal and then we could have a bite together at one of the restaurants. They, as you know, have good eating places. It will be a nice way to spend the evening together."

Shanker thought for a while and then said, "Alright."

Surya said, "It is perfect."

Shanker thought to himself that he just couldn't refuse Surya. He had a weakness for her and enjoyed meeting her despite his suspicious about her employers, whom he was investigating.

He reached about ten minutes late but, when he saw her, he wanted to hug her, which he couldn't do as there were many players of the show present.

Anyway, he took her hand and squeezed it affectionately and felt a response, which was difficult to describe. She also felt it, he was sure, but as she was being watched, she disengaged herself, and led him to the comfortable sofa in the front row and asked him what he would like to have, wine whiskey or coffee. He thought for a minute and then said, "Some white wine would be fine."

After the rehearsal, they crossed over and went to the deck of another restaurant serving continental food.

He ordered another glass of wine and was feeling a little tipsy, which made him smile a lot, and he led her outside to the swimming pool because he knew he had to kiss her. He took her behind some tall chairs where it was dark, and he kissed her with a passion that would make her toes curl and legs weak. This woman had tormented his thoughts during the day and his dreams at night leaving him in beads of perspiration and very aroused. There were many mornings of very cold showers. The amazing thing was the passion was equally returned by her … as if she was suffering the same faith as him. She caught him tightly and wouldn't let him go and kept on kissing him, as he responded. His breathing changed as he became aroused by this provocative sensual woman who had a body filled with desire and sexual awakenings that made you forget your own name. Shanker struggled to control his desires as lust threatened to take control of him. The restless aching in his groin made his organs grow as hot blood pumped through his veins. He held her waist with the intention of pushing her away, but he only drew her to him as he pressed his hot body to hers and ground his hips to hers. He cupped her breasts and her nipples stood to attention as she let a sigh of pure desire escape her lips as her sweet breath kissed his lips. He felt her shiver against him as she too began to lose control. She grabbed his butt and pressed into him; a low growl escaped his lips as he muttered, Surya .... babe .... s-t-o-p, babe. Honey, we need to stop. Surya's hazy mind barely heard Shanker as she was all caught up in the moment. They clung to each other trying to catch their breath and calm that raging fire within them. The breeze was cool as their breathing gradually began to return to normal. Shanker looked at himself and prayed that the evidence of his desire for her would subside very soon. He tried to look at her, but her head was bent on his shoulder as she tried to retain control. What was she thinking, he wondered?

The breeze blew softly and cooled them down. She thought of nothing at this moment but just like it be living in it. Held her in a loose embrace as she laid her cheek against his. They didn't speak, nothing needed to be said and they didn't want to break the magic. He smoothed her hair and kissed her forehead while she leaned again him with her hand on his chest. Surya refused to think she just enjoyed what it was ... what was it, anyway? Her flushed cheeks were cooler now and her rose-red face was almost normal now. Those lovely moments were broken when she heard her colleague calling out – "Where are you, Surya?"

They broke their embrace before the others could barge in and went inside, and he saw tears in her eyes and led her inside. The magical moments were broken, he was in another sphere and so was she. He knew he couldn't invite her to his house, maybe a farmhouse which he was resisting would be more appropriate.

She telephoned him that night and kept talking for a long time as she refused to put the phone down and he also was reluctant to end all, so he kept talking.

'Now what to do,' thought Shanker, he was definitely in love or totally infatuated with her and so was she.

Surya wasn't putting it on he was sure, they had to find a way forward, he would think seriously for a change.

He said goodnight, most reluctantly, and switched the phone off and deleted the conversation, in case somebody may hear it, as he, at times, absentmindedly left it on his desk.

Kathpalia telephoned Shanker and laughed. Shanker asked him what the joke was, he replied that the names you gave me we have identified, but I don't think the police have any role to play as this is our jurisdiction. "I shall be happy to proceed, but will require your help, you are more interested in the criminal side of the investigation as six persons have been murdered, five to be more accurate as the murder in the United Kingdom can't be taken as a murder. Hari Mohan died on the operating table, the medical council said it was death caused by medical factors and found no negligence on the part of the hospital."

"According to us, there were two attempted murders which luckily for the victims failed. The one in Goa is being investigated, but again we will not be able to prove anything."

"Vikram luckily escaped on the last flight to Toronto, otherwise he may not have survived as Ravi Mathew had put a contract on him. Again, it would be impossible to prove. You are right," he told Kathpalia, "we have to concentrate on the borrowers and find out where the money has gone. If it is being used by any borrower for criminal activities, then we come into the picture, and I am sure that there will be many such cases."

"I have some more news for you Shanker, we have managed from our records to get the names of another 25 borrowers, who have taken loans though they are medium-sized or small, but they all add up. Some of them were shady characters, which from your records you may be able to identify, and also, our Mumbai office can contact the police and get the required details." "That could be very useful," said Shanker. "I think now we are making some solid progress and the sooner we break this chain the better."

"I am concerned," said Kathpalia, "as I talked to the director general, and he was very unhappy to learn about the RML bank portfolio. He would have to answer the minister and secretary in charge and would ask '*what were you doing, why didn't you act sooner, you knew that RML was giving these loans to unrecoverable people.*' He will, of course, put the blame lightly on a previous govt. and minister, who blindly signed the papers put in front of him and could hardly understand financial issues, even the secretary was afraid to act. What a mess the whole thing is. I hope the press doesn't get hold of these deals that have gone sour. Our department will also be blamed. They will also ask '*what they were doing, why they didn't investigate earlier?*"

"The auditors were being bullied to give clean audit reports and did so knowingly. We will insist on a change of auditors and give it to a large international firm. That will have to be done," exclaimed Shanker, "but first you will have to act and cross question KBL and ask them what work they have done. They have given the consultancy, but no report is in sight."

"You can call Mr. Ramesh Pratap, the managing director of KBL Associate, and question him," advised Shanker. "I suppose I will have to do that," Kathpalia responded.

Shyamala was sitting in her office and was deep in thought when her mobile phone rang quite loudly. She snapped out of her dream world and stumbled to pick up the phone, which slipped from her hand and dropped down, luckily the carpet saved it and she saw the missed call from Somaya.

She telephoned her back, and after the customary courtesies, asked her if any progress had been made.

Somaya told her that they were able to trace the nurse who gave Ajit Kumar the injection, she gave it on the instructions of one of the junior ayurvedic consultants and was asked the next day to leave and was given Rs. 5000/- ex gratia payment, though she had just joined a few days earlier. They told her to go to a hospital on a small island, off the coast, which was owned by the same family.

She didn't know what was in the vial and gave the injection as directed. She was trained to give injections; she gave it very gently so that he would not even feel if he had been given the injection. The vial she threw in the large bin at the end of the corridor as the practice was, and it was emptied the next morning and loaded onto the garbage truck.

"So, there was no way they could trace it now, whatever was in the truck. Could she identify the doctor, who told her to give the injection?" Shyamala enquired.

She said, "Yes, but there are so many doctors, and they all looked the same, with their white clothes and heads covered."

"Anyway, we took her to the hospital, but she couldn't identify the young ayurvedic doctor, she said she was sure he was not there as she could identify him if she saw him."

"The doctor she described doesn't work in the hospital," said the head nurse. He must be a visiting doctor; we have them from time to time as trainees. But she couldn't recollect any trainee of the description."

"We let her go but told one of the staff whom we knew well and had helped in the past, to keep an eye on the old nurse."

Somaya related that the staff followed the old nurse one day in a scooter rickshaw in which she was traveling and saw her get off near the building where the office of Mr. Ravi Mathew was located. She hesitated to follow her inside as she would have been recognised.

It appears that she is also on the payroll of Mr. Ravi Mathew, so now they are keeping an eye on her every moment. She also followed her to her residence, which is located in a small colony, where the staff of Ravi Mathew resided. He had provided them with accommodation. We were able to trace her small residence where she lived with her son, daughter-in-law, and two grandchildren. The son was an employee with Ravi Mathew's company, may be a peon or typist.

"I must say Somaya, you have done a great investigation, but we have nothing we can pin on Mr. Mathew."

"That is correct," said Somaya, "but we will sooner or later find something important, leave it to me. Somaya felt optimistic that they would find something very important. Shyamala told Shanker when she briefed him about Somaya's call to her. Shanker looked a little disappointed that they had not found something that could lead directly to Mathew or implicate him. But, like Somaya, he was patient as they were dealing with a powerful and clever adversary.

It would be better if they concentrated on Ramesh Pratap, he was easier to deal with and now RML was going to be under attack from Mr. Kathpalia's department, with all their resources, and they would also have to question Ramesh Pratap.

Ramesh Pratap had been clever and had not seriously proceeded with the consultancy deliberately and made the excuse that he was not getting the required cooperation, and his two consultants who were doing the work in Cochin had left, and the team was leaderless. He was deliberately trying to delay, as Ravi Mathew was involved, and it would expose him.

Shanker telephoned Kathpalia and asked him if it was possible to terminate the consultancy on the grounds of a conflict of interest and give it to other consultants, preferably an international firm, with an office in India.

Kathpalia said he would try but it may not be easy as they signed a contract and KBL would not likely go to court.

Shanker agreed that it was a possibility, with no harm in trying.

Kathpalia called back a few days later and said that the secretary was not agreeing, and he had taken legal opinion on the proposal and showed the opinion to Kathpalia, which was negative.

Shanker was disappointed, but they had no choice, the minister would be guided by the secretary and would not agree.

'What were they going to do now,' thought Shanker. They would have to wait on Kathpalia's department, to proceed further, but to continue with the criminal cases maybe Shyamala could make another trip to Cochin, along with her friend and colleague Som, and work out a possible plan.

Shyamala caught a flight to Cochin, as suggested by Shanker, and was booked into a guest house for senior officers. It was maintained by the armed forces, who obliged the other services like IAS, IPS, IRS, etc. It was very nice and comfortable, and the food was good, particularly the seafood dishes. Somaya came and met Shyamala and they had breakfast together and tried to make a plan to confront Ravi Mathew.

It was a task of trying to figure out how to go about this issue since he was a very clever and resourceful person who had kept all her colleagues and even the superintendent and his deputy happy, even the state inspector general he had approached and called on him when he visited Cochin.

Shyamala asked Somaya, "How do we tackle him then?" As they tried to find a way to get information from Mr. Mathew knowing that he was very slick, and they had to move carefully.

"Maybe we could take an appointment with him and confront him."

"That does not appear to be easy. What will you ask him?"

"Well," replied Shyamala, "I will ask him about Ajit Kumar, and see his response because he was lucky to be alive. We traced the nurse who gave him the injection, who was giving the orders, and what was the reason for it?"

"I do not know if it will work but it is worth a try," said Som. "Let me fix an appointment with him, he may not meet us, and will probably ask some senior in his office to deal with us."

With that in mind, they made an appointment to meet Mr. Mathew, the following day.

His office was huge and had very expensive paintings and sculptures and some beautiful Greek pottery. It reeked of wealth. Even the light fixtures were expensive looking.

He personally met them when they entered and took them into his private chamber which was lavishly furnished and ordered coffee for them. He said that he had a very special coffee which he got from South America and that they would enjoy it.

They looked around and there were beautiful paintings from all over the world, particularly from Europe, and there were painted pottery and plates.

Shyamala complimented him and said, "You have a very good collection and amazing taste for *objet d'art* and appear to be a serious collector."

He simply smiled and offered them some chocolate truffles then got straight to business.

"Now, ladies, what can I do for you?"

"Well, we are doing an investigation into the RML bank and KBL consultants' case and thought maybe you could assist us."

"Well," he laughed "certainly. What do you want to know?"

"Plenty," answered Somaya.

She asked him if he knew about Ajit Kumar and why he was sent to that Ayurvedic Treatment Centre where they gave him an injection that almost killed him. Mr. Kumar had been saved because, it was she who had him shifted to the hospital. "We have traced the nurse who gave him the injection, but not the doctor who was behind it."

"Well," said Mathew without even blinking, "I don't know anything about it. One of my assistants was interacting with him and I didn't interfere much, I have more important matters to attend to."

Shyamala asked, "Could we talk to the concerned assistant?"

He picked up the phone and asked his secretary to call Pillai and send him to his office.

The secretary telephoned 10 minutes later and said that Pillai was in Dubai attending to some office matter regarding shipments. He won't be available for at least 15 days.

Som was disappointed and knew, and so did Shyamala, that Mathew had very cleverly sent him to Dubai.

"When did he go to Dubai?" asked Som.

"I think it must have been yesterday late evening. He must have gone on a chartered flight. We have arrangements for our senior executives to travel by chartered flights."

"Anything else I can do for you ladies? Why don't you have lunch with me tomorrow?"

"I shall be returning to Delhi," said Shyamala.

Shanker and Shyamala were sitting in his office and having hot masala tea in a glass.

Shyamala said, "We have not gotten very far, and, in fact, we are going further back though we should be moving forward."

Shanker nodded. "I don't know how we can proceed, when I think we are making some progress, we end up at a dead end, like your trip to Cochin. Mathew was too smart for you and sent Pillai to Dubai, whether he did or not we could verify."

"Why don't you telephone Som and ask her, which of the chartered flights left that late evening for Dubai, and was any employee of Ravi Mathew, called Pillai, in any of them. It is worth checking up as Mathew might be bluffing."

Shyamala telephoned Som and told her what Shanker was thinking and there may be a possibility that he was bluffing.

Som agreed, "It is possible."

In the afternoon, Som telephoned and told Shyamala that Shanker's intuition was correct, the airport controller checked records and no chartered flight had left on that day, and no passenger by the name of Pillai had boarded any evening flight for Dubai. "That means that Ravi Mathew was bluffing, as he didn't want us to interrogate his senior assistant."

Shanker spoke directly to Som and told her that he had spoken to the superintendent of police concerned and she can go ahead and send a team to pick up Pillai from the office or residence, wherever he can be located, and then you can take him to the police headquarters for questioning.

Before Mr. Ravi Mathew could act he was busy with other matters and was not in the office, the police reached his office and took control of Pillai and brought him to the police headquarters for questioning. He was interrogated by Som and the deputy superintendent and accused of conspiracy and attempt to murder Ajit Kumar. He was also questioned on who the doctor was who had given the nurse the vial for injection.

After intense questioning, he could not answer the question and said he didn't know at all the doctor or that person who most likely was not a doctor, but somebody directed by a doctor, but he didn't know by whom. His identity couldn't be verified as he was not at all aware of it. He was asked to play a certain role which he did, and he had no idea, that it was a plot to murder Ajit Kumar or grievously harm him.

The police made a charge sheet against him and took him into custody and put him in jail.

He would have to appear before session court, to answer his charges, and could, of course, try for bail, which Mathew would be willing to pay for, or he may not interfere as it may incriminate him.

As anticipated by Somaya, the lawyer of Pillai, he was a private lawyer and applied for bail.

The judge granted the bail for 5 lacs, which the lawyer said he would deposit before 3 p.m.

Pillai was free to leave and left the jail by 4 p.m. after the payment was made.

Now the police had a plan to question Ravi Mathew, as he had lied that Pillai had gone to Dubai in a chartered flight, which was untrue as he never left the city. On what basis had Mathew told Som and Shyamala that Mr. Pillai had left by a chartered flight?

The senior superintendent of police telephoned Mathews and asked him to come to his office the next day at 2:30 p.m. He asked Somaya to be present and, in case Shyamala wanted to be on the team, she could catch the morning flight and come.

Shyamala caught the early morning flight to Mumbai and caught the first flight to Cochin, reaching at 11 a.m.

Somaya picked up Shyamala from the airport and took her straight to the guest house where she changed quickly, and both had lunch together and left for the senior superintendent's office at the headquarter.

They reached the office early enough to be able to discuss the strategy in the line of questions The senior superintendent thought that Somaya could start and then Shyamala could take over and then, finally, if required, he would question Mathew, whom he had met several times in connection with his shipping matters and various irregularities for which he always paid the penalties and got away with.

He was not looking forward to interrogating Mathew, because he was a powerful person and had connections right up to the chief minister of the state, whose party he supported with donations.

It may be best if Shyamala does the main interrogation as she was from the Delhi police, and under the jurisdiction of the lieutenant Governor, who reported to the Home Minister. He was from a different party than the ruling party in Kerala and would be happy to nail Mathew.

Mathew showed his arrogance by arriving half an hour late, making the excuse that there was too much traffic. He was wearing a smart London tailored suit and had expensive rings on his fingers. His shoes were expensive Christian Louboutin black, red bottom leather loafers. He dressed the part of a '*Don*' and sat with the air of one too much to the amazement of the police officers.

Shyamala broke the ice by asking him, "How is your wife? Does she live in Cochin?"

He smiled and confidently stated, "No, she lives in Dubai, so does my son who is a student in the British school, and my daughter is studying at a well-known university in Scotland."

'So at least they knew about his family,' thought Somaya, who wasn't aware of it and nor was the senior Superintendent.

"Mr. Mathew," said Shyamala very politely, "you told us that Mr. Pillai had caught a chartered flight and gone to Dubai when we came to your office and wanted to question him regarding Ajit Kumar, the consultant from KBL. He was all the time in Cochin and had not gone to Dubai and had no plans to even go there. What is your reply to this?" she asked.

"Well," he said, "Ours is a large corporation and I delegate to my executives and don't interfere in case they do their work according to schedule and satisfactorily. I was under the wrong impression, I admit that. His boss, one of our senior executive directors, had asked him to go to Dubai on an assignment. I don't keep a track of everything that goes on in my organisation, every department has a head, and they manage their department. If I am not satisfied with their performance, I transfer them to another department or ask them to look for a job elsewhere." Leaning back in the chair and crossing his right leg over his left knee like he was a VIP guest, he continued speaking.

"In fact, after you left, I asked Pillai's assistant on the intercom whether he had heard from him in Dubai. He was quite surprised and said he is here, and he never went, no such instructions were given to him. Should I ask him to come to your office?" He looked so sincere like a scorpion in a prayer meeting. He continued his explanation as if at a meeting for new managers.

"I said no need, I made a mistake, I should have verified before telling you that he had gone. I apologised for my lapse, and charged him, he is now out of the bank. As far as I am concerned, I had no knowledge about Ajit Kumar being taken to the ayurvedic hospital for treatment and what subsequently followed." He continued with emphasis, "I strongly deny it, and, in fact, even when Ajit Kumar was here, I hardly met him more than two or three times, maybe for fifteen to twenty minutes. He had a list of questions, which I tried to answer. In case I couldn't answer them, I gave him the name of the concerned manager, who would be in a position to answer them."

"They were handling the KBL consultancy cooperation so that everything went smoothly. I was of course concerned as I am a director in KBL and a substantial shareholder and have a good rapport with Ramesh Pratap. We have known each other for a long time, and meet at the quarterly meetings, if not on more occasions, and we can do good coordination that is why KBL is so successful and is making a good profit. We hire the best consultants and pay them well."

Shyamala yawned and was bored with Mathew's lecture. Som and Shyamala went back to Shyamala's suite at the official guest house.

"Now we are stuck again," said Shyamala, "unless you can get something out of Pillai, which will not be easy as he has strong protection from Mathew. But the fact is he was injected and if you had not taken him to the hospital, he may have died. The nurse doesn't know who the doctor was. I am sure Pillai knows."

Chapter 15

Shanker was daydreaming thinking of Surya and, at the same time, was cautious, as he was still not sure where her loyalties were. She was able to do things to him that no woman has ever done; the power to arouse him and make him feel alive like a virile man. He was certainly strongly infatuated with her and was waiting for an opportunity to meet her and have intimacy with her. But would it calm the primitive beast in him or awaken a gallant knight with an unsaturable soul?

He initially hesitated, but then decided to telephone her.

She responded, he thought, a little cautiously. So, he said, "Please telephone me when you are free," and put the phone down.

She telephoned him back after she left the office, and said, "I was taking notes when you telephoned. I was waiting for your call; it took you a long time to call me."

"You were never out of my mind, Surya, I can assure you. Anyway, when can we meet again and where?"

"Ramesh has received some information about us and is suspicious. There are a lot of spies in the office, and he has cleverly put one against the other, and some of the girls in the office are envious of our relationship. They appear to know about it and are constantly chattering on their mobile phones. Nothing can be kept a secret these days."

"Why don't we restart by having late tea at *'The Yellow Brick'* and then work out something, maybe a place in the old city, a haveli which doesn't object to privacy. I don't know if there are any, but it would be ideal. That dinner at the Haveli, you took me to, I will never forget, it was straight out of a bygone era, which doesn't exist anymore. That culture has almost vanished in the 21st century."

Shanker was surprised at her appreciation for that evening. Such places were rare, he would have to do some police work and locate a haveli, if it does exist, where they could have intimacy. He knew that the old city was riddled with *kothas* which were nothing, but brothels and prostitution were rampant, despite laws against it, but it was something you could not stop. It was much worse in Mumbai and Kolkata, but Delhi was close behind.

He asked Surya to meet him at *The Yellow Brick* at 5:30 the next day.

She was waiting for him when he reached but wearing her smart office attire as she had come straight from the office.

He gave her a peck on the cheek as the restaurant was quite full, and he was sure that there was someone spying on them on the instruction of Ramesh and someone was clicking photos, maybe recording their conversation, by sitting at the nearby table, or even Surya could be taking a recording.

He got up and said, "Let's go to Lodhi Gardens for a walk. I love walking there and it is just five minutes from here."

They got into his car, and he looked to see if someone was following them but couldn't be sure.

They reached Lodhi Gardens and he took Surya to his favourite spot, a bench in the Rose Garden with a view of the pond and the ducks.

They talked and flirted and joked happily and she appeared to be very happy, which worried him, as, if she became very fond of him and they broke up, it would leave an emotional scar on her.

They caught each other's hand and she put her fingers through his and clasped it tightly. Shanker was worried that somebody may see him or recognize him, as he was a semi-public figure, and someone may just click on his mobile phone and take photos.

He disengaged and told her to be careful, but she ignored him and whispered sweet nothings in his ear. He got up and said, "Your idea of haveli would be worth exploring and I will find out." He didn't ask her anything about the office or what was going on, this was just a romantic diversion. She let go of his hand with great reluctance and wanted to hug him, but he discouraged her, though he would have also loved to do the same."

He then dropped her back at the *Yellow Brick*, where her car was parked. She has been given a Honda car by the company.

He quickly gave her a hug and kiss before she got into the car, to which she responded passionately. She appeared to be reluctant to leave him and he was sure it was genuine, and she was not acting.

Shyamala was sitting with Shanker who was slowly whistling away. So, Shyamala smiled and asked him, "Did you by any chance meet Surya yesterday and take her to Lodhi Gardens?"

Shanker was shocked. He looked up and asked, "How do you know?"

"Don't forget you are a public figure. One of my friends from our colony, who was walking there, saw you both sitting on a bench in the Rose Garden." Shyamala laughed and said, "You must take her out more often, but to a more private place, maybe Sunder Nagar Nursery and Humayun's Tomb. Not that many people go there, and it is very beautiful. The Aga Khan Foundation gave funds for its beautification."

"Yes. I read about it," said Shanker, "I must see it."

Shyamala's mobile phone on mute, vibrated in her purse.

It was from Som, she put it on loudspeaker so that Shanker could hear it also.

She said, "We used a pressure tactic on Pillai as we found a file on him. He had been convicted in the past for a minor crime and Mathew had got him out."

"He said that he didn't know from whom the order came, but he and a colleague Karim, were told to take Ajit Kumar to the Ayurvedic Treatment Centre or hospital and they got a room which was waiting for him when they arrived, as Mr. Mathew is one of the donors to the Ayurvedic Treatment Centre group, of which this is a unit, and so they checked him in."

He was told that the staff - nurses and others - would look after Mr. Ajit Kumar. One of the nurses was an older lady who was only a temporary nurse loaned from one of the other units and she sat outside the room. Later in the night, he received an injection which affected him very badly, and as they came to know he was shifted to the hospital.

She continued that the nurse did not know the identity of the doctor, but we managed to know, through interviewing the staff and threatening them, that he was not a qualified doctor but just a sort of a male nurse who gave the vial to the nurse to inject Ajith Kumar with. His whereabouts were traced, and a visit was paid to this residence, which was near the quarters of the nurse; he was not married, and he lived alone.

"And guess what Shyamala?" she asked.

"He was found dead after receiving a lethal injection, am I right?" she stated.

"Yes, dead right, Shyamala," replied Som.

"So, we have another murder to investigate," said Som. "Back to square one," she guessed.

"He was an ordinary worker - a male nurse. They dressed him up to look like a doctor and the nurse thought it was a doctor. We are questioning his neighbours about his family, etc. They don't appear to know too much as he kept to himself and was quite anti-social, except that he liked to play badminton and was a good player. There is a nice badminton court next to the quarters, part of the property."

"He was friendly with one or two nurses in the hospital, so we will question them and try to get some information about him."

"Bye for now," she said.

Shanker was amazed at the number of murders and that over a consulting assignment. It didn't make sense to him. There was more to it than they had deduced so far, after all, KBL was only a consultancy assignment for a bank that had not followed proper procedures and had lent large amounts allegedly to politicians in Maharashtra and Kerala under pressure, which were not recoverable. There was nothing unusual about it, as banks in India and abroad had gone under because they were not able to recover the loans, many of them loaned on genuine grounds but the companies went bankrupt, but others under pressure from politicians and criminals, which they were unable to pay back.

Why all these murders, it was not clear at all. What was behind it all? Shanker was not able to focus on the reason. Maybe they should meet Ramesh Pratap again and call him to Kathpalia's office.

He contacted Kathpalia, but since there was a murder involved, he didn't think it was appropriate to involve his department.

They went to meet Ramesh Pratap once again in his office, not at his residence but in the building in Barakhamba Road near Connaught Place. It was a large modern architectural, marble-finished building with many commercial offices, and their office was on the 8th floor.

Ramesh had a large office to which his secretary, the same lady they used to meet at his residence office, smiled and ushered them in. Surya, of course, would not be there, she was working from his residence office and mainly looking after hospitality.

Shyamala could sense the disappointment on Shanker's face and realized that he had a strong emotional connection to Surya.

After the customary formalities, Shanker asked Ramesh how the consultancy was proceeding and if he had found a replacement for Ajit Kumar.

Ramesh shifted in his chair, hesitated, then said that they were sending an executive from Chennai's office called Sampath Kumar. This individual was a highly qualified executive who had been with them for almost 12 years.

Shanker asked Ramesh if he had been briefed about what happened in Cochin and that now, they were investigating a third murder.

Shanker questioned Mr. Pratap on the reason for all these murders. After all, his company was only doing a consultancy job and wanted to know what was going on. It appears that there were criminal elements involved, particularly from Mr. Mathew's office. What was Mr. Mathew trying to cover up? It all seems very surprising to Shanker.

He pleaded with Ramesh, "I want answers, Mr. Pratap, otherwise, we will have to involve other agencies such as CBI or IB."

"If I do not hear from you within 10 days, I will act and, as you know, the Audit and Accounts office of the central government has also started their own investigation as the government is the single largest shareholder of RML Bank."

Ramesh replied, "Mr. Kathpalia's senior officer is doing the investigation. I know Mr. Kathpalia, we have dealt with him on other assignments before. He is a very hardworking and competent offer. However, he has not contacted me so far. I will see what I can do and contact you within a week."

Shanker telephoned Kathpalia and told him that he had spoken to Mr. Pratap who claimed to know him and that he has dealt with you.

"Yes, I know him, but I have not been able to break the barrier. He is very reserved and does not give out very much information. He will answer you only in monosyllables. But he is otherwise quite hospitable and has good staff at his residence, where he invites people to lunch or tea and nice-looking secretaries, particularly a lady called Surya, who is very good at entertaining guests."

"I have met Surya," said Shanker. "She is very attractive, I must admit, and I have taken her for lunch and also for dinner." Kathpalia laughed, "That is her job, and she is good at it. You are a bachelor, and she must have charmed you very easily, but be careful, and be a little reserved with her because she goes and tells everything to Pratap, but she does not like the other fellow – Mathew; and when he comes, she disappears - takes leave, annual vacation or whatever."

"So, you have also been entrapped by Surya, not the first. Pratap looks after her well. She is highly paid, and he also pays for the education of her brother, who is studying in a college in London. These are wheels within wheels, you are dealing with a very clever group, with two pillars- Mathew and Pratap. Each of them has their talents. Mathew is a 'Don', no different from a gangster, and has been charged in criminal cases, but always got away with it. He is too clever and has the money to pay off the authorities concerned."

Shanker commented, "Kathpalia, I am a policeman, but you have given information which I suspected but had not been able to come to terms with. Particularly,

Surya, I find her very attractive and dated her on more than one occasion, and she always gets my heart beating. To be frank with you, I have not made love to her, she cleverly finds an excuse."

Kathpalia laughed, "You policemen are not good at seducing women. Your mental makeup is different, and she takes advantage of it. You should put a handcuff on her and then, like in American movies, proceed with it. They, of course, also aim guns, but you won't need that. But if she fancies you, then I don't see why you are hesitating."

Shanker laughed. "Kathpalia, you have told me more than I as a policeman was able to figure out."

"That is because you appear to have fallen head over heels, as they say, for her," Kathpalia laughed.

"My wife judged her very accurately when we met her at Pratap's place. We had lunch with him, more than once. My wife used to insist on coming, for reasons you can guess." He laughed again.

"I suggest that you investigate, without him trying to divert your attention, through other ruses."

"Surya is nice, but never forget that she is working for him, he is paying her very well, and also educating her brother in a university in London - an expensive education."

Shanker was disappointed after talking to Kathpalia, but at the same time grateful for his caution. There was no doubt that Surya liked him, and he liked her, but to what extent was she prepared to go? There may be other secrets, which Kathpalia was not aware of, maybe she was in the past involved in something, and Ramesh helped her out. He didn't think that Surya and Ramesh were sexually involved, it did not appear so, he had plenty of other ladies in his office, which he could use for his activities if he so desired.

He telephoned Shyamala and she told him that she would be in the office after lunch. She was meeting some college friends, and they were having some sort of lunch party.

Shanker understood and did not admonish her for not attending the office where several officers were waiting for her besides a whole bundle of files.

She came before 3 p.m. and was swamped by the clerks and others, who had been waiting for her, but she cleverly went into Shanker's office and gave him a box of mithai, a very special *mithai* from a *halwai* shop in Lucknow. "There is only one who makes this *mithai*".

Shanker opened the box. The sweets smelled very appetizing, and he broke a piece from it and ate it.

He smiled and said it was delicious. "I am going to hide it and, in the evening, visit my mother and give her the box, she deserves it. I, of course, will keep some for myself."

So after about an hour, Shyamala came into the office swearing and shouting, "What a mess, we have to find some solution, we can't give attention to such minor matters. They have to be delegated to junior officers who must be given full authority to handle them and then back them on the action they take. This is becoming too much," she shrugged.

Shanker told Shyamala that he had talked to Kathpalia, and he seemed to know Pratap quite well though he was reserved and did not say much. Mathew, like everyone else says, is a different type of person and he would like to keep away from him.

"So, any news from Som," he asked Shyamala.

She said, "Let me telephone her, and find out."

Som came on the line and said that they were looking into the murder of the young male nurse-called Gopi, and also tried to contact his family without success. It appears that he was in an orphanage, and probably the manager knew the doctors in Ayurvedic Treatment Centre and persuaded them to give the young man a chance. He was, by all accounts, a very well-behaved and honest person and got along well with colleagues and had only one passion - badminton. It was his ambition to become state badminton champion, and so, in his spare time, he always practiced. He was good at the game. "We don't know anything more. Maybe it was a professional who was paid to do the job. There are many such criminals available in Kerala or for that matter all over India, who for a price will do the job of assassination. We are trying to find out and then further lead to who could have hired him. My guess is that Mathew's company is directly or indirectly involved in it."

"I will be in touch," said Somaya, and put the phone down.

Shanker heard her as Shyamala had put it on the speaker. He said, "We will have to wait for further development, of course, as it is a criminal matter, and we cannot interfere. It is for the state police to take action."

Shyamala entered Shanker's room and said that she had received a message from Som to telephone her at 11 a.m. Som had made a breakthrough in the murder investigation of the young man Gopi, the male nurse.

Shanker looked at Shyamala and said, "I am impressed with your friend. Let me hear what she has to say and put it on the speaker," and told her to speak on the landline.

Som responded saying, "I have some news for you. We have traced the killer of Gopi."

"Well, we started questioning the residents of the quarters, and they all liked Gopi and often invited him to eat with them as he had no servants to cook and could not afford anyone either. In return, he would do small favours for them like going to the post office for registering or depositing cheques or buying provisions from the bazaars, etc.

"There was a middle-aged lady, whose quarter was near his, and she was relatively friendly with him and was very upset with his murder. She had a good rapport with him and cooked for him. She had a young son, and he would babysit him. She said that on the night before they found out about his murder, she had gone out for some fresh air, as she had the usual family quarrel with her husband and wanted to cool off. She saw two men enter Gopi's quarter after knocking, and he opened the door for them. But he looked surprised as he didn't appear to know them, and she saw one of them push Gopi inside and close the door. She hid behind a wall not wanting to be seen, as they looked like bad guys. She didn't suspect that they had killed him. She caught a glimpse of them, and then, they drove off on a small motorcycle - black in colour, not so old, maybe a one-or- two-year-old Hero model. She couldn't note down the number as she didn't have a pen and paper, but she remembered the last three numbers.

"The next day, she had gone to the market to buy provisions and she saw the same scooter outside a cloth store and the two men inside. She had vaguely seen them as it was dark but could sort of recognized them. She telephoned the police constable who was investigating the murder and had given his number to the residents. He came immediately and went to the cloth shop with his assistant and arrested the two men, who tried in vain to run away. Their scooter was confiscated. They must have beaten them very badly as they got a confession from them. They were paid Rs. 20,000 each for doing the job. They confessed that they were professionals, but this was their first murder assignment- generally, it was just beating or robbing, etc. They were asked who the person was they were acting on behalf. They were most reluctant to answer but gave the name of a hotelier. He owned a midsize hotel, but also ran a sort of brothel there. The police knew about him but were unable to nab him as he provided women to politicians and other influential people.

"As this was a murder case, they got a warrant from the sub-judge and arrested him. He was most reluctant to reveal anything and kept dropping names, and every five minutes, the deputy superintendent got a call that he ignored. Eventually, he revealed that it was someone from Mr. Mathew's company, who had telephoned. Someone who worked there and knew him well. We now have to trace who had ordered the murder."

Somaya telephoned and sent copies of the major city newspapers that had made a big issue of the murder of a young and innocent boy, and the opposition parties spoke loudly about it in the state assembly. The State Home Minister agreed that a proper investigation will be done, and they were expecting a directive from him to the senior police authorities to investigate and report to him as soon as possible.

Som, it was decided, would be the key investigator, reporting to the Inspector General of the police and the State Home Secretary. She told Shyamala that it would be a difficult investigation; they would put hurdles in the way at every step. For, her it was a challenge, and if she succeeded, a step towards a promotion, or even a transfer to the IB was possible.

Shyamala had a long talk with her and wished her the best of luck, and, in case, any investigation had to be done at their end in Delhi, with the head office and the consultancy team based in Delhi, they would be only happy to oblige.

Shanker was happy to hear that now it had become a larger issue. It was always a needle in the haystack that created the maximum problem. The murder of an insignificant employee, in this case, had triggered it off, as there was widespread sympathy in the city about the murder of a harmless orphan, and the T.V. channels had made it into a big issue.

He decided that he would not telephone Ramesh, and, as the consultancy, would wait for him or Surya to telephone.

As anticipated, Surya telephoned the next day, late in the afternoon, and asked if he was free to have tea or preferably dinner with her. She said that she was really missing him and asked whether he was upset with her as he had not even telephoned her, and she was waiting for him to telephone. Shanker kept quiet despite what Kathpalia had told him; he had a very soft spot for Surya and just couldn't ignore her invitation.

They met at their favourite restaurant, *The Yellow Brick,* in the evening, and though he was in his police clothes, she was wearing a very stunning dress, exposing more than usual. The dress was armless, and the upper part of her dress clasped her erect breasts and erect spine. There were heart-shaped openings on both sides of the dress just above her hips exposing her slim waist and dazzling belly button. The heavy material of the skirt of the dress was brief to mid-thigh. It was then continued with a long sheer thin material to her ankles. Her well-shaped legs were visible as they ended in a beautiful pair of heeled glass slippers. Her hair was brushed until it was shiny, and the waves stayed in place as she moved. Her makeup was just right, emphasizing her natural beauty, angled jaw, and plump lips; making them look kissable. As she walked, her well-rounded backside swayed in time with her hips making him want to grab them.

All heads turned when she entered, and he could smell an exotic perfume he hadn't smelt before. Though she was very fond of French and European perfumes, this was quite different.

He complimented her on her lovely dress and asked where she bought it from.

She answered coquettishly that men were not supposed to ask such questions and just admire the dress. It was jealous women who asked such details about the dress, perfume, etc.

Shanker laughed and said, "You are dressed stunningly with a perfume to match."

She was surprised that he found the perfume enchanting.

"Anyway, Surya, now tell me why you suddenly remembered me, and no calls all these days?"

She replied, "I can say the same about you. It is generally men who take the initiative, am I right?" she asked.

"Yes, you are right Surya, but I was busy with the bureaucrats in the Home Ministry, they had given me so many files to go through. It is confidential so I can't tell you the details."

"Stop making excuses, Shanker. You could have easily found time to telephone me and flirt with me, at least."

"Surya, has Ramesh sent you to meet me? Don't forget I am a detective and can make deductions cleverly."

Her face fell and her smile disappeared as she said, "You don't trust me, I am surprised. Please tell me what you have in mind."

Shanker kept quiet and said, "Let me not spoil the evening talking and let me enjoy a nice cup of coffee with this beautiful woman, whom everyone is admiring and wondering if she is a Bollywood actress." And he caught her hand under the table and squeezed it passionately.

After flirting for a while, Shanker said, "I have another appointment and will be in touch, and I still have to locate a suitable haveli where I can take you for dinner and for an alluring night."

"Please find one soon," said Surya, "I am getting impatient."

As anticipated, the next day Ramesh Pratap telephoned Shanker and inquired if he was all right.

"I am fine," replied Shanker. "However, there are a lot of questions that need answers from you, Mr. Pratap, maybe we can meet over lunch at your residence to discuss?" Ramesh agreed.

Shyamala bought the note, typed on her computer, and showed it to him. He made a few changes and additions and asked her to print it out.

"This is not to be shown to Pratap, it is for us, we can memorize it and put it on our mobile phone and if we get stuck, we can always say that we have to make a call and look at it."

They reached Pratap's house at 1:30 p.m., deliberately half an hour late, to keep him waiting.

He was sitting in his office and, as soon as they entered, he got up and said with a forced smile, "Let's go to the dining room."

He noticed that Surya was not there and maybe he had sent her out for some errand. He didn't want Shanker to meet her.

They sat down, and Ramesh offered a drink to Shanker and Shyamala, and they both opted for a soft drink which the waiter poured, a sort of lemon cocktail which tasted quite nice.

He told the waiter to get him a beer and the waiter brought him a German beer, which looked quite mild.

"Are you sure Mr. Dayal, that you wouldn't like to have the beer? It is very nice and light."

Shanker nodded his head and said, "No thanks."

"Now, Mr. Pratap, we have a lot of questions for you."

"Firstly, we have another murder in Cochin, which has been traced to Mr. Mathew's office, the police will sooner or later find out who ordered the killing of this innocent young boy, which has shocked the city and got wide media publicity."

"Mr. Mathew is a compulsive aggressor, and whenever something does not suit him, he tries to eliminate him or her, which is unfortunate. He is like a trigger-happy Don."

"He was trying to hide the names of the borrowers and the status of the loans from us, and from you as well. When both Vikram and Ajit Kumar got close to it, he tried to eliminate them for reasons we don't understand."

"Both were lucky; Vikram caught the last flight to Toronto otherwise he would be dead, and Ajit Kumar was fortunate also that Somaya transferred him to the hospital.

Then the young man, a male nurse, who told the nurse to give the injection, poor boy he was murdered by the hired goons."

"What are you trying to hide? I am told you have made very little progress in your consultancy?"

"The names of the kin of the politicians who were given these irrecoverable loans are now with us. It is more or less complete. Mr. Kathpalia's department has traced all the names with details, as the government is the largest shareholder in RML bank."

"But there is more to it than this, and we have so far not been able to find out, as names of the loans cannot possibly be kept secret. Finding most of the money, and how it has been spent, is the job of Mr. Kathpalia's department; it is not our concern."

"Our concern is these murders and attempted murders. What is the reason for them? We intend to find out."

"If you know anything, please tell us, otherwise you would be an accessory to these murders."

"I am giving you two weeks, please decide and let me know."

Shanker was daydreaming in his office and when Shyamala came with two assistants, he didn't even notice that they had come. He was strumming the desk with his fingers, trying to play a classical tune, and seemed to be in a different world.

Shyamala made a polite noise, which woke him up, and he appeared surprised and said, "When did you come? I didn't hear you enter."

She laughed and said, "We didn't want to disturb you, it appeared you were in deep thought."

Shanker kept quiet, knowing what Shyamala was hinting at, and she was an intuitive person, so she guessed that he was thinking of Surya, which was right as he was thinking of her. The woman who has captivated this very emotional existence; smooth skin like velvet, lips that made you want to devour them all day and night, and her legs .... oh goodness, he was totally hopeless.

"So, you don't remember that you called a meeting at 12 p.m., and I had given you the agenda, which you approved?"

"Yes, I do recollect and clearly remember the agenda which appears to be outdated as circumstances have changed."

Shyamala looked at him in surprise. "I don't understand what has changed Mr. Dayal," she said formally.

"Well, to start with, Mr. Ramesh Pratap has left the country, and no one knows where he is right now. Last night, he caught a flight to London, and then when his office telephoned, he was not in London, and his mobile phone showed another location in the United States, but it appears that he caught a flight ostensibly from Miami to somewhere in Central America."

"I can only think of one country and that is Panama, which is known for keeping confidential accounts and has a favourable tax system for people who want to hide money."

"They have banks, law firms, and accounting firms which specialize in concealing ill-gotten wealth and recycling it to make it appear legitimate. Many rich Indians have hidden their wealth there, as have Europeans and Americans. Now, what has he gone there for, I have no clue or idea about. I doubt if he has that kind of money, which would require a trip to Panama, on the other side of the world."

Shyamala said, "He would have gone to track down RML creditors, those they had given large loans to, particularly the kin of politicians, after receiving a tip from someone in his organization."

Shyam added, "Shanker, Panama would never disclose the names or details of the money parked. For that, he would require a court order from some European country like Britain or Germany, and why would they give it as the Swiss Bank keeps secret accounts, why would they use Panama?"

"The USA has very strict laws and to get a court order would be impossible."

"The only reason I can think of is if he has parked money there, or if Mathew, most likely, has parked money. Let us wait and watch, my guess is that Mathew will reach Panama in the next day or two."

Chapter 16

As anticipated, Shanker got a call from Kathpalia that the counsellor in the embassy had telephoned him and told him that Mr. Ravi Mathew called on the ambassador that very day.

Kathpalia continued, "He is known to Mathew, as he is also from Cochin and was in college with him. The ambassador, I understand, is a highly respected individual and is married with two sons, who are studying in the USA at the University in Florida. Anyway, they are friends. However, I don't think he would help Mathew in any unlawful manner. The most he could do is to introduce him to a law firm which deals with such issues, the city has several of them, with British and American links."

Shanker was not at all surprised and said to Kathpalia, "You said this is to be handled by our department, but we have not been successful in the past, the authorities are not helpful, and I don't blame them. It is a big business for them and a major source of earning, as they have nothing much else in the economy, except the major earnings from the canal."

"Well," said Shanker, "let us be patient and see what we can do when they return. I don't know whether you can interrogate them on their return, as you have no grounds on which you can question them, except that they visited Panama City."

"Yes," said Kathpalia. "You are right, Shanker. Any progress on the murder case in Cochin of the young male nurse, where the evidence was leading to Mathew's company?"

"I don't know," said Shanker. "I will ask Shyamala to telephone Somaya tomorrow. I am not that confident about their investigation; Mathew is very shrewd and well-connected and has large pockets."

"Well, keep me informed," said Kathpalia.

Shyamala telephoned Somaya, as suggested by Kathpalia, and hoped that she had some news for them.

Somaya called her back and told her that they had made a breakthrough and arrested two executives of Mr. Mathew, who were identified by the hotel manager. One was Pillai and the other was his assistant. It was Pillai who had given the order to the hotel manager to hire the goons to kill the male nurse. He was being paid Rs. 1 lac for doing the job but bargained for Rs. 1.5 lacs as he had to pay the two goons for doing the job and, also, his share would be about 1 lac.

Pillai agreed and told him to go abroad, as he was also on bail for the offense of trying to kill Ajit Kumar through the nurse and the injection vial given by the male nurse, who had no idea it was lethal. He was too innocent and didn't suspect anything. He also trusted the old nurse and, therefore, had no suspicions. It would now appear that they will have to go back to court and appeal for a second indictment against Pillai and ask the court to cancel his bail, if possible, which will not be easy as Mathew will hire a top high court lawyer to represent Pillai.

The other concern is for the hotel manager, Ravi Shanker. He may be bumped off by Pillai's goons, as he is the only one to give evidence that Pillai had contacted him, and the orders came from him. It is certain that this is not the first murder and Mathew would not like them to open the can of worms, so that fingers are pointed towards him, for other criminal activities, which will eventually land up on the table of Mathew.

Somaya indicated that they had decided to provide security to Ravi Shanker as his life was in danger, but at the same time he didn't appear to be worried. Maybe he had something on Mathew, therefore he was not in position to act brutally against him. He had probably left some important documents implicating Mathew with a lawyer of the high court or in some bank locker.

Somaya added that she won't be surprised if he left the key to the locker with Ramesh Pratap as he mentioned his name prominently. He, more or less, admitted that he looked after the needs of Mr. Pratap whenever he was in Cochin. It is well known that he supplied women, and so he pleased Pratap in that way, and he is very sharp. He must have taken photographs from a camera, most likely of Pratap with one of his special women, and maybe he was keeping it as a security, knowing that one day he may need it.

Shyamala was quite shocked to hear it all and so was Shanker, who heard it from the speaker.

Shanker was feeling a little lonely and a little depressed, so he decided to telephone Surya. She didn't take the call but sent a message that she will telephone back.

He waited for her call, and then got into his car and saw a message from her. 'Waiting for you at the *Yellow Brick*.' He felt a little elated and it was always nice to see her, flirt with her and a little intimacy as well, but so far, no sex. Maybe it was better that way, as she was in the camp he was investigating.

He stopped at the florist at the Khan Market and bought a bouquet of mixed flowers. They didn't look very fresh, but the thought counted.

He entered the restaurant and saw her sitting on her favourite chair, near the window. She was wearing her office formal clothes as she had come straight from the office.

She looked nice in whatever clothes she wore and had probably gone to the well-stocked cloakroom at Ramesh's residence and to deck up and dab perfume, with her glossy pout in a shade of dark red.

He handed her the flowers and gave her a peck on her cheek. He was tempted to catch her tightly and kiss her passionately on her lips. She would absolutely sure have enjoyed it, more than him. She had a passionate nature but kept it subdued due to obvious reasons.

He sat down opposite her but didn't speak a word, waiting for her to say something. She blew a kiss towards him that made him smile.

"It is good to see you smile," she said, "You are always so serious and in thought, what do you keep thinking about?"

"You would like to know; I am sure and have probably guessed."

She laughed and said, "You have to locate that haveli so that we can do what is only in our imagination at the moment." Then she asked, "Have you come to flirt with me or is there another motive to do with KBL Associates?"

Sounding all enthused she told him, "By the way, I didn't tell you. I have got a promotion and am on the same scale as the consultants like Vikram and Ajit Kumar. So, I have been given a flat in an apartment house in Sunder Nagar, not a very large flat, on the top floor, but Sunder Nagar is Sunder Nagar - one of the best residential colonies in Delhi. I can see DPS, Mathura Road, from my bedroom window."

"Congratulations, Surya, you have done well! Now, what you need is a husband and children, so that you have a family."

"Yes, you are right Shanker. I do need to find a husband as I am getting on in age. Any suggestions?"

He laughed heartily. "You are not serious about hooking up with a policeman, are you? An executive with a multinational or a bank would suit you better."

"Always evading the issue. Shanker, you can never be serious."

"Give me time, Surya. I have to also think of many things, and I feel we have to get to know each other better. So far, our relationship has been superficial and more to do with a serious investigation."

"We have to get out of this so-called mess, and then freely get to know each other in a different manner. I admit I like you very much, but let's proceed cautiously so that there are no regrets later." She looked at him in a disappointed manner and said, "I will wait for our evening in the haveli."

Shanker now knew how to proceed. He had to nail Ramesh Pratap and Ravi Mathew. Beth was also their godfather in the ministry who was pulling the strings. It would be impossible to nail the powerful politician, but his name and reputation could take a hit.

He was not sure at all who was involved from the top. It had to be somebody very shrewd and clever, that he had stayed in the background but pulled all the strings.

Kathpalia may know, so he telephoned him and told him that they made progress on identifying the criminal elements but had no clue who was pulling the strings from the top, as eventually it was all related to making big money through wrongful means, and politicians needed a lot of it, to win elections.

Kathpalia kept silent and said, "Let us have lunch tomorrow at one of the five-star hotels in Chanakyapuri - Taj Palace - at the Chinese, and you will pay for it." Shanker laughed and said, "It will be my pleasure."

"Just the two of us, don't bring your assistant, though I have high regard for her intellect."

Shanker was there fifteen minutes before time and found a table that was a little isolated so that they would not recognize them.

One of the seniors recognized him and said, "You helped my aunt when she was injured in a car accident some years ago, took her immediately to the hospital, and saved her life."

Shanker remembered the accident. She was saved after being hit by a delivery van driving fast, which hit her Toyota car. The driver also suffered serious injuries but recovered.

She was forever grateful and sent him expensive gifts on Diwali and New Year's, and whenever she returned from an overseas trip. She was in the garment export business and had a large establishment in Okhla.

Shanker smiled, "Please give my regards to your aunt and I hope she is keeping well. Please also don't tell anyone that I am here as I am having a confidential meeting."

"In that case, why don't you sit in the enclosed cabin, then you will have more privacy."

Kathpalia came dressed in a brown suit, probably bought on an overseas trip.

The manager led him to the enclosed cabin and gave a bouquet of flowers to both of them.

"Why are we getting this VIP treatment? I thought it was confidential," asked a curious Kathpalia.

"The manager recognized me as I saved his aunt after an accident on Tilak Marg when a big delivery van hit her car. I rushed her to the hospital. My jeep was just behind her car."

"Lucky woman. So, she is eternally grateful?"

"Yes, she is a very nice and charming lady in her late fifty. She runs a successful garment business."

"You are not talking of Mrs. Khosla; are you Shanker?"

"Yes, I am, what a small world, do you know her?" replied now surprised-looking Shanker.

"Yes, she is my wife's cousin."

"Okay, now let's discuss business," said Shanker. "I am on a roll and have now sufficient evidence to indict Ravi Mathew for criminality, committed under his orders by a manager of his called Pillai, who murdered a young male nurse in Cochin. We also know that he almost killed Ajit Kumar of KBL, but luckily for him, Somaya saved his life."

"Now, Kathpalia, you know better who the big man behind all this is; loans were given to kin of politicians who have not repaid them. It must have been on the orders of some powerful person, most likely an important politician."

Kathpalia kept quiet, "Don't forget Shanker," he said, "I work in the ministry, and the bosses are the IAS-babus-secretaries, and all. Secretaries and, on top of the heap, the minister, his minister of state, and other familiar ministers.

Now, the minister will never expose himself. He will tell one of the junior ministers, who directs the secretary of the ministry, and they will direct us, and others concerned. They deal directly with the chairman etc. of the banks and big businessmen and industrialists. The really big industrialists deal directly with the ministers, and he is open to them, as they contribute generously to their election funding.

So, tell me, Shanker, in this scenario, who would you try to point fingers at?"

"Certainly not the minister. He wouldn't bother about the loans to relatively small politicians' kins, though they are helpful during elections.

The final order comes either from the minister of state or his deputy to the secretary, who passes it on to his joint secretary and down the ladder to the bank chairman or managing director.

So, it is very difficult to trace who gave the orders and, sometimes, the managing director refuses to put it on record, then another route has to be found.

I will try and find out from the joint secretary, who is a friend of mine and was in college with me if he can assist. He is a very straightforward and honest civil servant. I hope he will cooperate. If he does, then I will let you know."

They got up, the manager refused to give Shanker the bill and said it was, with his compliments, on the house.

"I wouldn't even dream of charging you, Mr. Shanker," he said, "after what you did for my aunt."

"Please give her my regards," said Shanker.

Shyamala was busy dictating some letters when she received a call from Somaya. She didn't pay attention as she was busy dictating, but when she heard Pillai's name, she asked the stenographer to go and said that she would call her later.

"Sorry Som, I was dictating some official letters and got a little absorbed in them."

"Shyamala, we have got Pillai's bail cancelled and now he is in the city jail along with the two boys who murdered Gopi." A warrant was arranged for the arrest of the hotel manager, Ravi Shanker. The lawyer had to approach the high court in Trivandrum, as the session judge was not prepared to give a warrant and politely and cleverly made his arguments for the same. The senior public prosecutor was asked to approach the high court, and they overruled the session judge's order and granted our request. He is now also in jail, and has applied for bail, pleading that he was not involved with the two boys who murdered Gopi and that there was no proof, though the two boys had confessed that they were paid by him. He, however, said the police got a confession through brutal methods.

Ravi Shanker has contacts with powerful politicians and ministers and had obliged them in some manner or the other and these secrets and information could be damaging to them.

The fear is that he may be murdered in jail as he poses a danger to these powerful politicians and, also, some senior bureaucrats, including maybe senior police officers. A lot of his clients were foreigners as well, but they do not come into the play. Arabs from the gulf and Saudi came routinely for treatment in Kerala.

"Well," Shyamala assured, "I agree with you Som, you will have to have him guarded well."

"I will definitely try and let us see what happens."

Shyamala was worried that Som may be a target, but then thought they would not try to harm her, as the entire police force would descend on them. They protected their own.

Two days later, Som telephoned Shyamala informing her that their fears have been realized. A powerful bomb exploded in the jail, killing Ravi Shanker and Pillai, it was so powerful that it made a big hole in the building and the two boys tried to escape but were caught.

So, they were back to square one. All they have now are the two boys who murdered Gopi for a price, and the main players who would have led them to the masterminds are dead.

Shyamala went and told Shanker what had happened.

He replied, "I was expecting something like this, but not so soon and the manner in which it was done points towards the involvement of some senior officer in the jail complex.

There will be another investigation," he laughed. "We seem to be stumbling from one hurdle to another. These people are extremely clever and well connected."

Shanker asked the operator to get him the commissioner of income tax on the telephone.

He knew him well since they had worked together in the past. He was from the IRS, a few years his senior.

"It is nice to hear your voice, Shanker. What is it you want me to investigate?"

"Well, I called to tell you that both Mr. Ramesh Pratap, Managing Director of KBL Associates, and

Mr. Ravi Mathew from Cochin, who is a large shareholder in the company, were in Panama recently."

"Shanker, we have informers who told us about their presence. So, what do you want us to investigate?" asked the director.

"I don't know, maybe they are parking some money there, ill-gotten gains," said Shanker. "It is your line of work, so you would know better. We have been in touch with Mr. Kathpalia from the Audits and Accounts department and are working with him. For the loans that were given by RML bank, the KBL Associates have been given the consultancy. RML is in a bad financial situation and the government is the largest shareholder in the bank. The loans are not recoverable as you may be knowing. However, it is not the police's headache. We are concerned about almost 6-7 murders that have taken place since the consultancy started. Most of them are in one way or the other connected to Mr. Ravi Mathew.

The Cochin police, with whom we are closely working, had arrested a senior executive of Mr. Mathew, and he was murdered in jail along with another associate."

"This is news to me. I didn't know about the murders, and the seriousness of the irrecoverable loans amounting to some crores of rupees. I did get a whiff that some powerful politicians were involved, therefore, the money may have been siphoned off to Panama, which is a safe haven for these deals.

Let me talk to Mr. Kathpalia also and some others and I will get back to you."

It was getting murkier by the day, and the murder of Ravi Shanker and Pillai was a serious matter. Matthew was clever, as he was in Panama at that time, so no fingers could be pointed at him. He must have gotten it done from gangsters and paid a heavy price for it. Probably, a Mumbai-based gang, which specializes in such killings. Mumbai was famous for such gangs, and so was Kanpur, but it was a little far-fetched to think that they would give an assignment to somebody in UP or Jharkhand, though it was possible. Most likely, it was somebody from inside the system, maybe the jail itself.

Shyamala spoke to Som the next day and asked her if there was any progress in the investigation of the murders. "Both Pillai and Ravi Shanker were not entities. Ravi Shanker, in fact, had obliged many politicians and businessmen who visited his brothel, and they are worried that he kept some records or even photographs secretly taken," said Som.

Somaya related that Ravi Shanker's house was ripped open as only his servant was there. He was tied up in the dark and could not identify anyone. All his drawers and cupboards were broken into; the steel cabinets were broken, and files were missing. Investigations are ongoing as to who may have done this.

Ravi Shanker's wife, son, and two daughters left him a long time ago and went to live in Bengaluru, with his wife's family. He sends money to them regularly. His son is studying to be an engineer at a well-known college. The wife is from a decent family; her father who is retired worked with the PWS and later, after retirement, with a well-known builder. His wife had not divorced him and technically they were still married.

Som explained that she had a long talk with his wife, Sakshi, on the telephone and she admitted that their marriage was a failure. When she found out what he was doing while running the hotel, she left him and took the children with her. He was upset and wanted his son to stay on and live with him and help him in the business. The estranged wife indicated that she very strangely put her foot down and threatened to expose him. He was very close to Mathew, who gave him a lot of business, particularly from his customers from the UAE. She told Somaya that more than that she doesn't know or want to know.

Somaya thought it was a big relief for her, though financially I don't know the implications. But she did mention that he left his properties to her and his son, so they can sell them and manage, I suppose. He was very fond of his son and would visit Bengaluru regularly. It is just a one-and-a-half-hour flight. He would catch the early morning flight and return by the 11 pm flight. He didn't like staying in Bengaluru. He gave expensive presents to his daughters; saris and gold jewellery and promised to give them a good dowry on their marriage, Sakshi expressed.

She said she believed him because he was very fond of his children and even her, he was always polite and kind to her and sent enough money for them to live comfortably. He paid the fees of the daughters' schools and son's college fees including a trip abroad to England, whenever he wanted to go.

'He made a lot of money from a relatively middle-level hotel – 3-star - I think, I don't know how, but he was always flush with cash, which he literally gave to them when he came to Bengaluru,' she admitted. The wife related, 'It was Mathew who put him on the wrong track in life and he was greedy enough to follow that shameful track - greed for money through any means. We knew what was happening in the hotel, but never talked about it. My children will miss him, particularly my son, as he was very fond of him.'

Shanker tapped on his desk and tapped it in deep thought. He was thinking of a plan to proceed further. His job was to expose the criminality and find the person or persons who were behind the murders. Were they individuals, or was it one of the organized gangs, in all the states in Delhi, Kerala, and particularly Mumbai? He did not think any gang from UP was involved, though it was the most lawless state with the maximum number of such murders.

It was very unlikely that Mathew would engage someone from outside his circle, on the other hand, the gang had contacts in London, as it gave a contract to someone to eliminate Vikram, which, of course, failed.

How to trace this gang? He thought he would ask some known people, and even some gangsters in Tihar prison if they could give information on the gangs that may be involved. It would be a difficult job, but they had to try.

He telephoned the prison warden in Tihar prison and asked his permission to interrogate a well-known criminal, who was well informed and may be of assistance.

He received a call from the warden who told him to come the next day around 4 pm.

He went and met this criminal, who was on life imprisonment. Shanker had helped him from getting hanged and instead persuaded the public prosecutor to plead in court to give him life imprisonment though he deserved to be hanged.

He was quite feared in the prison and had good contacts to give information. Shanker had used him effectively in the past.

Shanker went the next day and met the warden, had a cup of tea with him, and then went into a private chamber to interrogate him. He appeared to have lost weight and was looking a little rundown.

"Tell me Shanker sir, what do I owe the honour of your coming to meet me? I suppose you want some information about some gang or criminals. If I can help you, I will certainly do so."

Shanker quietly related to him briefly about the murder he was investigating. He said there must be more than one gang involved and he had heard about Ravi Mathew, and that he used a particular gang when required. But the attempted murders in London and in Punjab, had no connection with Mathew, he thought.

"The murder inside the jail is probably an inside job with outside assistance, Mathew is certainly behind it, but I am not sure about others. I will try and find out. Give me ten days and then come and meet me again."

Shanker gave him a present of dry fruits and sweets which he liked and left.

Shanker thought that if Mathew was not involved, then it must be someone else, the only other person could be Ramesh Pratap, who was leading the investigation and had the agenda of career up, that no politicians would be indicted if their kin didn't pay up, or to find some other way of deflecting that issue. Ramesh was the managing director and dealt with senior bureaucrats and ministers, unlike Ravi Mathew, whose role was different. He had to somehow find the link of Ramesh who was creating all these problems so that they could proceed further.

He received a call the next day from the prison warden, who requested him to come, as the concerned criminal whom he had met in prison, had some information for him. Shanker immediately got into his car and proceeded to the prison.

He requested a special room, where he could interrogate Ganga Ram, otherwise, he would not talk and also did not want it recorded through the special equipment they had. He told the warden he would inform him of the relevant details. The warden reluctantly agreed. He offered some special mithai (Indian sweets) to Ganga Ram, who was thrilled as he had not tasted such sweets in years, the badly cooked food in the prison was only fit for the criminals.

Ganga Ram told Shanker that Mathew's ring only runs in Kerala and mainly in Cochin and the surrounding areas and he did not have the talent to deal with sophisticated and important people. He was a rough type of person, but with good contacts with certain types of criminals and was dangerous too, as he would not hesitate to even put on the block people who may have helped him in the past, like Ravi Shanker. He could not be relied upon for any form of loyalty. He was not capable as a person to deal with people in high positions, with his background and education, he felt incapable of dealing with senior officials.

He was told that the Managing Director, some Pratap person, who was highly educated and moved in high circles, had excellent contacts with the bureaucrats and ministers and knew how to deal with them. He was the real boss, and Mathews coordinated with him and listened to his advice.

Everything was controlled by Pratap, and he had some very attractive ladies working for him, whom he used when required to ensnare the officials and ministers. One of them was very close to him, and he had helped educate her brother abroad and done favours for her and she was very clever in her work. And knew how to trap men and set their co-operation. Shanker got cold on the inside as he continued to listen to Ganga Ram.

Everything is planned and controlled by Mr. Pratap, who is extremely intelligent and totally ruthless, much more than Mathew, who is crude. Pratap is different and does everything in a planned and sophisticated way.

Ganga Ram spoke all this in colloquial Hindi, which sometimes made it difficult for Shanker to understand. Where he got this information from, Shanker did not ask, and gave him a large box of his favourite mithai (sweets) and left saying he will help him get an early discharge if it was possible.

Shanker was in deep thought as he returned to his office. He had been on the wrong track, particularly regarding Surya. He would have to really rein in his emotions and feelings, but he would play along with her giving her no indication of what he knew about her. He had to admit that he was slightly disappointed, but he was told by more than one person what she was up to and to whom she reported. So, why not start with her? He telephoned her and chatted with her. Of course, she did most of the talking. He put in a word or two and was a good listener.

He proposed that they meet the next evening at the Chhatarpur temple at 7.30 p.m., then have dinner at her favourite restaurant at the farmhouse. He encouraged her by mentioning that they can enjoy the music of the lovely band and it would be fun to meet, have dinner, and then dance a bit.

She agreed immediately. He didn't notice any hesitation in her tone or voice.

He reached early as usual and went to do the darshan and meet *panditji* and receive his blessings. Panditji invited him for a cup of tea served in a mug which was very sweet, and the mithai was very tasty.

He had used his personal car without a driver. He drove to the farmhouse and found a table on the side and two chairs. The was music being played from a recorder as the band was not there. He ordered a soft drink, and a non-alcoholic cocktail, which he asked the waiter not to make it too sweet.

Shanker did not see Surya approaching. She must have come from behind him as she put her hand over his eyes and said, "Guess who," jokingly.

He caught her hand and pulled her to the side, giving her a soft kiss on her lips, whilst she sat down. She smelt good and looked great as always. Her soft, well-manicured hands were smooth under his touch. He smiled at her saying, "I was thinking of you and waiting patiently for you to get here."

"Here I am," she replied. She was dressed like a film star in a fashionable designer dress- a luxurious pink georgette cigarette dress with *resham* work. She must have gotten it as a present, as it would be very expensive to purchase. Her accessories were sterling silver drop earrings and a thin matching chain that clasped her beautiful neck with two tiny hearts at the centre. She also had the same pattern bracelet on her wrist and around her ankle. The colour of her makeup matched her dress. The heeled silver sandals on her feet matched the outfit. Maybe Pratap arranged it for her compliments of *Andaaz Fashions*.

"You look very stunning," he complimented, "and look at me, I am simply dressed in clothes police officers can afford." He was dressed in a light chocolate coloured suede jacket with a white crew-necked T-shirt, and black jeans. This was complemented by black leather loafers on his feet.

"Not everyone is honest like you. There are others who take advantage of their position," she said jokingly.

"I am sure you know some," he said with a smile.

She smiled politely then teased, "Now, Shanker, you didn't call me here to make polite conversation, so what do you have in mind?"

"I have plenty in my mind, but don't know how and where to start." He sat back in his chair admiring her but more in an observant way, then continued speaking.

"Firstly, Surya, you forget that I am a detective and have so many sources of information. For example, I know that you are very important to KBL and particularly to Mr. Pratap. He is educating your brother in a well-known college in London, and the company is paying for it, or there are special funds at his disposal for such purposes. He has given you a promotion and a flat in Sunder Nagar, which is one of the posh colonies of New Delhi. Now, let us stop playing games Surya. I have an investigation in hand and have also to prove my abilities. You are his trusted executive, and your company is in quite a mess with so many murders that have taken place, particularly in Cochin.

Now, tell me, what is this all about?" "I am sure you know much more than you are admitting."

Surya was quiet for a minute before she replied, "You don't trust me Shanker." she said and made a sad face.

"It is very difficult for me to tell you what you want to know, as I myself don't know what the whole plan is. I am only a small player and told to do what they want me to do. Yes, I admit that it was Pratap's plan that I get close to you and find out as much as possible about the investigation. You were clever enough to have sensed it or detected it and have got a fair amount of information.

I am not in their inner circle and don't know much, and they have obliged me, so I am grateful for that and follow their orders. Beyond that, I am not privy to the type of information you want.

Mr. Pratap, Ravi Mathew, and a senior officer in the ministry are closely involved besides some politicians who deal through this senior officer. I think you know him; he is a very clever operator and, by telling you about me, he won your confidence."

"I know whom you are talking about, and my intuition was wrong, as I have known him for many years, but his behaviour was suspicious which I noticed, last time we met."

"Anyway, you have given me an important lead."

He got up and Surya followed him, and they left the venue. They were both disappointed that the evening had been an anti-climax.

Chapter 17

Shanker called Shyamala and asked her to sit down and ordered some coffee.

"I don't know where to start, Shyamala, but the last two weeks have been a big eye opener for me."

Shyamala looked at him and smiled, "I did not want to discourage you, as you were quite besotted with Surya, and why not, she is a very attractive and charming lady, and you are a lonely bachelor, and she was willing to play along with you. It was all an act, I could sense as a woman from the beginning, but was reluctant to say anything. I did some checking with friends from my circle, who knew her, and they did not trust her and said that this was not the first time. Her company uses her for such assignments as she is very attractive and charms the men and uses them or gets information from them. She has done such assignments with overseas clients of KBL and been quite successful."

Shanker was disappointed as he had started liking her even more; he thought he was in love with her and had fantasies about her. He even thought that one day he would propose to her and marry her if she agrees and settle down as he was getting on in age and wanted a family and children.

That was all shattered now, she was just baiting him for KBL who wanted her to get information from him. He knew she would agree to go to bed with him if it helped her in the assignment.

Shyamala looked at him, "Mr. Dayal, don't feel disappointed. There are many women who find you very charming and you would have no difficulty in finding a nice lady, maybe not so attractive, but looks are not everything."

Shanker kept doodling and said, "We have to move on, Shyamala. This investigation has gone on for too long, it is time we finished it." He continued, "I frankly don't know how to proceed; my brain is not working right now," he said and gave Shyamala the look of a lost person.

"You work out a strategy Shyamala, as I have failed and don't know how to proceed." He looked at her and said, "Take up the challenge, I will assist you in whatever manner possible."

Shyamala looked at him. "I am prepared to take the challenge, give me time to work out a practicable strategy."

With that, she got up and walked out of his office with the mindset of doing what needs to be done. Shyamala was as determined as ten elephants. She took her time making a list of possible approaches and plans.

Shyamala telephoned Mr. Kathpalia and requested him for an appointment. She didn't know him well but had met him with Shanker at two or three meetings they routinely had with the ministry.

He agreed to meet her and invited her for an evening tea session at his club.

Shyamala gracefully agreed and said she would be there by 5.30 p.m. Shanker had warned her that he was an extremely clever and perceptive person and he had known him for many years and had attended his lectures which were held periodically at the ministry in which the police officers also participated. This was a common practice and Shanker had also been a speaker at these sessions.

Shyamala was on time, but the hall porter told her to wait for him in one of the enclaves with sofas in the main hall. He came about 20 minutes late, apologizing that he was held up by his seniors on some important issue they were discussing.

Shyamala did not complain, knowing fully well that senior officers in the ministry have these issues of being summoned by their superior officers or junior ministers.

He was dressed in his office suit and was looking a little hassled, but he smiled and asked if she would have some tea or coffee along with snacks.

She opted for tea, with a plate of vegetable pakoras, a popular item in the club.

"Now, Miss Tripathi, how can I help you?"

"You can certainly help us solve the present riddle, which is getting more complicated every day, and is becoming a game of chess, every move of which is being cleverly planned and we do not think we have made much progress."

"You gave an important clue to Mr. Dayal about Surya, and he is crestfallen after that, as being a detective, he made his enquiries and found them to be true. He had become very fond of her, and she had cleverly ensnared him to the extent that he was preparing a proposal of marriage to her. In the office, he would just sit and look at the wall, and everyone wondered why he was in such deep thought. He was fantasizing about her; I could make out. I feel sorry for him," said Shyamala, "he is very disappointed."

Kathpalia just smiled and said, "I know Shanker since he joined the IPS and also knew his father who was in the IAS. I felt it was my duty to warn him before he got deeper into it. Now, what help do you want from me, Shyamala, if I call you by your first name?"

"Please do, Mr. Kathpalia. Surya also gave us some information that you are very close to Mr. Pratap and most likely were responsible for KBL getting the consultancy contract and that Mr. Pratap would not give any report contrary to your plans. She said that the whole consultancy was a sham including your ministry's senior officers and the deputy minister, in particular, who is heavily involved."

"She could not have said that," claimed Kathpalia. "I know Surya well; she is far too shrewd."

"No, you are right. She didn't say it, but her actions and hints indicated that Mr. Dayal is a very clever man and so deduced the meaning behind them."

Kathpalia sat back in his chair, paused for a minute, and quietly observed Shyamala thinking he had underestimated her intellect. He then asked, "What do you want me to do?"

"You could in some manner whatever you think possible, assist without anyone knowing that you are doing so, and we will keep it absolutely confidential, and never betray your trust. You have our word for it. What we are asking is something that is fair justice of a kind from your end. The ministry will not come to know if it is done confidentially."

Kathpalia looked at her over his cup of tea which he held in his hand. He was in deep thought. 'If they can guarantee that nothing would be said, or no fingers would be pointed his way … after all Shanker is my friend.' 'I did warn him about Surya. I didn't know he was *that* sweet on her.' He kept quiet and sipped his tea and didn't answer. 'I do know more than they do, and Shyamala looked very determined … hmmm if she could be confidential … there are many of wrongs that I want to be made right in the system … this could be my only chance. If the ministry or anyone asks me anything about divulging information, I will deny it to my death. I must move smartly and without anyone knowing or this could blow up in my face and affect my family and image or get me killed. On the other hand, I am close to retirement so ....'

After five minutes, he got up and nodded and said, "Tell Shanker I will try."

Shyamala saw Shanker sitting alone as she passed his cabin. She knocked and went inside and found him in deep thought. She flicked her fingers and he smiled and said, "I was not thinking of Surya, I was thinking of something else, about Vikram and how he managed to escape through sheer luck.

"Do you hear from him, Shyamala? Does he ever telephone to say hello or whatever and send an email?"

"Well, he has sent me emails but nothing romantic," she sighed. "It is about his work, studies, and environment. He has still not settled down and is finding the transition not easy at all, despite the fact that he is good at making friends, particularly girlfriends, maybe he has not found anyone to his liking."

Shanker laughed, "Maybe he thinks of you that's why."

Changing the subject, she told him, "Where were we, yes you met Kathpalia, he said that he will try. He has not communicated anything to me so far, but I believe the minister of state is being changed, and then I suppose the new incumbent will bring in the junior of his choice, and most likely the Secretary in the ministry will also change, the present Secretary in the ministry will possibly go back to his home state on a promotion."

"This is likely to happen in the next one month, with a major cabinet reshuffle."

"So, we have to wait and see who comes. It won't make any difference to Kathpalia's position because he is almost at his peak and would not find it to go higher also, he has only a few years left till retirement, so now he may decide to help us as he has nothing to lose."

"If the new minister is someone from Eastern India, then both Ravi Mathew and Pratap will be in serious trouble, without their godfather, there will not be anybody to protect them."

Shanker was right, he got a call from Kathpalia that a minister would be taking over. "He is from Madhya Pradesh, and I don't think there is any link with Mathew or Pratap and their companies." Kathapulia said, "He will ask for a briefing, and I will most likely, as the old hand here, be guiding him. I know this minister very well, his brother is in the same service, and we are good friends. He is presently posted in Maharashtra, Mumbai. I don't know much about the civil servants or their advice. He is his own man and will get him changed if he doesn't fall in line, and bring his own man from Madhya Pradesh, where he is very close to the chief minister."

Kathpalia said, "Let us be patient and wait. I am quite hopeful of getting a promotion and I think I will be able to play a far more important role than at present."

Shanker was optimistic once again and hopeful that the police would play an important role. Somaya telephoned Shyamala the following morning saying, "I have some very interesting and important news for you."

She explained, "this Chief Minister has announced that the term of the present state assembly is coming to an end and elections will be held after two months and has given the tentative dates, subject to the Election Commission's approval.

"Now, the Chief Minister is a very shrewd politician and the opposition parties had been making allegations against him, that he was corrupt and had links with the crime syndicates in the state, and was close to some shady business companies; Ravi Mathew's name was mentioned by the opposition in the assembly on more than one occasion, and they wanted an enquiry into his dealings, by a committee.

"The Chief Minister sensed this as a serious problem for himself, as he had been protecting Ravi Mathew, who was a major contributor to his party's election fund.

After the explosion in the jail, in which Ravi Shanker and Pillai were killed, there was an uproar about an investigation, and the prison superintendent was suspended. He pointed fingers at Mr. "Ravi Mathew and his company. The Chief Minister could not ignore this and asked our department to do a proper investigation and give them a report.

"My boss, the superintendent, and a colleague of mine did the investigation very thoroughly and came to the conclusion that there was enough evidence that Ravi Mathew was the person who had hired the goons within the prison to kill both Ravi Shanker and Pillai by planting a bomb supplied through Ravi Mathew's trusted employee, who has been identified and confessed. The man testified that he was just following orders as a good employee and didn't know what was in the big parcel, he delivered to one of the convicts in prison, who along with another convict carried out the bombing in the prison. They think the lower category of prison wardens was probably paid off. It was a very powerful bomb and killed two convicts as well in the adjoining prison rooms. Ravi Mathew is now in a high-security prison in Trivandrum and will be prosecuted, and the courts will decide his punishment.

"So, now Ravi Mathew's company will probably collapse, unless they find a buyer, as there is no one to run it. His wife and children live in Dubai and are not interested in coming to Kerala.

"The wife was contacted but showed no interest in the assets of Ravi Mathew and told them that she was not involved in any of his businesses and was running a restaurant chain of three outlets in Dubai and

Sharjah, which were popular with the South Indian community.

"They had separated and both, her son and daughter, were studying in the British schools in Dubai and after completing school, could join some university in the UK."

Shyamala was happy to hear all this, and now, KBL Associates, of which he was a substantial shareholder, would be in trouble.

"With Kathpalia on our side, hopefully, KBL would be in trouble, and with the new minister, he would like a proper audit and report to take appropriate action."

Chapter 18

Around 8:30 pm, while she was eating dinner alone in her flat, Shyamala was quite surprised when her home phone rang; it was a long-distance call. Except for her family and some close friends, very few calls came on the landline. So, she was quite surprised when it rang. She answered it and recognized the voice immediately, the voice of Vikram. 'Why on earth was he calling her?' she wondered.

After the initial polite talk, he asked, "Please tell me what is going on in the KBL Associates case?"

Shyamala cautiously asked him, "Why are you concerned, you have left the company so of what interest is it to you? You must have already heard from your former colleagues about Ravi Mathew's arrest and the murderers in jail, I am sure."

He replied, "Yes, my former friends in the company keep me fully informed. I was very happy that Mr. Ravi Mathew has been arrested. I hope he gets the punishment he deserves, though, knowing the corruption and his clever manipulations; he may get off lightly, which is a pity."

Shyamala said, "I agree with you on that, but the Chief Minister is determined to see him punished for political reasons."

He changed his tone saying, "Mr. Pratap had telephoned me and asked me if I could locate suitable accommodation for him in Toronto. It is quite obvious that he is going to resign and leave the country before they start investigations against him. The next senior Director, Jagjit Jaiswal will most likely take over and he is very different and known for his integrity and no-nonsense attitude. He will make a good Managing Director."

"Anyway, I have to now look for a place where Ramesh Pratap can settle down and lead a retired life. He doesn't have any financial problems, I believe. He has settled away funds illegally and parked them in Panama and maybe also in Switzerland. He took bribes from companies for their good reports so that they could borrow from banks and financial institutions.

He and Mathew were very clever on that account, and as far as the RML consultancy is concerned, I think it will probably take a different direction. I don't know how and which direction it will take."

Vikram suddenly said, "I think of you often, and regret that our relationship didn't work out. I am sorry about it. It was my fault. I know you will never leave your job and come to settle down in Canada."

Shyamala had tears in her eyes, and said, "I miss you Vikram, but we are not on the same road and have taken different avenues. I don't think you would ever decide to come back and settle in India."

Vikram was silent for a minute before replying, "Shyamala, it was nice talking to you, and you wouldn't mind if I telephone you to keep in touch, right?"

Shanker was sitting in his office and looking at Shyamala, who entered very meekly and sat down.

"Any problems Shyamala, you look depressed." He took a chance and asked, "Did Vikram telephone and say he was getting married or engaged or something?" She looked at him in wonder.

"How did you guess that he telephoned?" asked Shyamala.

"Oh, I know you well enough and you know I am quite intuitive."

"Yes, he telephoned," and Shyamala told him word for word all about the call, except the last few minutes of the call which was personal, and between her and Vikram.

"So, Pratap is going to run away abroad. I suppose with Ravi Matthew behind bars he has no choice, and KBL Associates has not even given a preliminary report so far, or anything regarding their consultancy. I think they have not proceeded with it. Seriously, trying ways to evade issues and delay it, until the next government comes or ministry changes."

"They have no intention; I think the award of the consultancy contract was manipulated very cleverly in their favour."

"Now, the new minister heading the audit and accounts division of the ministry will have to decide how to proceed. But I also heard that Jagjit Jaiswal is likely to take over and he is known for his competence and integrity. He was side-lined because of that, and because of the influence of the shareholders, Ravi Matthew mainly, who is very close to Pratap. I am awaiting a call from Kathpalia for a meeting on how to proceed further. He has taken over and heads the division and I believe he may get an extension of two years. He had overnight, very cleverly, changed his colours and now has dumped Pratap, and tells everyone that he hardly knows him and has only a few minor dealings with him."

"I wonder what will happen to his personal staff and Surya. Take her out, without worrying that she is spying on you," teased Shyamala.

Shanker laughed and said, "I had thought of it, but I don't know whether the company will keep her, knowing her closeness to Pratap. She may be sacked unless she is clever enough to change her loyalties, which she is good at, and they would benefit from her knowledge of the previous regime, particularly Pratap. I doubt whether they will pay for her brother's education in England."

Shyamala said, "I am sure she will telephone you as soon as Pratap packs up and departs and the new managing director takes over."

"Let's be patient and see how things play out and then we will make our strategy," stated Shanker.

Shanker was thinking about Surya and her plans now that the godfather had to leave the company - KBL Associates. 'What was Kathpalia planning now,' he thought. Several thoughts came to his mind, and he was overwhelmed by them.

He took a pain killer as his tooth was aching and telephoned the dentist for an appointment. He left a message as he must have been busy, and his telephone kept ringing.

His fingers touched Surya's telephone number, and he dialled it. She was quick to answer and said she was anticipating his call and was surprised that he did not telephone earlier.

Shanker said, "Let us have lunch at *Yellow Brick* and we can chat." She suggested tea in the evening, and he agreed.

He was looking forward to meeting her and had put on some aftershave lotion someone had given him as a present and reached 10 minutes earlier and sat at their favourite table near the window. She came punctually and dressed in office clothes, except that she had put on make-up and deep red lipstick as she always did, as it made her look more attractive. She had chewed some peppermint, as he could smell it when he kissed her on the cheek. He waited for her to talk and she, as usual, started the conversation.

"Mr. Ramesh Pratap has resigned after the board meeting where they passed a no-confidence vote against him. Out of eight directors, only one supported him. Jagjit Jaiswal, the senior-most director was appointed as the Managing Director. He is competent and properly qualified for the position and is known for his integrity. He will take the company in the right direction and reinstate its high-calibre position before the consultancy business had taken a dive in the last year or two. I am sure the company will regain its positive image under his guidance."

"What about you, Surya? Where do you stand now, Pratap had given you a special position, and also, they were paying for your brother's education through a special fund."

Surya stated she cannot answer as she did not know what Mr. Jaiswal will decide but she had good relations as an employee with him always and he had entrusted important work to her in the past.

"I can request him for my brother's grant. He has only nine months left before he graduates. I hope he will agree. My brother looked after him when he visited London two years ago."

"What about our relationship?" asked Shanker with a smile. "It appears to have taken a dip as you were directed by Pratap to please me in a benefitting manner or whatever he meant, and you played your role very well." He continued with a smile on his face, but he had the feeling she may not be interested in a long-term relationship.

"I am still very fond of you, Surya, but don't know whether and what type of relationship we can have now."

"Let's give it time. Mr. Pratap, as you know, is going to Canada and planning to settle down there. He has relatives in Toronto and his wife's brother is an executive in a well-known company. Anyway, he was reaching his retirement age and I believe he has plenty of funds abroad in tax havens, which should sustain him, and he can live a comfortable life there and come to India in winter and stay in his flat in Magnolia's in Gurugram, which is a very nice place to live."

Shanker got up and took Surya to the end of the corridor and, after looking around, gave her a passionate kiss and said, "Look after yourself Surya and keep in touch." He had to have closure and he needed to be at peace with himself. He saw tears in her eyes as he left.

Kathpalia telephoned Shanker and asked him if they could meet for lunch. Shanker willingly agreed and they met at the Taj Hotel in the Chinese room, where the manager, as usual, went out of his way to please them with his best dishes and made something special for them.

"So, what is being planned now?" asked Shanker. "Your new minister is very active and constantly in the news."

"Well, you know that the elections are around the corner, and everyone, including our ministry, has to show results. We have to show that we are making efforts to collect bad loans and debts, from politicians and their kin."

"I have orders that all those who were given loans by RML and haven't paid a rupee so far, their assets should be confiscated and to that extent, we have passed orders to take over some of the properties they acquired and auction them to pay back their debts. They have hired lawyers and gone to court. So, now the proceedings will start, and you know courts take their own time to pronounce judgments, and then, if they lose, they will appeal to a higher court."

"Of course, the tax department has been more active and has conducted raids and found a lot of cash hoarding in some properties and plenty of gold bricks, which they have confiscated. This will be a quick process and the recovery of loans will be faster, but I don't think they will be able to recover more than 40-50%, the rest will be irrecoverable, it may have been sent abroad and deposited in tax havens.

The government is planning to ask one of the larger public sector banks to take over RML and I think that, eventually, that will happen. It has happened in the past.

What about Pratap?" asked Kathpalia.

"My information," indicated Shanker, "is that he is going to Toronto and settling down there. His daughter is studying at a university in New York which would be convenient for them. I understand that he has plenty of money settled abroad in Panama and other tax havens, made in collaboration with Ravi Mathew, who is now behind bars on serious, criminal charges."

"Let us see what happens," said Kathpalia and he got up and left. Shanker went back to his office and wondered what the next move would be. It appears that KBL could continue with their consultancy as the management had changed and even the ministry had confidence in Mr. Jaiswal and was confident that it would be a fair report, with Ravi Mathew out of the way.

Later, he was sitting in his chair with a piece of paper in front of him and drawing triangles and squares, with a red pencil, and making some sort of notes. He didn't hear the knock on his door until he saw Shyamala enter and she said, "I knocked but there was no response, so I opened the door wondering if everything was all right."

"Any urgent problem?" he asked. "Yes, she said. We got a call from the residence-cum-office of Mr. Pratap at around 5 p.m. One of his assistants told us that Pratap had been shot and they had called an ambulance and rushed him to Safdarjung hospital. However, he had died on the way and his body is lying there, to be taken by his family, after the post-mortem procedure by the doctors, for the cremation."

Shanker was shocked and could not believe what was happening. He thought the killings were all over now. He rushed to the hospital where the senior doctor took him to the examination room where his body was being kept.

"We have to do a very thorough post-mortem and give a comprehensive report, but the preliminary findings are that he was shot by a revolver and three bullets were found in his body. The bullet in the heart must have killed him instantly. There was not much bleeding. It must be one of those latest types, imported most likely, as the bullets had foreign markings. He was shot at a short distance, not more than 10-15 feet, and fell down and injured himself. Whatever the other injuries are, he was killed by the bullet in his heart, and the other two bullets hit his left shoulder and left arm. It appears to have been an amateur who fired the gun, as at such close range, the person got the third bullet in his heart. It could be a man or a woman, which is for you to determine after your examination."

Shanker had sent Shyamala to his West End residence-cum-office and told her to cordon it off. Shanker proceeded to his residence and the police constable told him that Shyamala was in the office where the murder had taken place. He went to the office, which he was familiar with, and saw Shyamala directing the homicide team to take photographs and fingerprints, etc., so that they may identify the killer. They appeared to be doing a thorough job patiently so as to not miss a thing.

"What about the servants and office staff, including his wife and other relatives?"

"His wife left two days ago for Canada. His daughter is studying abroad in the U.S. and is presently living in a hostel there."

"She said she will come for the cremation of her father along with a male cousin, his younger brother's son, who lives in Delhi and works in a bank.

His younger brother and his wife will organize the cremation and the *Chauth*. He is an executive with a multinational and travels a lot on businesses and is based in Navi Mumbai."

Shanker told Shyamala, "You carry on with your work and we will discuss the details after we get the post-mortem report along with your investigation report with details of fingerprints and also interviews with the office and house staff."

They met in the office, Shanker and Shyamala, with the other investigative officers.

The post-mortem report was very lucid, that he had been shot from a range of about 10-15 feet, with a revolver, the bullets indicated that it was of eastern European origin, most likely made in the Czech Republic. It was a medium-sized pistol with large bullets.

They were unable to identify the fingerprints, though they took them from the office staff and the sweepers and cleaners.

Whoever did it must have worn glasses. However, there was a whiff of perfume in the air, and was identifiable on the chair seat as well, which indicated that most likely it was a lady who used the pistol. Someone who was familiar with pistols or guns and owned a pistol.

They checked with the registry of the area and surrounding areas, but no one from their office staff had a shotgun or revolver licence registered.

"Who was it that gained from his death?" His law firm partner, Ranjit Kumar showed his will that he had left for his wife and daughter. Both of whom were abroad when the murder took place.

They, however, would find it difficult to trace his will for assets kept abroad in Panama and other tax havens. They would be with the respective banks, which they would have to trace and that would be a difficult job, and, in any case, they would not disclose the contents to them and were not required to do so.

Now with his wife and daughter abroad, they would appropriate the overseas assets, which he must have told them about, and probably a firm of solicitors in London was dealing with the matter.

They had no means, or interest in this part of his assets and were concerned with only who had murdered him. It did not appear that it was for money, but in vengeance for having broken a deal or a promise to some lady perhaps.

'Who could this lady be?' thought Shanker.

Suddenly, it struck him that it could be Surya. He may have made promises to her that he was not willing to fulfil; for favours done, or maybe even that he should leave his wife and marry her though he was much older than her. Many men did marry younger and prettier women especially in these recent times. He may have been sleeping with her. He may have been having an affair with her as she was easily available to him and would do his bidding, maybe he rewarded her regularly with gold and diamonds, as she always wore expensive jewellery when they went out at night. She was his mistress and he never suspected her. 'What a slip-up,' thought Shanker.

He discussed it with Shyamala who agreed with him and said that she always suspected that there was something between them. The way they had vibes between them, she could sense them when they were in the room together. But she also wondered what Surya would gain by killing him.

"We will have to investigate and talk some more to other members of his personal staff and residence staff, and also his lawyer about his will."

Shyamala went the next day and questioned the staff about who came during the afternoon, they must be keeping a log of it in some register at the entry gate, and, of course, the normal office staff who reports for duty in the morning.

She got the list, but his secretary told us that it may be incomplete as not everything is recorded, particularly with regard to known and regular staff, who go on assignments throughout the day and come in and out of the office, like any other busy business office.

She made a list and there was nothing unusual in it as no outsiders had visited him and Surya's name was not there.

She asked if any staff from Ravi Mathew's Cochin office visited Mr. Pratap.

There was no record of any such persons. In fact, it had been a dull day, and Mr. Pratap had gone to the main office near Parliament Street and came back at lunchtime. After that, as it was his practice, he took a nap for an hour and then sat at his office desk.

He called his secretary and dictated some official letter and then she did some filing and left at about 4:30 p.m. He said he was planning to go to the club and chat with friends and later go to the bar and have drinks.

After 4:30 p.m., he was sitting alone in his office when he was shot, but no one appears to have heard any shots. When the office peon went to his office to ask him if he could leave if there was no other work, he saw that he was bleeding. He raised an alarm and other house staff rushed to the office and called the ambulance and police. Immediately, two of his senior assistants who were always on call, as well as his secretary, came rushing to the office.

They too were called to the office and questioned, and their version was the same as the others." The head peon was very alert and had called everyone to the office, he was an old and trusted hand - Rameshwar Chand. He knew everyone by name and had been in service with them for more than 10 years.

No one could give a clue as to who could be involved, and they spoke as concisely as possible, avoiding any gossip or theories of who could be responsible.

"So, here we are, stuck, and our main suspect, we have to find out how she entered without anyone meeting her entry, including the gate's entry. He said he was there all the time; however, he could have gone to the toilet or for a smoke, but on questioning, he did not waiver from his original statement," Shyamala concluded.

Shanker said, "We will discuss it tomorrow in the office."

Chapter 19

That evening, when Shanker reached his house, his mobile phone vibrated. It was on mute, the name of the caller indicated Surya. He was surprised that she had called.

She said, "Hello, is that you Shanker?" she sounded distant.

He answered, "Yes, it is."

"I am speaking from Nairobi, Kenya. I arrived here yesterday evening."

"What are you doing in Nairobi?" he asked.

She paused for a minute then she answered, "I guess you want to know about the killing of Mr. Pratap?" "Let me tell you everything, I know you are going to record it, but it doesn't matter now."

So, she related to him that evening she went to his office to ask him if she could leave for home.

He had his head on the desk and was looking crestfallen, I could see the tears in his eyes. Mr. Pratap looked up at me and said, 'Surya, 'I don't deserve to live. I have done some very bad, unforgivable things because I got ensnared by Ravi Mathew. Involvement in murders, done by him, which I can't deny, I was in some manner an accomplice. The young boy in Cochin and several others, Vikram and Kumar were lucky to get away. Poor Hari Mohan, who was a good friend and a very decent person. I'm involved in money laundering by keeping foreign accounts in Panama and other tax havens. I can't put all the blame on Ravi Mathew. I could have easily stopped him, but I did not do so.'

She related that he told her everything. Then he suddenly retrieved a strange looking revolver from his drawer and aimed it at his temple. She was shocked and scared. She did care for him and begged him not to do it. She claimed that she pleaded with him. He suddenly gave the pistol to her and told her that he could not shoot himself. He then complicated things by begging her to please shoot him. She related that she didn't know what to do and in reaction, claimed that in her confused state, she pulled the trigger. She said that she had no idea how to use the revolver, so she missed. She related that she pulled the trigger three times. The third bullet apparently killed him. She related that she did not know what to do and was so shocked at what she had done. She added, "I thought for a minute or two and then, as I had seen in British movies, with my dupatta I wiped my fingerprints from the revolver. Where to hide it now, I thought I would go up to the roof and hide it there. I opened the lid of the water tank and put it in there, you will probably find it there at the bottom of the big water tank."

She related that she was so worried, but soon calmed herself down. She then telephoned her aunt, her mother's sister, and told her that she had done something wrong and wanted to leave the country and will explain everything. Her aunt sounded worried but told her to catch a flight to Dubai by Emirates and from there catch a connecting flight to Nairobi. Surya followed her instructions and went to the airport, to the counter of Emirates Airlines. Fortunately, the flight was not full, and paid using her credit card and reached Nairobi late the next morning. Her aunt was there to meet her, along with her cousin Ranbir. They both welcomed her and were happy to meet her and were able to get her a visa on arrival. She said she explained everything to them, and they said that it is certainly not my fault. It was a forced accident of sorts. Her aunt was in the process of getting her a job in a consultancy firm or a bank. Her uncle is quite a successful businessman, and their family has been in that country for three generations. They have a lovely house in the Westland area of Nairobi. She told Shanker that she will not be returning to Delhi anytime soon, but she will miss him. "Shanker, I have become very fond of you. Keep in touch. I will be changing my mobile phone but will contact you. Good luck with your investigation."

Shanker deleted the recording and poured a drink for himself. He was numb on the inside and his emotions were all over the place even though he appeared calm on the outside. He just sighed, leaning back in his favourite chair just steering at his drink; not seeing the liquid but the beautiful face of a woman whom he fell in love with.

www.ingramcontent.com/pod-product-compliance
Lightning Source LLC
LaVergne TN
LVHW041013150826
845672LV00001B/83

* 9 7 9 8 8 8 7 0 4 8 8 9 5 *